*THEY'R[...]*
*TROU[...]*

*LUKE TRAVIS:* It's up to the marshal to keep the peace in Abilene when the prizefighter comes to town . . . and a big-time gunfighter follows in his wake!

*CODY FISHER:* The young deputy has his job cut out for him with Abilene primed and ready to explode . . .

*SEAMUS O'QUINN:* Witness to a murder in Chicago, the heavyweight fighter is the only man who can put two big-time mobsters away for good—unless they get him first . . .

*INSPECTOR JACK MCTEAGUE:* The veteran Chicago detective brings his star witness to Abilene under cover before the grand jury convenes. But how long can he protect O'Quinn before the truth is out and the killers are on his trail?

*DARIUS GOLD:* The Chicago crime kingpin is dead meat if O'Quinn lives to testify against him . . .

*MITCH RAINEY:* His surface charm belies a ruthless, violent nature. Gold's right-hand man, he's gunning for O'Quinn in Abilene—and planning to bury him in lead . . .

*EMILY BURTON:* She didn't expect to find love with the prizefighter—or to be swept into the violence that dogs his every step . . .

**Books by Justin Ladd**

Abilene Book 1: The Peacemaker
Abilene Book 2: The Sharpshooter
Abilene Book 3: The Pursuers
Abilene Book 4: The Night Riders
Abilene Book 5: The Half-Breed
Abilene Book 6: The Hangman
Abilene Book 7: The Prizefighter

Published by POCKET BOOKS

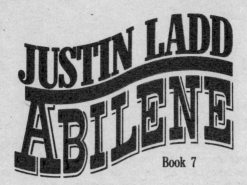

# JUSTIN LADD
# ABILENE

Book 7

# THE PRIZEFIGHTER

Created by the producers of
**Wagons West, Stagecoach, Badge,** and **White Indian.**

*Book Creations Inc., Canaan, NY · Lyle Kenyon Engel, Founder*

**POCKET BOOKS**

New York     London     Toronto     Sydney     Tokyo

An *Original* Publication of POCKET BOOKS

 POCKET BOOKS, a division of Simon & Schuster Inc.
1230 Avenue of the Americas, New York, NY 10020

ISBN: 0-671-66992-3

First Pocket Books printing April 1989

10  9  8  7  6  5  4  3  2  1

POCKET and colophon are trademarks of Simon & Schuster Inc.

Printed in the U.S.A.

# THE
# PRIZEFIGHTER

# Chapter One

A COLD AUTUMN WIND WHIRLED THROUGH THE DIMLY lit Chicago streets, and heavy clouds, threatening an icy rain, scudded across the crescent moon. Pedestrians unfortunate enough to be out on this bitter, damp night cast envious glances at the closed carriages that occasionally rolled by them on the cobblestoned avenues. They pulled their caps down farther on their heads or drew their jackets closer to them to ward off the chill. But not Seamus O'Quinn. He was still too excited about the fight he had just won to feel the biting cold.

"I knew you had it in you, O'Quinn!" exclaimed Dooley Farnham. The small man walking beside him was struggling to keep up with O'Quinn's long strides. "I knew you could take Packard, he's nothing but a big tub of lard. But a knockout! *That* will make people sit up and take notice, my boy. Mark my words, you keep punching the way you have been, and you'll be fighting for the heavyweight title before another year is out!"

O'Quinn grinned at the smaller man's enthusiasm. Clapping him on the back, he said, "I never could have done it without you, Dooley."

Dooley staggered a bit from the exuberant blow, regained his balance, and then caught the derby that was about to fly off his plastered-down, carrot-colored hair. "I'll start setting up the next fight right away," he declared, returning O'Quinn's grin. "We'll have you back in Gilmore's Garden before you know it!"

O'Quinn laughed at the idea of returning to the famous New York exhibition hall. "I hope you arrange that before they change the name to Madison Square Garden the way they're threatening," he chortled. "People won't know where they're going otherwise."

The prizefighter was a tall, brawny man with wide shoulders that stretched the fabric of his cheap suit. His thick black hair was rumpled and unruly, but his heavy black mustache was neatly groomed with the tips lightly waxed. The hearty laugh rumbled from his broad chest as if it were coming from a deep well.

"But don't get carried away, Dooley. I want to celebrate tonight's win for a while before I start training for the next fight."

"Sure, sure, celebrate all you want." Dooley rubbed his palms together in anticipation as he bounced along at O'Quinn's side. "Because tomorrow morning, you'll be doing road work again, laddy buck!"

O'Quinn groaned. He had better have a good time tonight, he decided, because he knew Dooley meant every word he said. The little man was quite a taskmaster. He was also Seamus O'Quinn's best friend and had salvaged his once-failing boxing career.

Dooley Farnham had been O'Quinn's manager for a little over a year. In that short time he had taken a down-on-his-luck slugger who had served mostly as a punching bag for other prizefighters and turned him into a legitimate boxer who would soon be a contender for the heavyweight crown. Dooley had worked him mercilessly, never settling for any less than O'Quinn's absolute best effort, both in the prize ring and in the training sessions that preceded the bouts. Nursing O'Quinn's career along, he arranged matches that had taken them from small, but tough, New Jersey towns to tonight's important fight in Chicago.

This evening in a waterfront hall, O'Quinn had faced Vinnie Packard, a powerful fighter who had once fought for the championship himself and was still highly regarded. The bout ended in the seventh round with a knockout. O'Quinn's knuckles still ached from the blow that did the job—a solid right cross that slipped past Packard's guard and caught him in the jaw. Packard almost flew out of the ring. The crowd went wild, shouting and cheering as the referee lifted O'Quinn's hand in triumph. Even now, over an hour after the fight had ended, O'Quinn's heart pounded at the memory.

He had heard such acclaim before from an even larger crowd, but then the cries were not for him. At the very start of his career he had fought at the Garden in New York and lost. After that defeat he went from bout to bout in a spirit-dampening succession of losses. His manager at the time had been more concerned with where his next bottle of whiskey was coming from than with guiding the career of his boxer.

In despair O'Quinn resigned himself to his status, halfway between a has-been and a never-was. Then Dooley Farnham came along and changed his life.

In this neighborhood near the docks the lights from the many saloons glowed invitingly in the dark, windy streets, and the two men could walk into any one of them to have a celebratory drink. But Dooley insisted on going to a place called Red Mike's that he remembered from a previous visit to Chicago. The little man had been in the fight game for most of his forty-odd years and knew practically everyone involved with it, as well as the dives and bars they frequented. He assured O'Quinn they could make some good contacts at Red Mike's.

A carriage pulled to a stop ahead of them beneath one of the infrequent street lamps that lighted the waterfront. A tall man wearing a soft felt hat and an expensive overcoat leapt gracefully to the cobblestones. As he paid the driver, he glanced toward O'Quinn and Dooley, who had moved into the pool of lamplight, and a quick smile of recognition brightened his lean face.

"Ah, Mr. O'Quinn!" he said as he strode to meet the approaching pair. "I was in the hall tonight when you disposed of the unfortunate Mr. Packard. What a magnificent performance!" He extended a hand toward O'Quinn.

The heavyweight shook it as he nodded his thanks for the compliment. Dooley said, "Hello, Rutherford. How are you?"

"I'm doing fine, Dooley." Another smile creased Rutherford's face. "Especially since I had a wager riding on your boy here."

Dooley put a hand on O'Quinn's arm. "Seamus, I

want you to meet Mr. Mel Rutherford. Mr. Rutherford is a . . . sporting gentleman, shall we say?"

Rutherford chuckled. "I prefer to be more straightforward, Dooley. I'm a gambler, Mr. O'Quinn. And I expect to make a great deal of money on your fights in the future."

O'Quinn moved his shoulders awkwardly. He felt a bit uncomfortable in the presence of swells like Rutherford who obviously had a great deal of money and spent it lavishly. Having grown up in one of the poorest sections of New York as one of several children in a penniless immigrant family, O'Quinn was awed and ill-at-ease with the large sums of money that floated around the boxing business. He said nervously, "I hope I don't disappoint you, sir."

"I'm sure you won't, Mr. O'Quinn." Rutherford placed both his hands on the silver head of his walking stick. "Are you gentlemen going anywhere in particular? I wouldn't mind buying you a quick drink."

"We're on our way to Red Mike's," Dooley offered.

"Perhaps some other time, then," Rutherford said, shaking his head. "I had some place a bit closer in mind. I'm in a bit of a hurry tonight. Wouldn't want to keep a young lady waiting too long, now would we?"

"No, sir, we certainly wouldn't." Dooley leaned closer to the gambler and lowered his voice. "Say, Mr. Rutherford, I was talking to some of the boys around the hall earlier, and they were telling me something you might want to know."

"And what might that be, Dooley?" Rutherford asked absently. He slipped a large gold watch from his vest pocket, flipped open the case, and glanced at it.

"I heard Darius Gold is upset with you. He seems to think you're moving into his territory or something."

In the pool of lamplight O'Quinn saw Rutherford's head snap up and his eyes suddenly narrow with worry. Then the gambler shook his head slightly and said in a hearty voice, "I appreciate your interest, Dooley, but I'm afraid I have more important things to concern myself with than an old man like Gold. His day is past. He's no threat to me."

Dooley shrugged. "I just thought you'd like to know."

"Of course." Rutherford nodded rather curtly and went on airily, "Well, good evening to you, gentlemen. Congratulations again on your victory, Mr. O'Quinn."

"Thanks," O'Quinn muttered. He watched thoughtfully as Rutherford turned and strolled down the street.

Dooley tugged at O'Quinn's sleeve. "Come on, Seamus," the manager said. "I want to find Red Mike's and see if his whiskey is still as good as it used to be."

O'Quinn nodded absently and let Dooley lead him in the direction opposite that which Rutherford had taken. As he kept pace with his manager, the prizefighter shoved his hands in his pockets and remarked, "I don't care what that fellow said, he looked worried when you told him about Darius Gold."

"He has good reason to worry," Dooley replied with a shake of his head. "I've tried to keep you away from that side of the business, O'Quinn, but you know how those gamblers are. Gold is an important man in this town. He doesn't just control the betting. His influence is widespread; he's got a finger in every crooked deal in Chicago. And he doesn't like it when somebody like Rutherford comes in and tries to take over part of the action."

"Well," O'Quinn said, "it's none of our business, after all."

"No, it certainly isn't," Dooley agreed. "Why don't we try this alley? I think it's a shortcut to Red Mike's."

They had just turned into the dark alley when they suddenly heard the patter of running footsteps behind them. There was a smacking sound that reminded O'Quinn of someone hitting a sandbag, then a cry of pain ripped through the night.

O'Quinn whirled around and took a step back toward the sidewalk. Peering from the mouth of the dark alley into the street, he saw several men clustered around a lone figure a block away. It was the gambler, Mel Rutherford, who was being attacked, O'Quinn realized. The assailants, swinging fists, blackjacks, and clubs, swarmed around him. Although Rutherford tried to fight back, he fell to the sidewalk in a matter of seconds.

A growl rumbling in his throat, O'Quinn started forward. But before he could leave the alley, Dooley Farnham clamped both hands on his arm and pulled him back. "Don't, Seamus!" Dooley hissed. "Don't be a damned fool! There's nothing we can do."

O'Quinn stared at the brutal scene. Some of the thugs began to kick Rutherford, and the clubs were still rising and falling. There had been no further outcry from the gambler since that first pained yell.

Rutherford was probably long past crying out now, O'Quinn thought bitterly as he watched the men beat the gambler to death.

"Take it easy, lad," Dooley whispered. "There are too many of them, and we can't help Rutherford." The small man sighed. "I tried to warn him about Darius Gold."

At last the men gathered around Rutherford's body

stopped their assault. They stepped back slightly, and one of them waved toward a darkened area farther down the street. A moment later two men moved out of the shadows and walked toward the figure sprawled on the pavement.

As they passed beneath the street lamp where O'Quinn and Dooley had met Rutherford only moments before, O'Quinn could see that these two newcomers were not roughly-dressed toughs like the men who had just murdered Rutherford. Both of them wore expensive overcoats. While one man was small and had a dapper hat tilted rakishly over his forehead, his companion was taller and wore a derby pushed back on his blond hair. They stood for a moment staring down at Rutherford's bloodied form, then the smaller of the pair nodded in satisfaction. The larger man pulled a wad of money from his pocket and began passing bills to the thugs.

In the gloom of the alley, Seamus O'Quinn clenched his big fists. He had not met Rutherford until tonight and had no great fondness for the gambler, but to see a man murdered so callously, then to watch as his killers were paid for their bloody deed . . . It was all O'Quinn could do not to charge into the street and lay into the two well-dressed men who were paying for the dirty work.

"The little one is Darius Gold," Dooley said softly. "The fellow with him must be Mitch Rainey. I've heard of Rainey, but I've never met him. He's Gold's right-hand man, handles a lot of the details of the operation. From what I hear, he's even more vicious than Gold himself."

"They probably enjoyed that little show their men put on, then," O'Quinn whispered harshly.

Dooley tugged at his arm. "Come on. We're not doing any good here. We might as well go on to Red Mike's."

O'Quinn shot a surprised glance at his manager. "You mean we're not going to the police and tell them what we just saw?"

Dooley grimaced. "You don't understand, Seamus," he said earnestly. "Men like Gold are a part of this business. We have to accept that. If we get on his bad side, you'll never be able to fight in Chicago again."

"But he just had that man killed!"

"Seamus . . . if we cross Darius Gold, he'll see to it that you don't fight *anywhere* ever again." Dooley jerked a thumb toward the waterfront a couple of blocks away. "We'll wind up out there with the fishes in the lake. That's what'll happen if we go against Gold and Rainey."

After a long moment, O'Quinn nodded. "I suppose you're right," he said.

"Of course I'm right. Now let's go." Dooley turned to start down the alley once more.

He had taken two steps, O'Quinn at his side, when he bumped into something in the darkness. A sudden crash echoed in the alley as the object overturned. Dooley yelped and dropped to one knee before he caught his balance. O'Quinn bent quickly and grasped his friend's arm to steady him. With his other hand, the prizefighter reached out and felt the barrel that Dooley had just knocked over.

"Hey! Who the hell's down there?" someone shouted from the street.

Clutching at O'Quinn's coat, Dooley scrambled to his feet. "Oh, my God!" he cried. "They heard us!

Now they know somebody was watching! Come on, Seamus, we've got to get out of here!"

O'Quinn chanced a look out the mouth of the alley. He saw Darius Gold pointing in his direction, heard the little gambler snapping orders. With Mitch Rainey in the lead, the group of toughs started toward the alley. In seconds the men had broken into a run.

O'Quinn, still clutching Dooley's arm, began to run, dragging the terrified, smaller man with him. Dooley's feet seemed to touch the rough paving stones of the alley only every few yards.

Except for the slap of shoe leather on pavement and the harsh breathing of the running men, the deadly pursuit was carried out in silence. While O'Quinn's training gave him the advantage of being in better shape than any of the thugs chasing them, he did not know these dark streets and back alleys. Rainey and his men did.

"Down there!" Dooley cried, waving frantically as he tried to direct O'Quinn through the dimly lit maze of alleys and back streets. They raced past several people who ducked out of the way and scurried into the concealing shadows rather than offering to help. The inhabitants of this part of the city knew well enough to mind their own business.

Nowhere in their flight did they see a policeman. And even if one had been around, O'Quinn doubted that one man would be much help against the brutal mob that pursued them.

Cold, wet air stung his face as he ran. Gradually he became aware that they were running toward the docks. He glanced over his shoulder and saw Rainey and the others emerge from a narrow street and come pounding after them. The street-wise thugs had closed the gap, and O'Quinn realized that their lead had been cut by more than half. As he looked ahead of them, he could see they had nowhere left to run.

"Oh, no!" Dooley wailed. "We took the wrong turn back there!"

The street they were on led between two long rows of warehouses that were dark and deserted at this time of night. The buildings ran straight to the waterfront. At the end of the avenue were several piers that jutted out into the icy waters of the lake.

Rainey and his thugs had the street behind them closed off now. There was no escape in that direction. And once they reached the piers, there would be nowhere else to run. They were going to have to stand and fight, O'Quinn decided.

Dooley was slowing down, his feet weighted by weariness and despair. O'Quinn tugged him forward, urging, "Come on! We'll be better off on the pier."

The prizefighter's heavy shoes clattered on the planks of the dock as Dooley and he ran onto it. When they had gone several yards, O'Quinn slowed and turned. The pier was only ten feet wide. Dooley and he could spread out enough so that Rainey and the others could only come at them from one direction.

"They're going to kill us!" Dooley whimpered.

O'Quinn shook his head. "Maybe not," he growled. His fists were bunched, and he stood lightly on the balls of his feet, waiting.

If none of the men in the group was armed, they had a chance, O'Quinn thought desperately. The pursuers had slowed down now that they saw their quarry was trapped. Rainey fell back slightly, letting the hired musclemen ease forward. O'Quinn counted them quickly, saw that there were six of them.

Dooley was not going to be much good in this fight, O'Quinn knew. Could he handle six rugged, back-alley brawlers by himself? To his surprise, a grin tugged at his wide mouth. It was going to be a hell of a fight.

Suddenly the thugs charged. O'Quinn roared defiantly and leapt forward to meet them, swinging his deadly fists with every ounce of speed and strength at his command.

The next few minutes were a nightmare of thudding fists and flailing clubs. O'Quinn took blow after blow, shrugging them off as best he could while continuing to throw punches of his own. Fists came at him from every direction, but he did not try to block them. Instead he concentrated on inflicting as much damage as he could. Noses broke and jaws shattered under his hammering fists. His bony knuckles were slick with blood, a crimson mixture of his own and that of his attackers.

Lost in the throes of his fierce battle, O'Quinn suddenly heard Dooley scream in pain and snapped his head around in time to see one of the thugs slam a club into his manager's stomach. He groaned as he realized that, while he had tried to occupy all of them, one man had managed to slip past him. Roaring again, the heavyweight swept his powerful right arm around, clearing two of the thugs away from him. Then he started to go to Dooley's aid, but before he could reach him, someone landed on his back, wrapped his legs around his waist, and began clawing at his eyes.

O'Quinn reached back, grabbed the man's hair, and heaved. The man screamed as O'Quinn hauled him over his shoulder and slammed him onto the dock.

Blood dripped into O'Quinn's eyes, blurring his

vision. But through that red haze he saw Dooley's attacker raise his club and savagely smash it on his friend's head. Dooley fell forward onto the planks, blood and bits of bone spattering the dock, and the man standing over him brought the club up and continued to batter his skull viciously. Within seconds what had been Dooley's head was a gruesome mass of scarlet and gray.

"Dooley!" O'Quinn screamed wildly. Witnessing the horrible murder of his friend enraged O'Quinn. No longer was this fight a matter of self-defense. In a frenzy of blind madness he whirled among the attackers, his fists shattering bone and scattering the thugs around the pier like tenpins. Now he wanted to pound Mitch Rainey, and then, when the man was pulp, he would destroy Darius Gold.

One tough still stood in his way. He grabbed the man's coat and flung him to the side. The thug sailed out over the lake, uttering a frantic cry, then splashed into the water. The path to Rainey was now open.

O'Quinn shook his head to clear the blood from his eyes and took a step forward. In the dim light he saw Rainey's hand rising and something glinting in the man's fingers. O'Quinn recognized the gleam of a pistol barrel and started to lunge toward him, hoping to tackle Rainey before he could fire.

The gun cracked, flame spitting from its muzzle. O'Quinn felt the slug slam into his shoulder, but he willed himself to continue forward a few steps. Rainey triggered two more shots. This time the impact of the bullets spun O'Quinn around. He clutched at the sudden fiery pain that exploded in his side while he kept staggering on the planks of the pier.

Suddenly there was nothing under his feet. He felt

himself falling and knew vaguely that he had walked right off the dock. The few seconds it took to plunge into the water seemed to last forever, then abruptly the icy waves closed over him, wrapping him in a frigid embrace that took away all his pain.

Mitch Rainey watched the big man's body disappear into the lake and the familiar thrill he always felt at the sight of sudden, violent death coursed through him.

"I was beginning to think you were going to wait all night to shoot the bastard," a voice behind Rainey observed dryly.

Rainey turned to see Darius Gold ambling toward him. "I wanted to see if the boys could handle him by themselves," he told his boss. "They took care of the little one all right."

Gold stepped over to the corpse lying on the pier and regarded it dispassionately. His ageless face was lean, the features almost delicate, and it reflected little of the depravity he had witnessed over the years. He said, "From what I can tell of the mess that's left, I think that was a scruffy fight manager named Dooley Farnham. That would make the big one some Irish boxer he's been handling. I can't remember his name. Well, neither one of them will cause us any trouble."

"Neither will that damned Rutherford after tonight," Rainey commented. He watched as the bruised, bloodied thugs scrambled to their feet. A few yards away, the man the Irish prizefighter had tossed into the water hung onto the dock, gasping for breath, his teeth chattering from his dip in the icy lake.

"Give them a little extra money," Gold sniffed as he looked at the thugs in disdain. "They didn't do much to earn it, but we have to keep them happy, I suppose."

"Sure. Should we throw the manager's body in the lake?"

Gold shook his head. "Just leave it where it is." He smiled. "As a warning. It's dangerous to venture out into these streets after dark, you know."

Rainey chuckled. He flipped a few coins to the battered toughs, then followed Gold, who was strolling to their carriage. The thugs slipped off into the night to ease the pains of this fight with the whiskey that the blood money would buy.

Silence reigned once more on the waterfront street. Dooley Farnham would never utter another sound again.

Then a huge splash shattered the quiet night, and Seamus O'Quinn surged out of the water. Grasping the rungs of a ladder that led to the pier and hanging on for dear life, he gasped for breath desperately. He was numb all over, but some spark within him had refused to let him die. He had fought his way to the surface of the water under the pier, lifted his head high enough to drag air into his tortured lungs. The few minutes he had waited in the icy lake until Gold, Rainey, and the others were gone had been the longest of his life.

He was thankful for the cold; he knew it had kept him alive. At least two of Rainey's bullets had hit him, but the frigid water had kept the wounds from bleeding much. Now, as O'Quinn clung to the ladder, gathering what little strength he had left, he knew he would have to move quickly. Otherwise the bitter wind that was ravaging his soaked body would strip the very life out of it. With agonizing slowness he started to pull himself up, rung by rung.

Long moments later he sprawled onto the pier. He drew several deep, ragged breaths, then pushed himself to his feet and lurched over to Dooley's body. When he saw what had been done to his friend and manager, he heaved a great sob. Drawing on all his remaining strength, O'Quinn bent, scooped Dooley's limp form off the pier, and lifted it.

"I . . . I'll even the score, Dooley," O'Quinn rasped in a voice he did not recognize as his own. "Gold and Rainey . . . they'll pay. I swear they'll pay."

Cradling Dooley's body in his arms, O'Quinn, concentrating on putting one foot in front of the other, began to walk aimlessly away from the docks. Surely somewhere there was someone who could help him—

"Here now, what the divil is this?"

O'Quinn blinked and shook his head, trying to focus on the figure that had loomed out of the darkness. He saw the high peaked hat, the blue uniform with its brass buttons, the nightstick clutched in the man's hand. *Finally,* O'Quinn thought bitterly, *a policeman.*

He opened his mouth to tell the copper that he was too late, but the words never came out. O'Quinn felt his legs buckle, and he was falling, plunging into a blackness that was darker and colder than the waters of Lake Michigan.

"Well, now, finally going to wake up, are we?" said a faint voice that seemed to be coming from miles away.

Slowly, O'Quinn moved his head from side to side. His fingers moved a bit, and he was aware of the crisp fabric under them. Suddenly, one of his eyes was pried open, and he recoiled from the burst of bright light.

Blinking rapidly, O'Quinn jerked his head away and moaned as the slight movement shot pain through his midsection. He managed to force both eyes open, and when they had adjusted to the light, he saw that he was lying in an iron-framed bed in a narrow little room. High on one wall was a single window. O'Quinn stared at the bars on it.

"He'll be all right," a gruff voice said. "You can't hurt an animal like that, short of killing him."

"Thank you, Doctor. Can I question him now?"

"Certainly. Try not to tire him too much."

O'Quinn forced his eyes to move from the barred window toward the two men who had been talking. They stood on each side of the bed. The one on his right was a sour-faced, middle-aged man who was holding a black medical bag. That had to be the doctor. The other man was younger, probably in his thirties, with closely cropped dark brown hair that was parted in the middle. On his upper lip was a well-trimmed mustache. His gray eyes peered at O'Quinn.

"About time you decided you'd gotten enough sleep, Mr. O'Quinn," this man said as the doctor left the room. "You've been unconscious for over two days now."

O'Quinn tried to speak, to voice the questions that were exploding in his brain, but all he could utter was a strangled croak. A stern, gray-haired woman appeared in a crisp nurse's uniform. She held a glass of water and, lifting his shoulders, pressed it to his lips. He choked down several swallows and shook his head as a signal to her to take the glass away. Then O'Quinn lowered his head to the thin pillow and stammered hoarsely, "Wh-where am I?"

"You're in the prison ward of Mercy Hospital, Mr. O'Quinn," the man said. He inclined his head toward the door of the room, and O'Quinn looked and saw a uniformed policeman standing guard. The man next to the bed went on, "I'm Inspector Jack McTeague, and I've been waiting to talk to you for quite a long time."

"T-talk to me . . . about what?"

"I want to know whether or not I should charge you with murder," McTeague said bluntly.

At the inspector's words O'Quinn remembered that awful night on the docks. He closed his eyes and groaned. "Dooley," he muttered bleakly.

"Indeed," McTeague said crisply. "Your manager, Mr. Dooley Farnham. I understood that the two of you had a fairly successful business relationship. Did you kill him, Mr. O'Quinn?"

O'Quinn opened his eyes and stared in shock at McTeague. Anger quickly replaced the shock, and he struggled to sit up. He discovered then that his midriff and his right shoulder were tightly bandaged and that he was too weak to pull himself to a sitting position. He fell back and gasped, "You can't think that I killed Dooley!"

McTeague shrugged. "What else are we to think? You staggered out of the night carrying the body, and no one else was in the immediate vicinity. We had to account for those bullet wounds of yours, but Farnham could have shot you before he was killed. Until you woke up, we could only assume that you murdered him."

"That's a hell of an assumption," O'Quinn snapped, feeling some of his strength returning. But abruptly he felt weary and realized that his anger at McTeague's accusation had prompted the surge of energy. As he fought the sudden urge to go back to sleep, he knew his reserves were limited.

He would use his remaining strength to tell this policeman what he had seen two nights earlier. McTeague looked like a competent man; he would have to take care of the real killers. O'Quinn was in no shape to do it himself.

"If you didn't do it, O'Quinn, who did?" McTeague asked, his tone cold now.

"Gold," O'Quinn said simply.

McTeague suddenly leaned forward. "What's that? What did you say, man?"

"It was . . . Darius Gold. He ordered it. His men killed Dooley. That other fellow . . ." O'Quinn cast about in his memory for the name. "Rainey, that's it. Rainey, he's the one who shot me. But Gold ordered it done. They killed some gambler, too. . . . Rutherford, I think."

McTeague's eyes grew wide with excitement. He glanced at the officer at the door and then asked in a low voice, "You saw this happen, O'Quinn?"

"Of course I did."

"And you'll testify to it?"

O'Quinn lifted a trembling hand and gestured at the bandages wrapped around him. "If these don't . . . don't kill me first."

McTeague shook his head. "They won't kill you. The doctor assured me of that. You lost quite a bit of blood, but the bullets missed all the vital organs. You'll be fine with a bit of rest." The inspector looked at the uniformed policeman and went on, "Step outside for a moment please, Officer Brown. And take the good nurse with you."

"The doctor said I was to stay here," the nurse protested.

"I shouldn't leave you alone with the prisoner, sir," the officer added.

McTeague looked sternly at them. "I'll take the responsibility, both of you. Now please, step outside." His tone, though polite, made it clear he would brook no more argument.

Looking uncomfortable, the officer and the nurse stepped from the room and closed the door behind them. O'Quinn stared at McTeague, baffled by the inspector's behavior.

"What was that all about?" O'Quinn asked.

"I'm fairly certain I can trust Brown," McTeague replied. "But I don't want to take any chances. Gold has informers scattered throughout the police force. We can't afford to let him know that you're alive, not yet anyway."

"I . . . I don't understand."

McTeague smiled broadly. "Thanks to you and what you've just told me, my friend, Darius Gold is finally going to get what he deserves. The bastard's going to hang for the murders of your friend Farnham and Melvin Rutherford."

O'Quinn took a deep breath, ignoring the pain it caused him. "That's what I wanted to hear you say, Inspector. You believe me when I say I didn't kill Dooley?"

"I believe you, all right. I doubted all along that you would murder your own manager, Mr. O'Quinn, but we had no other suspects. Now, considering where we found Rutherford's body, what you tell me makes sense. He was discovered only a few blocks from where you and Farnham were found."

O'Quinn nodded. "Gold is responsible for all of it."

"And he'll be brought to justice for it, I assure you.

The honest members of the force have been trying for years to get some specific evidence against him, and now you've given it to us." A worried look suddenly passed over McTeague's ruddy face. "Now all we have to concern ourselves with is whether or not you'll live to testify to his evil in court."

"What do you mean? I thought you said I wasn't in danger from these bullet wounds—"

"You're not." McTeague looked grim as he went on, "But Gold is sure to find out that you're still alive and planning to testify against him. We'll issue warrants for his arrest and for Rainey's, but Gold is slippery, O'Quinn, and his organization is like a many-tentacled monster. He'll try to have you killed. He'll probably send Rainey himself after you."

Even though he was weak, O'Quinn clenched his hands into fists. "Let him," he growled. "I'd like another chance at Rainey."

McTeague shook his head. "No, no, we can't have that." He rubbed his chin thoughtfully. "We can keep your presence in this hospital secret for a few more days, until you're well enough to travel. But then we'll have to get you out of Chicago. Do you have any friends living some place far away from here where you might be able to hide out for a while?"

O'Quinn pondered for a moment, then said, "I've still got some family back in New York."

Once again McTeague shook his head. "No, Gold has too many contacts there. It would be too easy for him to locate you. We need some place more isolated."

The idea of hiding went against everything O'Quinn believed in, but he knew that McTeague was probably right. He thought for a moment more. "I do have a friend," he finally said, "a boxer I knew in New York. He doesn't live there anymore, gave up the prizefight game and moved away from the city."

McTeague nodded. "That sounds more like it. Who is this fellow, and where is he now?"

"His name is Leslie Gibson," O'Quinn growled, remembering the last time he had seen the man. "We went twenty hard and painful rounds in Gilmore's Garden one night before he knocked me out. The last I heard he had become a schoolteacher, of all things. Moved to some place in Kansas called Abilene."

# Chapter Two

AUTUMN WAS CERTAINLY AN EXCITING TIME OF YEAR, Leslie Gibson thought as he walked down Texas Street. School had started again, bringing both old and new students and all the same challenges. To Leslie, nothing was more fulfilling than seeing the light of understanding dawn in a child's eyes. It was definitely a better life than being battered in some smoky hall. He did not miss the prizefighting game at all.

The teacher stopped in front of the Northcraft Apothecary and frowned. He wondered why he had thought of his days as a professional slugger. He had put all that behind him months ago when he came to Abilene to begin his new career as a teacher, and everything that had happened to him since his arrival had reaffirmed his decision. He was at peace here, a peace he never would have found in the prize ring.

After school had been dismissed on this crisp autumn afternoon, Leslie decided to stroll down to the business district to pick up a few supplies. He had already stopped at Karatofsky's Great Western Store and was carrying his purchases in a small bundle under his arm. Now he was going to the drugstore to pick up some headache powders.

He would need them eventually, he knew, since he worked for Thurman Simpson, Abilene's thoroughly unpleasant schoolmaster. Simpson was the only blight on his happy existence in Kansas. There were times, Leslie mused, when a solid right hook to Simpson's jaw might be more effective than a headache powder.

Suddenly, high-pitched yelling coming from somewhere nearby snapped him out of his reflection. About a block away a small boy darted out from the narrow space between two buildings. The lad cast a frightened glance over his shoulder, lost his balance, and went sprawling in the dusty street.

At least a half-dozen boys, all of them larger, burst from the alley behind the smaller boy. Evidently they had been chasing him, and, now that their quarry lay in the dirt trying frantically to scramble away, they pounced on him.

Leslie watched, his eyes narrowing, as the largest boy in the group grabbed the small lad's shirt and, ripping the garment, hauled him to his feet. Shaking his captive like a rat, the leader of the gang said harshly, "So, you think you can laugh at me, do you, Burton?"

"H-honest, Roy, I never laughed at you!" the boy replied jerkily. "I never did!"

Leslie recognized the small boy as Avery Burton, one of his students. He knew the others, too. The leader was Roy Summers, and he was the worst bully the teacher had ever seen. Leslie was not surprised to see Roy and his toadies take pleasure in torturing someone younger and smaller.

Roy pushed Avery away. The boy bounced off one of the other members of the group, who also shoved him. For several moments the gang thrust Avery back and forth among them before Roy grabbed him again and pulled the lad to him.

"You ain't got nothin' to laugh about, Burton," Roy snarled, his face only inches from Avery's. "Your pa's a drunk, and your sister's a whore!"

Avery's already pale face became even more ashen. "Th-that's not true," he stammered timidly.

"Of course it is," Roy sneered. "Ever'body in town knows about your old man, and my big brother says your sister goes with anybody who's got a nickel! Now, are you callin' me a liar, Burton?"

"I . . . I . . ." Avery squirmed in Roy's grip, but his head was bent in defeat.

Roy spat in the boy's face. "You're nothin' but trash, just like the rest of your family. I reckon it's time somebody taught you that good and proper." He cocked his fist and drove it into Avery's stomach.

"That's enough!"

At the sound of the deep, rumbling voice Roy Summers jerked around. Leslie Gibson stepped off the boardwalk and strode toward the knot of boys. Roy swallowed, then abruptly released Avery's collar, and the boy slumped into the dirt. The gang scattered, no longer interested in tormenting Avery, but as he backed away, Roy called out to Avery, "I'll see you again sometime, Burton, when you ain't got the teacher to hide behind!"

The youngsters feared Leslie Gibson not only because he was their teacher, but also because he presented an imposing figure in the late afternoon sunlight.

Leslie Gibson stood several inches over six feet tall, and although he was dressed in a sober dark suit, it could not conceal the powerful shoulders, muscular arms, and narrow waist of a fighting man. His thick black hair was lightly touched with gray, and the short beard he wore gave him a grim, fierce look. Only in his blue eyes could the man's gentle nature be seen, and at times, even his gaze could be stormy and dangerous —as it certainly was at this moment.

Leslie had watched Roy and the other boys assaulting Avery longer than he should have, but he had been hoping the lad would stand up for himself. Leslie knew that fighting seldom solved anything, but it was not right to let someone ride roughshod over you, either. Even the insult to Avery's sister had not provoked much of a reaction from the boy.

Leslie bent, grasped Avery's arm, and lifted him to his feet. As he brushed the dirt off the lad's ripped shirt, he asked, "Are you all right, son?"

Avery wiped a shaking hand across his nose. Tears streaked the dust on his pale face. "I . . . I reckon so," he mumbled. "Thanks, Mr. Gibson. I thought they was going to kill me for sure this time."

"This time?" Leslie echoed, ignoring Avery's bad grammar. "Have Roy and his friends bothered you before, Avery?"

"Well . . . I guess they just like to hoo-raw folks a little. I've had a few run-ins with 'em since school started."

"I'm sorry to hear that. Why haven't you told Mr. Simpson or me that they were bothering you?"

Avery frowned at Leslie as if he could not believe what he had just heard. After a moment, he said, "I don't figure Mr. Simpson would care much. And if I told on 'em, Roy and the others'd hate me that much more. A feller's supposed to take care of his own fights out here, Mr. Gibson."

Leslie nodded. "So I've heard. But it didn't look like you were doing anything to stop them."

Avery dropped his head. "I ain't much of a fighter," he said softly.

"You *aren't* much of a fighter." This time Leslie corrected the boy's grammar.

"Shoot, that's what I just said," the boy muttered. Suddenly, he looked up at Leslie again and went on, "I've heard tell that you used to be one of them prizefighters back East, Mr. Gibson. Is that true?"

Leslie grimaced. He had purposely said very little about prizefighting since coming to Abilene, trying to put that part of his life behind him. But Orion McCarthy, the burly Scotsman who owned Orion's Tavern, had seen him fight several years earlier and told quite a few people about Leslie's background. It was inevitable that the students would hear about it.

"It's true," he told Avery now. "I fought in the prize rings for several years. But I gave all that up once I decided to become a teacher."

"You still know all about boxing, though, don't you?"

"I'm not sure I ever knew *all* about boxing," Leslie replied with a slight smile. His record included only a few more victories than defeats. He had been a good, solid boxer but never a contender for any titles.

"I'll bet you know enough to teach me how to fight," Avery said, his boyish enthusiasm growing by the second.

Leslie shook his head slowly. "I don't know about that, Avery—" he began.

33

"I just want some pointers," Avery cut in excitedly. "I hate it when Roy and the rest of them push me around, Mr. Gibson. I hate it."

Leslie could understand that. He rubbed his bearded jaw thoughtfully for a moment. "All right," he agreed. "I suppose I could show you a few things."

"Right now?"

"Well, I was about to do some more shopping."

"But I've got to get back to our farm by dark," Avery protested. "I've got our old mule to ride, but it'll take me a while."

Leslie shrugged. "All right, come on. There won't be time for much, but at least we can get started." He would get those headache powders another time, he decided.

With Avery bouncing happily at his side, Leslie walked to the small house he rented on South Second Street near the school. A scrubby tree grew in the front yard surrounded by a little grass. Leslie stepped onto the porch, placed his package on a chair that stood there, and took off his hat and coat. He put the hat on top of the bundle from Karatofsky's, then hung the coat over the back of the chair. As he rolled up his sleeves, he said to Avery, "The first thing you have to remember is that you don't want to fight."

"But I thought—"

Leslie shook his head. "If there's a way of solving a problem without your fists, always try that first. And if that doesn't work, you try to think of something else, and then something else. Fighting is only a last resort."

"You fought all the time, didn't you?"

"That was different. Prizefighting was my business, the way I made my living." Leslie hoped the boy could understand that distinction.

"But if you try ever' way you can think of and none of them work, what else can you do but fight?"

Leslie hesitated for a moment, then said, "If you've got to fight, then you have to be prepared to win. There's no point to it otherwise. That's why we're here." He put his hands on his hips and went on, "Now, let me see how you'd get ready to fight somebody like Roy."

He watched Avery ball up his fists and lift his arms awkwardly. The boy certainly did not look like a fighter, he thought. Avery was twelve years old, but he was small for his age. Dark brown hair framed his narrow face. As his teacher, Leslie knew the boy was intelligent, but he was definitely not imposing physically. Avery had developed muscles from his chores on the family farm, but Leslie could see the lad had no idea how to use them.

The teacher raised his big hand, the palm facing Avery. "Hit my hand," he ordered.

Avery frowned slightly. "You're sure?" Clearly the idea of trying to hit an adult, let alone his teacher, was foreign to him.

"I'm sure." Leslie nodded. "Go ahead."

Avery took a deep breath and swung his right fist toward Leslie's hand. Without seeming to move fast at all, Leslie slid his hand to the side so that Avery's blow missed badly. Thrown off-balance, the boy staggered.

"Try again," Leslie told him.

For several moments, they repeated the maneuver, and Avery continued to punch futilely at Leslie's hand. As they practiced, Leslie recalled what he knew about Avery Burton and his family. He knew the boy's mother was dead; she had passed away before Leslie came to Abilene. Charlie Burton, Avery's father, was indeed a drunk, just as the bully named Roy had said. Leslie had seen him stagger around town often enough to know that. There were also two daughters in the family, one younger than Avery named Nora, whom Leslie knew from school. The other girl was considerably older. While Leslie had seen her before, he did not know her. He had no idea if there was any truth in Roy's slurs concerning her virtue. Nevertheless, the boy had no right to say them.

"That's enough," Leslie said after another of Avery's punches sailed past its target. "You're just swinging at my hand as if it wasn't going to move. You're not thinking about what I'm going to do with it."

"You told me to hit it!" Avery protested.

"Watch where it goes when you try."

Avery swung again, then twice more, paying attention now to the way the teacher's hand moved easily out of the path of the blows. The boy took a deep breath, started to throw another punch, then suddenly altered its angle slightly. His fist grazed the side of Leslie's hand before the teacher could flick it away.

"Much better," Leslie observed encouragingly. "You've got to develop both a quick eye and quick hands. But most of all, you've got to think. The first step in outfighting a man is outthinking him."

As the sun sank toward the horizon, the man and the boy worked together in the front yard under the tree. This was teaching, too, Leslie Gibson thought, as important as spelling and geography and arithmetic. And in a town set on the frontier, what Avery Burton was learning now might mean more to him than any of those academic subjects.

\* \* \*

Seamus O'Quinn peered through the window of the passenger car and watched the Kansas plains roll by. He had never seen so much open space in his life. Just the sight of that much land with the blue sky looming over it made him slightly nervous.

Even though he had been born and raised in New York, he had not spent his entire life in cities. But neither was he accustomed to the vast openness of the frontier. He reflected on the journey thus far and realized he had not seen a building over two stories high since leaving Kansas City.

In the seat beside him, Inspector Jack McTeague was dozing, his derby tilted over his eyes. O'Quinn glanced at him and thought that the detective had relaxed considerably in the last few days. When they first left Chicago, McTeague was on edge constantly, always alert in case one of Darius Gold's henchmen tried to kill O'Quinn.

Now, however, they were evidently far enough away from Chicago for McTeague to believe they were safe. They had taken a roundabout route that required twice the time it would normally take to reach Abilene. At last they were on the final leg of their journey and would be pulling into the town in less than an hour.

North of the Kansas Pacific tracks were seemingly unending plains and gently rolling hills occasionally dotted with scrubby trees. Looking across the aisle and through the windows on the south side of the train, O'Quinn caught a glimpse of a line of bigger trees that marked the banks of the Smoky Hill River.

Every now and then he moved his right arm slightly to ease the sore muscles in his shoulder. Rainey's first bullet had punched through his body there, luckily

missing the bones. The shoulder was stiff, but
O'Quinn knew that would go away eventually. The
second slug had slammed into his side, causing him to
lose quite a bit of blood but once again missing
anything important. Bandages were still wrapped
around his middle, but they did not hamper his
movements too much.

During O'Quinn's stay in the Chicago hospital,
McTeague had watched over him like a mother hen.
The detective brought in a clerk to take down
O'Quinn's statement concerning the murders of Dooley Farnham and Melvin Rutherford. Then warrants
were issued for the arrest of Darius Gold and Mitch
Rainey. McTeague kept O'Quinn up to date on the
progress of the investigation, reporting the futile
attempts to locate Gold and Rainey so that they could
be taken into custody.

As soon as O'Quinn was strong enough to travel,
McTeague appointed himself O'Quinn's bodyguard,
and the two men left Chicago in great secrecy. No one
on the police force knew their ultimate destination.

Just before they left, McTeague received word that
Darius Gold had been picked up as he attempted to
leave town in a private carriage. O'Quinn thought that
was good news, but McTeague shook his head.

"Gold can pull just as many strings from inside the
city jail as he can when he's free," McTeague told him
bleakly. "And Rainey is still at large. As long as he's
on the loose, you're not out of danger, O'Quinn. We're
going through with our plan."

That was all right with O'Quinn. Once he had
reconciled himself to the idea of hiding out, he found
that he was looking forward to seeing Leslie Gibson
again. They had never been close friends, but they
shared the camaraderie of men in a hard, demanding

profession. O'Quinn respected Gibson, although it was beyond him why anyone would want to give up prizefighting to become a teacher.

Beside him, McTeague awoke from his nap, yawning and straightening up in the hard wooden seat. Blinking, he peered past O'Quinn out the window. "That looks like the same place we passed an hour ago," he observed.

"Everything out here seems to look the same," O'Quinn said. "I suppose you have to live with the land to be able to see its differences."

McTeague glanced at him through slitted eyes. "Waxing philosophical, are we?"

O'Quinn shrugged his heavy shoulders. "I'm just a dumb boxer, Inspector, but I like to look at things and think about them sometimes."

McTeague grunted. He twisted his head to look around the car, keeping an eye out for anything suspicious. But O'Quinn knew that all he would see were the usual travelers: immigrant families, businessmen, gamblers, prostitutes, and cowboys.

"Right now all I'm interested in seeing is this Abilene place," McTeague grumbled. "It seems like we've been riding one train or another for ages. I'm tired of breathing smoke and spitting out ashes. But it's better than ducking bullets, I suppose. And don't call me inspector. I'm your new manager, remember?"

O'Quinn nodded. "I think we'll be reaching Abilene soon. I hope Gibson is still there. We should have wired him we were coming."

McTeague shook his head. "I didn't want to take any chances that some telegraph operator might be working for Gold. I'd rather be too cautious than dead."

"I have to agree with that," O'Quinn admitted with a smile. Then he returned to watching the passing prairie and listening to the endless clatter of the train's wheels on the rails. A half hour later, the blue-uniformed conductor strolled down the aisle calling, "Abilene, five minutes! Five minutes to Abilene!"

O'Quinn leaned forward eagerly. Like McTeague, he was more than ready to end this journey. As the train rounded a bend, he saw the town still far down the tracks. At this distance, the only landmark that was clearly visible was the water tower at the depot, but as they drew closer, O'Quinn could make out some buildings and trees. Abilene appeared to be a sizable community.

The railroad tracks led through a large area of stockyards on the east side of town. According to a sign over one of the gates, the property belonged to the Great Western Cattle Company. The pens were not full at this time of year, but O'Quinn saw quite a few cattle—more than he had ever seen in one place before. McTeague, who had worked in the Chicago stockyards before joining the police force, identified some as Texas longhorns and others as Herefords. Most of them would be loaded onto eastbound trains to be shipped to the Chicago slaughterhouses. Looking at them more closely as the train passed, O'Quinn felt it was a shame to have to slaughter such handsome creatures, even though he enjoyed a good steak as much as the next man.

McTeague wrinkled his nose at the distinctive odor. "Smells like we're back in Chicago," he grumbled.

The train chugged slowly toward the station. Through the window on the north side of the tracks,

O'Quinn could see several tree-lined avenues. Neat, whitewashed houses gleamed in the autumn sun. As they neared the depot, the train slid past brick warehouses and a row of saloons and businesses that fronted on the street. Then the massive redbrick depot itself loomed into view. With a squeal of brakes, the locomotive came to a stop, leaving the cars next to the long platform.

"Here we are," McTeague declared, putting his hands on his knees and pushing himself to his feet. "Are you ready, O'Quinn?"

O'Quinn took a deep breath. Now that they had reached Abilene, he suddenly felt unaccountably nervous. It had been agreed that they would say nothing to anyone about the real reason they had come here, but O'Quinn doubted his ability to be convincing. McTeague had worked out a story to explain their presence and had gone over it with O'Quinn many times during the trip. *I'm a prizefighter, not some actor,* O'Quinn thought as he stood up.

"I guess I'm as ready as I'm going to be," he rumbled. Settling his derby on his head, he followed as McTeague started toward the door at the rear of the car.

Quite a few passengers were disembarking in Abilene, and O'Quinn and McTeague had to wait in line for a moment before they could approach the steps that led down to the station platform. McTeague was watchful, his hand near his pocket in case he had to reach for the little pistol concealed there. It was a .41 caliber Remington Number Four revolver, a weapon that packed considerable power despite its small size, and McTeague handled it with practiced ease.

At last the two men stepped off the train and turned

toward the baggage car, joining the crowd of passengers who had come to collect their bags and boxes. Again they had to wait, but after a few minutes they claimed their bags. McTeague led the way through the depot with its vaulted ceiling, and a moment later they got their first good look at Railroad Street.

On this bright autumn Saturday Abilene's dirt streets bustled with traffic. As they passed, buggies, wagons, and men on horseback raised a cloud of dust. Even though it was only the middle of the day, the hitchracks in front of the saloons across the street were lined with horses, and the establishments seemed to be doing a booming business. McTeague nodded toward them and suggested, "Why don't we wet our whistles first, then look for this friend of yours?"

"Sounds like a good idea to me," O'Quinn agreed. During the time he had been traveling with McTeague, he had discovered that the detective enjoyed an occasional drink. O'Quinn would not mind having a beer himself. The dusty air made a man thirsty. Dodging a wagon, they started across the busy street.

McTeague led the way, angling toward a place with a crudely painted sign above its doors that read: THE COWBOY'S REST SALOON. They stepped onto the boardwalk in front of the establishment and pushed through the batwing doors.

The interior of the Cowboy's Rest was very similar to the saloons and dives O'Quinn had known all over the East coast. The air was full of smoke, whiskey fumes, and raucous laughter. Several square wooden tables surrounded by chairs were scattered around the narrow, low-ceilinged room. In the dim light,

O'Quinn noticed that the occupants at three of the tables were playing poker. At the bar that ran along one wall stood quite a few men drinking beer or downing shots of liquor. A layer of sawdust covered the floor.

O'Quinn assessed the saloon's customers, judging their occupations by their attire. Most of them appeared to be cowboys wearing range clothes. A few others, dressed in coats and ties, were townsmen or travelers. No one seemed to be paying much attention to them. McTeague headed for the bar, and O'Quinn followed.

The bald-headed bartender, a soiled apron wrapped around his ample stomach, came over to them and nodded a greeting. "Howdy, gents," he said. "What can I get for you?"

"Two beers," McTeague grunted. "As cold as you've got."

"Sure." The barman drew the beers and slid them across the hardwood. "Here you go. That'll be a half-dollar."

McTeague dug in his pocket, drew out a coin, and flipped it to the bartender. O'Quinn picked up the mug of foaming liquid and took a long sip. The beer was just cool, not cold, but it went down smoothly.

McTeague drank from his mug and, licking the foam from his mustache, nodded his satisfaction.

The bartender poured drinks for some other customers, then drifted back to them. He leaned his elbows on the bar and said, "You gents just get off the train?"

"That's right," McTeague answered.

"Just passin' through?"

The man's curiosity seemed to spring more from

boredom than anything else. McTeague said, "I believe we'll be here a while. It all depends on how our business goes."

"And what business is that?"

"Ours," McTeague snapped.

The bartender shrugged. "Suit yourself, mister. I ain't nosy."

O'Quinn took another drink of his beer and then leaned forward. "Actually, you might be able to help us," he said, trying to counter McTeague's abrasiveness. "We're looking for a man named Leslie Gibson."

The bartender frowned. "Gibson . . . Gibson. Let me see. I don't recollect the name right off."

"He's supposed to teach school here. At least that's what he planned to do."

The bartender nodded abruptly. "Sure, I remember now. Say, it caused quite a stir when that fella showed up last year. We was all expectin' a gal—I mean a young lady, judgin' from the name and the fact that she—I mean he—was a teacher and all." The man threw back his head and laughed. "I hear ol' Thurman Simpson was fit to be tied."

"Who's Simpson?" McTeague asked.

"He's the schoolmaster. Likes runnin' everything his own way. I hear that him and that Gibson fella don't always get along too well."

O'Quinn could believe that. Leslie was capable of being strong-willed at times.

"Do you know where we could find Gibson?" O'Quinn asked.

The bartender considered again. After a moment, he suggested, "You might try Orion's Tavern over on Texas Street. Orion usually knows where most folks can be found around here. If he don't, there's always the marshal's office."

"Thanks," O'Quinn replied with a nod. He drained his mug as McTeague did the same. Then they picked up their bags and headed out of the saloon.

Texas Street was clearly Abilene's main thoroughfare; it was even busier than Railroad Street. Moving among women shopping or chatting, youngsters running and playing, and men loading wagons, they strolled along the boardwalk that fronted all the buildings and peered into shop windows on their way to Orion's Tavern.

As they passed the marshal's office, O'Quinn said, "Maybe it would be a good idea if we went in and talked to the local authorities, Inspec—Jack. You know, tell them who we are and why we're here. They might be able to help in case there's trouble."

McTeague snorted. "Bring in some bumbling frontier lawman who's not good for anything but locking up drunks and breaking up saloon fights? I don't think so, O'Quinn. From everything I've heard, the marshals and sheriffs out here aren't real lawmen. They're not much better than the criminals they arrest."

O'Quinn did not feel like arguing with the detective. He walked beside McTeague, taking in the sights. Diagonally across Texas Street from the marshal's office was a restaurant called the Sunrise Café. Colorful curtains adorned its sparkling windows, and it looked like the kind of establishment whose proprietors would serve a good meal in simple, clean surroundings. He had traveled so much during the last year with Dooley that he now made a habit of looking for good places to eat whenever they came into a town.

Tears stung his eyes; he quickly blinked them away. The pain had nothing to do with his bullet wounds. This was the pain of memory, hurt fueled by vivid images of Gold's thugs beating Dooley to death, just as they had killed Rutherford. O'Quinn hoped that when the time came he could watch Darius Gold hang.

McTeague spotted Orion's Tavern across the street in the next block. Once again, the men had to dodge wagons as they crossed Texas Street. The Grand Palace Hotel, which was a great deal seedier than its name indicated, stood in the middle of the block. Next to it was a small, well-kept house, set back from the boardwalk behind a tidy yard. Hanging from a lamppost set in the yard was a neatly lettered sign that read: DR. AILEEN BLOOM, PHYSICIAN. O'Quinn frowned and exclaimed, "They've got a woman doctor here!"

They had hoped Abilene would have a physician, in case O'Quinn's wounds needed any medical attention, but neither man had expected to find a woman doctor.

McTeague shook his head. "Maybe we'll be lucky and won't need any medical help. I wouldn't trust a frontier doctor to do much more than pry out a bullet, and that's probably all this woman is qualified to do."

O'Quinn hoped the Chicago policeman was right. He knew he would feel uncomfortable if he had to be examined by a female physician.

Next to Dr. Bloom's office was the long narrow building known as Orion's Tavern. The two men pushed through the batwing doors and found that the interior of the saloon was very similar to the Cowboy's Rest, from the sawdust on the floor to the shelves full of liquor bottles lining the wall behind the bar. There was a mirror on the backbar wall, though, which the other saloon did not have.

O'Quinn had to look twice at the backbar before he saw that it contained something besides bottled goods. A wooden perch was nestled among the liquor bottles, and on it sat a brilliant green parrot. The bird seemed to stare at them for a long moment with its beady black eyes before it suddenly screeched, "Dinna be daft, man! Dinna be daft!"

A brawny man whose muscles stretched the fabric of his dark shirt stood behind the bar. He turned toward the parrot and snapped, "Hush up, ye great feathered noo-sance. Tha' will be enough out o' ye." The man was a little below medium height, but the breadth of his burly shoulders made up for it. He had a tangle of reddish-gray hair and sported a majestic beard of the same hue. The authority with which he carried himself said that he was probably the proprietor of the tavern.

O'Quinn and McTeague went to the bar. The detective regarded the red-bearded man for a moment, then said, "You must be Orion."

"Aye." The man stuck a big hand across the bar toward them. "Orion McCarthy, at ye service, lads. Wha' kin I get f'ye?"

Before either of them could answer, the parrot squawked, "Enough grog t'choke a horse!"

Several of the tavern's customers laughed out loud. Orion waved at the bird and told the two newcomers, "Dinna mind Ol' Bailey there. Damned if I know where he comes up wi' all his nonsense. Now, ye were about to tell me wha' ye want t'drink?"

"Actually, we were looking for some information," McTeague replied as he shook Orion's hand. "We were told you might be able to tell us where to find a man named Leslie Gibson?"

"The slugger? Aye, I know where he might be found." Orion peered at them, his eyes narrowing slightly. "The lad's a friend o' mine, though. What be ye business wi' him?"

"We're not out to cause him trouble, I promise you," O'Quinn said. "He's an old friend of mine—"

He broke off as Orion suddenly pointed a finger at him. "Ye be a prizefighter!" the Scotsman exclaimed. "I thought ye looked familiar when ye came in! I saw ye take on Battlin' Billy Crawford four, no, five years ago. Wha' a fight tha' was! Ye was quite a fighter . . . f'an Irisher."

O'Quinn had to laugh. "Battling Billy gave me all I wanted, that's for sure," he declared.

"I'm sorry I kinna remember ye name, lad—"

"O'Quinn, Seamus O'Quinn."

Orion nodded enthusiastically. "O' course, tha' was it. Well, I want ye and ye friend t'have a drink on me, Mr. O'Quinn."

"Thanks," McTeague said, "but we're looking for Leslie Gibson."

Orion jerked his head toward the saloon's entrance. "Then ye be in luck. Here comes the lad now."

O'Quinn turned around and saw the man pushing through the batwings. Even though it had been several years since he had seen Leslie Gibson, O'Quinn recognized him immediately. Leslie's appearance had changed very little other than the simple, conservative suit he now wore. Grinning, O'Quinn strode toward him with his hand thrust out. "Hello, Slugger," he said.

Leslie stopped in his tracks, frowning for a moment

as he studied O'Quinn's face, then he cried, "O'Quinn? Is that you?"

"It certainly is!" O'Quinn grasped Leslie's hand and shook it firmly. Leslie reacted to the hard grip, returning it with an equal amount of power. O'Quinn's grin widened. "I see you haven't changed much."

"Neither have you," Leslie replied. "What are you doing in Abilene?"

McTeague appeared at O'Quinn's side, slapping him on the shoulder, taking care not to hit the injured one. "We're in training," he cut in before O'Quinn could reply. "Isn't that right, Seamus?"

"That's right," O'Quinn answered, recalling the story McTeague had prepared. "I've got a bout coming up, and Jack and I figured it might be a good idea to get away from the city while I trained. Jack thought it might be easier for me to keep my mind on the work." He nodded to McTeague. "By the way, this is my new manager, Jack McTeague."

The teacher shook hands with him. "Glad to meet you, Mr. McTeague," he said. Looking back at O'Quinn, he went on, "I thought I remembered reading that Dooley Farnham was handling you now."

O'Quinn's jaw tightened, and a small cheek muscle began to jump. But he forced himself to relax and said, "Dooley passed away not long ago, Leslie. I don't suppose you heard about it, all the way out here on the frontier."

Leslie shook his head and grimaced. "No, I didn't know," he said solemnly. "We don't get much boxing news out here. I'm sorry to hear about it. Dooley was a good man."

"That he was," McTeague intoned mournfully.

For a moment, all three men were silent. Then Leslie broke the silence by saying, "You said you have a bout coming up, Seamus. Is it a big one?"

O'Quinn nodded. "The biggest one of my life," he replied. And that was no lie, he added to himself. Staying alive to testify against Darius Gold and Mitch Rainey would be the most important thing he would ever do.

Orion had come from behind the bar and was listening to the conversation. Now he announced, "Leslie here is the perennial challenger f'me arm-wrestling champeenship. Would ye care t'watch this week's match, Mr. O'Quinn?"

O'Quinn cocked an eyebrow at the burly saloon-keeper. "Is there any wagering allowed, Mr. McCarthy?"

"Call me Orion. And if there was no wagering, 'twould not be much point t' the match, would there now?"

"Then I'll bet a round of drinks on Leslie," O'Quinn declared.

"F'the house?" Orion asked.

"Why not?" O'Quinn saw the warning look in McTeague's eyes as he responded to Orion's challenge. McTeague had cautioned him about drawing too much attention to himself. But for the first time in weeks, O'Quinn felt really alive. He was enjoying this reunion with Leslie Gibson, and he sensed that in Orion McCarthy he had found a kindred spirit.

"'Tis a bet!" Orion responded. Grinning broadly, the Scotsman began rolling up his sleeve.

# Chapter Three

———◆———

SPECTATORS AWAITING THE START OF THE ARM-
wrestling match were cheering so loudly that even
more men were drawn into Orion's Tavern from Texas
Street. Cowboys, townsmen, and railroad workers
crowded around the table where Orion McCarthy and
Leslie Gibson were seated. Bets flew through the air
along with laughter and jeers. In the forefront of the
crowd were Seamus O'Quinn and Jack McTeague.

O'Quinn was grinning broadly, while McTeague
still looked worried, but both men were engrossed in
the spectacle that was about to take place. As the two
participants in the match locked hands at the center of
the table, a silence fell over the room, broken only by
an occasional shrill piece of gibberish from Old Bailey, the parrot.

Orion glanced up at O'Quinn. "Start us, will ye, Mr.
O'Quinn?"

"Sure," O'Quinn replied. He looked at each man and asked if he were ready. After both nodded in affirmation, he paused, then suddenly slapped the table sharply. Orion and Leslie pitted their weight and strength against each other, concentrating all the power they commanded in their brawny arms.

As the spectators yelled their encouragement to the two men O'Quinn joined in the shouting. He glanced over at McTeague and saw that the detective was not participating in the excitement. McTeague was scanning the room, his eyes darting around the group looking for any sign that someone might want to hurt O'Quinn. The relaxation that had seemed to finally settle over the Chicago policeman while they were on the train had vanished.

O'Quinn realized that he was more exposed here than he had been during the journey and that it was harder to keep track of everyone around them. In the future, he decided, he would try to cooperate more with McTeague and avoid situations like this one. Being in the middle of a crowd was probably the worst thing he could do right now.

The batwings at the tavern's entrance swung open, and two men strolled in, drawn like everyone else by the cheering spectators at the weekly arm-wrestling contest. Something about them, however, made Seamus pause to examine them. The easy way they carried themselves spoke of their quiet confidence in their abilities, but the attitude did not edge over into arrogance. It was the same sort of bearing the best of champions possessed.

The older of the two men was in his forties and was dressed in a dark suit and a brown vest. A broad-brimmed, flat-crowned black hat sat squarely on his thick sandy hair, and a heavy mustache drooped past the corners of his wide mouth. Around his lean waist was a shell belt; a walnut-butted Colt rode neatly in its holster. As he ambled closer to the crowd, O'Quinn saw the star pinned to his vest, just under the lapel of his coat.

The man's companion wore a dusty brown Stetson pushed back on a thatch of black hair. He was probably about twenty years younger than the lawman, but his dark, watchful eyes showed that he had packed a lot of living into that relatively short span. His denims, work shirt, and scuffed boots made him look like a ranch hand, as did the bright bandanna tied around his neck. But he was no simple cowboy; the badge pinned on his shirt and the twin Colts in tied-down holsters at his hips told that eloquently.

The two men glanced through the crowd at the straining, sweating, red-faced combatants at the table, then turned and went to the bar. Evidently they were accustomed to seeing matches like this. As they ordered drinks from the gangly, aproned youth who had taken Orion's place behind the bar, O'Quinn turned his attention back to the arm-wrestling.

Orion had Leslie Gibson's arm bent far over. Leslie was struggling valiantly to keep his hand from touching the tabletop, but barring a dramatic turnaround, it was a matter of time—probably only moments—before Orion won. The muscles in the teacher's shoulders bunched and rippled as he channeled all of his remaining strength into one last effort. For a few seconds, he was able to force Orion's arm back up several inches, but that was all he could do. Orion grunted as he overcame Leslie's final attempt and slowly forced his opponent's hand back down. A shout went up as Leslie's knuckles grazed the table.

Leslie relaxed, letting his arm fall limp. With a

beaming smile on his bearded face, Orion raised both hands and locked them together over his head as he stood up.

"Winner and still champeen!" he proclaimed. As the men who had bet on him crowded around and slapped him on the back in congratulations, Orion turned toward O'Quinn and went on, "I believe ye said something about a round o' drinks, Mr. O'Quinn?"

O'Quinn joined in the laughter and reached out to shake Orion's hand. "I sure did," he replied. "Set 'em up!"

Orion headed for the bar, still surrounded by his admirers. Leslie remained seated at the table, massaging his reddened hand. He grinned ruefully at O'Quinn. "Guess I cost you some money," he said. "Maybe if you're still around next week, you can win it back."

"You do this every week?" O'Quinn asked.

"When I have time. It helps keep me in shape. Besides, I've beaten him a couple of times. He just keeps winning the so-called title back the next week."

O'Quinn slapped his friend on the shoulder. "Well, it looked like you gave him a good run for it. Come on, I imagine you could use a drink yourself, and since I'm paying for them . . ."

"I won't turn that down," Leslie grinned.

McTeague had said nothing during the match or its aftermath, but now he spoke quietly to O'Quinn. His voice was insistent enough to cut through the clamor in the room. "We have to see about finding a place to stay, Seamus. Don't forget that."

O'Quinn nodded. "I know, Jack, I know. We won't stay long, just to have that drink. If I'm going to be paying as much as I am, I want to sample some of Mr. McCarthy's whiskey myself."

"You'll find it's the best in Abilene," Leslie said as he shrugged into his coat. Together, the three men turned toward the bar and made their way through the crowd of people. When they reached the hardwood, they found themselves standing next to the two men O'Quinn had seen enter the tavern during the match.

The older man glanced over at them with the keenly appraising gaze of a lawman. He nodded and said simply, "Hello, gents."

His young companion leaned past him and said to Leslie, "That was a good fight you put up. Maybe you'll take Orion again next time."

The parrot squawked, "Dinna be daft!"

Leslie laughed. "Old Bailey doesn't sound convinced of that, Cody," he chortled.

Orion had gone behind the bar to help his assistant pour the drinks O'Quinn would be paying for. Now he made his way down to stand in front of the little group. "Did ye see the match today, Lucas?" he asked.

The older lawman nodded. "I saw enough of it, Orion."

Leslie leaned in from the other side. "Seamus, I want you to meet our marshal. This is Luke Travis. Marshal, this is an old friend of mine, Seamus O'Quinn."

Marshal Luke Travis extended his hand to O'Quinn. "Pleased to meet you, Mr. O'Quinn. From the looks of you, I'd say you used to be in the prizefighting business, too."

"Still am, Marshal," O'Quinn replied as he shook Travis's hand. "I've come to Abilene to train for a match of my own. I don't think it'll be as entertaining as the one I just saw, though."

Travis smiled. "Around here, Orion and Leslie are famous for their contests." He inclined his head toward his companion. "This is my deputy, Cody Fisher."

"And this is my manager, Jack McTeague," O'Quinn indicated, continuing the introductions.

When they had all shaken hands, Travis asked, "Well, Mr. McTeague, what do you think of Abilene so far?"

"I suppose it's all right, as far as frontier towns go," the detective replied.

"Shoot, this isn't hardly the frontier anymore," Cody told him. "It's downright civilized."

"That's right," Leslie added dryly. "It's been months since the last Indian attack, hasn't it, Cody?"

The deputy grinned and went back to his beer without responding.

Travis drained his mug and then said, "If there's anything we can help you with while you're here, just let us know. Nice meeting both of you." He turned to Cody and went on, "I'll head back to the office."

Cody nodded. "I'll be in later."

Travis left the tavern with a casual wave to the others. The place had settled down considerably now that the arm-wrestling contest was over, and the crowd began to thin out as people left the tavern to attend to their Saturday errands.

O'Quinn turned to Leslie and asked, "What's the best place to stay around here?"

"If I had the room, I'd ask you to stay with me," Leslie replied. "I'm just renting a small house, though."

"I don't want to put you out. A hotel will do fine for us."

"The Drover's Cottage has good accommodations,

but it's pretty close to the stockyards, as you can imagine. Other than that, there's always the Grand Palace. It's close by, and it's actually nicer than it looks. There are several rooming houses down on South Second Street, too."

McTeague spoke up for the first time in several minutes. "We'll also need a place to conduct our training sessions. Some place where we won't be disturbed."

"I imagine one of the livery stables would be glad to let you rent some space. With the doors closed, that ought to be private enough."

McTeague nodded. "Come on, Seamus. You'd better pay for those drinks, and we'll get started looking around."

"Sure. How much do I owe you, Orion?" O'Quinn asked the saloonkeeper.

Orion screwed up his face in thought for a moment. "Twenty dollars will cover it, lad," he finally said.

O'Quinn was surprised; he had been expecting Orion to ask for at least fifty dollars, considering the number of men who had been in the tavern when the match was over. But evidently Orion's victory made him feel generous, and O'Quinn did not mind accepting the rare generosity of a Scotsman. He pulled a double eagle from his pocket and slid it across the hardwood to Orion. "And it was well worth it," he said with a grin.

Orion scooped up the money, bit it out of habit, then returned the grin and said, "Thank ye, lad. I trust we'll be seeing ye again?"

"You can count on it," O'Quinn promised him.

Leslie put a hand on O'Quinn's shoulder. "Come on," he said. "I'll show you around town and make sure you don't get lost in this big city."

"I'm not sure if you're joking or not," O'Quinn grunted, "but I know that if I got out of town, I would get lost. I never saw so much flat land in my life."

Together, O'Quinn, Leslie, and McTeague strolled out of the tavern. They went down the boardwalk, past the Grand Palace Hotel. McTeague studied the establishment for a moment, then said, "I think we'd prefer one of those boardinghouses you mentioned, Mr. Gibson."

"Make it Leslie," the teacher replied. "Come on. I'll take you over to Hettie's. When I first came to Abilene, I stayed there until I found a house to rent. The rooms are clean, and Hettie Wilburn sets a mighty good table."

O'Quinn grinned. "Lead on, Slugger."

A grimace pulled at Leslie's mouth. "I try not to use that old nickname too much around here," he said. "Most of the folks in town know I used to be a fighter, but I'm trying to get them to look upon me as a schoolteacher, not an ex-boxer."

"Sure," O'Quinn agreed with a nod. "I understand. Don't worry about a thing, Leslie. We're not here to cause trouble for anybody, are we, Jack?"

McTeague shook his head. "Peace and quiet, that's what we're after."

Just as Leslie Gibson had said, the rooms in Hettie Wilburn's house were clean—scrupulously clean, in fact. O'Quinn looked at the starched spread on the bed, the hooked rug on the floor, the lace doily on the dresser, and the chintz curtains on the windows and reflected that this was just about the most wholesome place he had ever seen. It was a far cry from some of the flophouses where he had stayed in leaner times.

They were in luck. The widow Wilburn had two vacant rooms that were even next door to each other, which was more than either O'Quinn or McTeague had expected. Maybe that was a good sign, O'Quinn thought. Since leaving Chicago, they had been very lucky, and maybe that good fortune would hold until they returned to see that Darius Gold and Mitch Rainey were brought to justice.

Leslie had left them to get settled in, but before he went he made O'Quinn promise that they would have dinner together at the Sunrise Café.

As O'Quinn finished stowing his clothes in the dresser, the door opened and Jack McTeague stepped in. The inspector went over to the window and pulled the curtain aside to study the view. They were on the second floor of the rooming house, which was located at the corner of South Second and Buckeye. Across the street were private residences, and although Abilene's business district and the courthouse were only a couple of blocks away, the neighborhood seemed to be fairly quiet. That suited McTeague just fine.

"I don't think anybody's going to take a shot at you through this window," he grunted, "but try to stay away from it as much as you can after dark."

O'Quinn nodded. "I don't think we have anything to worry about, Jack. Gold's men won't be able to trace us all the way out here."

"You start thinking like that, and you'll wind up dead," McTeague said harshly. "Keep assuming that the worst is going to happen and maybe you'll stay alive."

O'Quinn shrugged. There was no point in arguing with McTeague; he realized that already, even though he had not known the policeman for long. He remarked, "Those two lawmen didn't strike me as being the kind of rascals you said they probably would be."

In fact, O'Quinn added to himself, Luke Travis and Cody Fisher appeared to be as thoroughly professional as any of the police O'Quinn had met back East, including Inspector Jack McTeague. He had not seen them in action, of course; then it might be an entirely different story.

"They seemed all right," McTeague admitted grudgingly. "From the way that deputy was carrying his guns, he struck me as a bit of a show-off. Marshal Travis looked reliable, though." He put his hand on his pocket where his pistol was concealed. "As long as they don't get in my way, I won't worry about them. I don't need their help, and maybe they're honest enough that whoever Gold sends after us won't be able to buy them. But I'm damned if I'm going to rely on some frontier lawman for anything."

Both men had finished unpacking, and it was still an hour or so before they were supposed to meet Leslie for supper. O'Quinn reached up with his left hand and gingerly rubbed his wounded right shoulder. "I'm pretty tired, Jack, and these bullet holes are hurting a little bit. I think I'll stretch out for a while."

"That's a good idea," McTeague conceded. "I'll come back later and get you when it's time to meet your friend." He went to the door and ordered, "Be sure to lock this behind me."

"All right," O'Quinn replied. He waited until McTeague had left the room, then turned the key so that the detective could hear him locking the door.

The bed was as comfortable as it looked, he discovered when he lay down on it. Sleep came surprisingly quickly, but it was not a restful slumber. It seldom was these days.

Too many dreams raced through Seamus O'Quinn's slumber, dreams of violence and blood and death.

When Jack McTeague and Seamus O'Quinn reached the Sunrise Café, they found Leslie Gibson waiting for them on the boardwalk. He led them inside to a table near the large front windows. As they sat down, McTeague skillfully maneuvered things so that Leslie was seated with his back to the window. That way McTeague could keep an eye on the boardwalk through the glass.

The red-and-white checked cloth covering the table and the delicious aromas coming from the kitchen gave the place a homey feel. O'Quinn brightened as a pretty, young, redheaded waitress came up to the table and said, "Hello, Mr. Gibson. What can I get for you tonight?"

"Hello, Agnes," Leslie replied. He glanced at O'Quinn and McTeague and asked, "Why don't I order for all three of us?"

"By all means," McTeague answered.

"We'll have three of the specials," Leslie said, nodding to the menu that was written in chalk on a board over the counter. The evening's special was ham, sweet potatoes, greens, and deep-dish apple pie.

"Three specials," Agnes replied with a nod. Smiling at the men, she turned to go back to the kitchen and convey the order to the cook.

"Nice-looking girl," O'Quinn commented. "She must be an Irish lass, with that red hair."

"Her name is Agnes Hirsch," Leslie explained. "She and her brother Michael came to Abilene last year with a group of orphans. They were brought by a Dominican nun who established an orphanage here. That was before I arrived, but Mr. Simpson told me all about it." Leslie smiled. "In fact, that orphanage is one reason the town council decided to hire another teacher, that and the arrival of quite a few settlers from the South. There were just too many children for one teacher to handle."

"So you took the job." O'Quinn nodded. "I had heard that you'd given up the ring and gone to college to become a teacher. Didn't believe it at first, not when I thought about that right cross of yours. Seemed like a waste."

"I'm much happier doing this than I ever was boxing," Leslie said sincerely. "I think this is what I was meant to do all along—"

He broke off abruptly as he saw the way McTeague stiffened. McTeague was staring at the doorway, and when Leslie glanced over his shoulder, he saw a clean-cut, earnest-faced young man coming toward them, carrying his hat in his hand.

McTeague rested his hand on the butt of the pistol in his pocket. The young man did not look threatening, but if he was a killer that was probably the edge he counted on.

"H-Hello, M-Mr. Gibson," the young man stammered a little nervously as he approached the table. "I-I heard there were some friends of yours in town."

"That's right," Leslie replied. "O'Quinn, Mr. McTeague, this is Emmett Valentine. Emmett's a reporter for the *Abilene Clarion*."

"And you're Seamus O'Quinn, the Irish heavyweight," Emmett Valentine said excitedly, holding out his hand to the prizefighter. "This is an honor, sir, and a privilege. I heard that you've come to our fair town to train for a bout, and I'd like to do a story about your visit to Abilene if I might."

Before O'Quinn could say anything, McTeague shook his head sharply. "No," he snapped. "No interviews, no story. I'm sorry, son, but Mr. O'Quinn has a great deal of work to do, and we don't need the distraction."

Emmett looked at O'Quinn. "Are you sure of that, sir?"

O'Quinn shrugged. "Jack is my manager, Mr. Valentine. A good fighter always does what his manager tells him."

The young man looked crestfallen. "Oh. Well, if you're sure . . ."

"We're sure," McTeague asserted.

"In that case, it was nice meeting you, Mr. O'Quinn. I've read about your fights, but I never expected to see you in Abilene."

"I guess you never know who'll turn up, son," O'Quinn said kindly, trying to take some of the sting out of the rejection.

"Enjoy your dinner, gentlemen," Emmett mumbled, and he nodded and backed away.

Leslie frowned as he watched the young reporter leave the café. He had not known that Emmett was planning to approach O'Quinn, but McTeague's refusal to have a story written for the newspaper was surprising. Leslie had been part of the fight game long enough to know publicity was vitally important. Boxing matches were still illegal in most states, but they went on all the time as tolerant authorities looked the other way. To the common man, prizefighters were heroes, and many of them worked hard to build up that image. Leslie found McTeague's curt behavior and O'Quinn's acceptance of it downright strange.

But before he could comment, Agnes appeared

carrying platters piled high with steaming food. With a cheery smile, she placed the dishes in front of them, and delicious aromas filled their nostrils.

If this appetizing meal was any indication, O'Quinn thought, his visit to Abilene was getting off to a grand start.

The restaurant was one of the finest in Chicago. Crystal chandeliers, heavy and ornate, diffused their glow on the sparkling silver and china on the tables below. Elegant men and women in expensive evening dress were dining at those tables. The murmur of softly-spoken conversation and an occasional polite laugh filled the air; delightful scents emanated from the kitchen.

At one of the tables sat a handsome young man and a stunning woman—a girl, really—who gazed at her companion with adoring eyes. This was the first time they had dined together, and she counted herself lucky to be with such a charming man. Obviously he was wealthy, or he would not have chosen this restaurant for their meal.

The man glanced up, a look of annoyance crossing his face as a waiter approached and bent over to whisper something to him. He gave a curt nod, slipped the man a coin, then turned to the young woman and said, "I'm sorry, darling, but I have to step out for a moment. Something about an urgent message, but I'll wager it's really nothing."

She smiled at him and said softly, "Hurry back."

"Oh, I will. You can count on that." He pushed his chair back and followed the waiter out of the dining room, his face becoming more annoyed with every step. Considering the way he hoped this evening would conclude, this message had better be important, he thought.

In the lobby of the restaurant he found a blue-uniformed policeman waiting for him.

The man's face tightened for a moment until he recognized the officer. Then he hurried forward and rasped, "What is it?"

The policeman spoke quickly, in a low-pitched voice that could not be overheard. The young man paled as he listened to the message. Then he nodded again and demanded, "How soon?"

"Any minute now, sir," the officer answered. "I've got to get out of here. I can't risk being seen—"

"I know. Go on." The man threw a glance back at the dining room as the policeman hurried out of the building. It was a shame to desert a young lady of such . . . potential, but there was nothing else he could do. He summoned the waiter who had brought him the message, pressed a bill into his hand, and then ducked outside without bothering to get his hat and cape.

As he stepped onto the sidewalk, the clatter of hoofbeats on the cobblestoned street made him jerk his head around. He saw a police wagon turning into the avenue a block away. The officer driving the wagon spotted him standing in the glow of the restaurant's lamp, let out a cry, and whipped his team to greater speed.

The man turned and dashed toward the mouth of a nearby alley. A gun blasted somewhere behind him, but the bullet came nowhere near him as he darted into the welcome shadows of the alley.

His pulse pounded in his head. At first he had not believed the warning that the police were closing in on him, that they were going to charge him with murder. It was insane!

But it appeared to be true. They would have his apartment covered; he would not even be able to go back there and pack a valise. He would have to flee with only the clothes on his back—and the small, deadly gun tucked under his coat. That would be enough.

Mitch Rainey's lips pulled back from his teeth in a grimace as he ran through the night. Someone was going to pay for this—going to pay in blood.

# Chapter Four

———⊷———

THE NEXT FEW DAYS PASSED QUIETLY, AND SEAMUS O'Quinn had to admit that Jack McTeague's idea of getting him out of Chicago was starting to look like a good one. The town's initial curiosity about them died down fairly quickly, and they were left to carry out their masquerade in peace.

As Leslie had suggested, McTeague rented one of the local stables for several hours in the middle of each day. Wearing tight trousers and a loose shirt that concealed his bandages, O'Quinn accompanied McTeague to the barn. With the doors closed and the horses in the stable as the only witnesses, the two men hung a burlap bag filled with sand from one of the rafters. They would leave it there to convince anyone who bothered to look that O'Quinn had been using it as a punching bag. That done, the detective proceeded to light his pipe and relax on a chair left by the stable's owner.

O'Quinn wandered around the stable, looking at the horses. He had never been an animal lover, but during that first day he found that several of them were gentle creatures, and he befriended them. Others snorted and bared their teeth at him. He quickly backed away.

By the second day, boredom had set in. McTeague had brought a copy of the *Abilene Clarion* under his coat. O'Quinn watched him reading it for a few minutes, then strolled over to the sandbag. Idly he tapped it lightly with a fist, but the heavy bag did not budge. O'Quinn drew back and hit it again, harder this time. Then, instinct taking over, he whipped a left hook into it. This time the bag shivered satisfactorily.

"Here now," McTeague scolded, looking up from his newspaper with a frown. "You don't have to do that, O'Quinn. This whole business is only for show, you know."

"I know," O'Quinn replied. Cocking his right fist, he drove a straight jab into the bag. The impact felt good until it reached his shoulder, where he felt a slight twinge of pain. Still, most of the stiffness had gone, and he was not worried about opening the wound. "I need the workout, Jack. I'm getting soft, just sitting around."

"What you need is to take care of yourself until it's time for Gold's trial, mister," McTeague snapped. "I don't want you starting more trouble with those bullet holes."

"Don't worry," O'Quinn assured him. He began to dance lightly around the bag, his hands up in the boxing style he used. Darting forward, he peppered the bag with his left. "I'll be careful. I just need to be doing something again."

McTeague snorted and went back to reading his paper, but he kept sneaking disapproving glances around it as O'Quinn sparred with the sandbag.

O'Quinn was sore the next morning when he climbed out of bed. Even though he had been inactive for only a few weeks, it had been long enough for him to get out of shape. But it was a good soreness, and he decided to continue working out. When he and McTeague went to the stable that afternoon, he found an old lariat in one of the stalls and fashioned a jump rope out of it.

"Got to get my wind back," he explained to the scowling policeman.

"Hmmmph!" was McTeague's only response.

That evening, tired and aching, O'Quinn felt better than he had since the deadly encounter in Chicago with Darius Gold and Mitch Rainey. He stood before the mirror in his room at Hettie Wilburn's and unwound the bandages from his shoulder and torso. When the wounds were uncovered, he saw that scar tissue had formed, leaving the skin reddish and somewhat sore-looking, but he was very pleased. He would leave the bandages off from now on, he decided.

Someone rapped lightly on the door. O'Quinn made no reply, following McTeague's instructions, and a moment later the detective called softly, "It's me, O'Quinn."

O'Quinn went to the door and unlocked it. McTeague slipped into the room, stopped short when he saw that O'Quinn had taken the bandages off, and stared. "Are you sure that's a good idea?" he asked.

"I think it is," O'Quinn declared. "I'm tired of

acting like an invalid, Jack. Rainey came damned close to making me one, but not close enough. I'm alive, and I want to act like it again."

McTeague took a deep breath, preparing to say something, then shook his head instead. Finally he said, "All right, but just be careful, O'Quinn. After all we've been through, I don't want anything happening to my star witness."

O'Quinn grimaced. "Sorry, Jack," he said coldly. "I suppose I thought I was your friend now, not just your star witness.'" He started to turn away.

McTeague reached out and grasped O'Quinn's arm. "Dammit, O'Quinn, don't talk to me like that!" he snapped. "I'm just trying to keep you alive—"

"Until I can testify against Gold and Rainey," O'Quinn shot back.

"Yes. Until you can testify."

"Fine. Just so we both know where we stand."

McTeague made no reply. He walked over to the window, pushed the curtains aside slightly so that he could look out. Night was falling, cloaking the streets in shadows. McTeague's keen eyes searched the gloom, looking for anything unusual, anything that might be potentially threatening.

When he turned around a few moments later, O'Quinn had donned a shirt and was shrugging into his coat. "Where do you think you're going?" McTeague asked sharply. Both men had already eaten supper downstairs at Hettie's table.

"Thought I'd go over to Orion's for a drink," O'Quinn answered. "Maybe I'll hunt up Leslie and talk to him for a while. I was wondering if he'd like to spar a little with me while I'm here."

"I'm not sure that's a good idea."

"Going to Orion's or sparring?"

"Either one," McTeague snapped. "I don't like you going out at night, and if you mix it up with Gibson, he's liable to notice that you've been hurt. That could lead to some awkward questions."

"Leslie Gibson is no threat," O'Quinn declared flatly. "I still think we're making a mistake by not taking him into our confidence, him and that marshal both."

"We don't need their help."

O'Quinn laughed humorlessly. "I just hope you're right, Jack." He started toward the door.

"Hold on." McTeague sighed. "If you're determined to do this, at least let me come with you." Out of habit, he slipped his hand in his pocket and touched the butt of the Remington. The gun was there, as it always was.

The two men walked one block north to Texas Street, turning left when they reached the busy avenue. The saloons were doing their usual busy trade. Music and laughter floated out of the Alamo, the Bull's Head, the O. K., the Pioneer. Several of the mercantile stores were still open, their evening business brisk. The street was well lit by the yellow lantern light that washed out of the businesses lining it. Wagons rolled by, along with quite a few men on horseback.

O'Quinn glanced across the street as he and McTeague strolled along the boardwalk. He spotted Luke Travis leaning against one of the posts that supported the awning over the walkway. The marshal lifted a hand in greeting, and O'Quinn returned the wave. Quietly he said to McTeague, "It looks like Travis keeps a pretty close eye on his town."

"Perhaps," McTeague replied, obviously unwilling to share O'Quinn's confidence in Abilene's lawman.

As they passed the Sunrise Café, O'Quinn saw Leslie Gibson walking toward them. At Leslie's side, was a much smaller man with thinning hair and a narrow face that was screwed into a pinched, sour expression. Leslie spotted the two visitors from Chicago at the same time and grinned.

"Hello, Seamus, Mr. McTeague," he said warmly as the four men met on the boardwalk at the corner of Texas and Mulberry. "It's a pleasant evening, isn't it?"

O'Quinn smiled. "It will be as soon as I get some of Orion's good whiskey in me," he replied. "Who's your friend?"

Leslie glanced down at the scowling man, who had begun to tap his foot impatiently. "Ah, this is Thurman Simpson, Seamus. Mr. Simpson is Abilene's other schoolteacher."

"Schoolmaster," Thurman Simpson corrected. "I've been in charge of the school here for several years." His pale eyes played over O'Quinn and were evidently not very impressed with what they saw. "And you must be the pugilist I've heard about, sir."

"That I am." O'Quinn extended a hand to Simpson. "Seamus O'Quinn, at your service."

Simpson's hand felt like a lump of biscuit dough as O'Quinn pressed it. The schoolmaster said, "No offense, Mr. O'Quinn, but I've always considered pugilism the most barbaric of pastimes."

"Oh, no offense, Mr. Simpson. 'Tis indeed barbaric. That's why the people enjoy it so much."

Simpson sniffed. "The hoi polloi must have their spectacles. Bread and circuses, you know."

O'Quinn nodded solemnly. "Exactly," he said, wondering what the devil Simpson was talking about. "Bread and circuses, that's just what I was thinking."

McTeague glanced around nervously, unhappy that they were standing out in plain sight on a street corner. He said to O'Quinn, "We'd better go on if we're going to get that drink. And just one, Seamus; remember you're in training."

"You're not likely to let me forget, are you, Jack? Mr. Simpson, this is my manager, Jack McTeague."

Simpson and McTeague nodded at each other, neither man offering to shake hands. Leslie said, "We'd better get going, too, Mr. Simpson, if we're going to be on time for the meeting." To O'Quinn, he explained, "We're going to a town council meeting. They're going to discuss how much money will be allocated to the school this year. I don't suppose you'd like to come along?"

O'Quinn laughed. "I'm afraid we'd be out of place at such a meeting, Leslie. But come on down to Orion's afterward and I'll buy you a drink. You, too, Mr. Simpson."

Simpson sniffed. "I don't drink."

That came as no surprise to O'Quinn. He slapped Leslie on the shoulder as they moved on. "Good luck," he said. "Get as much money as you can out of them."

Leslie grinned. "We'll try."

O'Quinn and McTeague continued down the street toward Orion's. As they passed the doctor's office, O'Quinn noticed a young woman stepping through the front door of the house. In the light of a lantern on the porch he saw she was a young, attractive brunette and wondered if she was the doctor. He would have thought that a doctor, even a woman doctor, would be older. The sight of her strengthened his resolve not to seek any medical attention unless it was absolutely necessary.

The bar at Orion's was full, O'Quinn saw as he and McTeague pushed through the batwings, but several of the tables were vacant. They took one of them. O'Quinn caught Orion's eye behind the bar and held up two fingers. The burly Scotsman nodded and a few moments later came over to their table carrying a tray that held two glasses and a bottle.

"How be ye this fine evening, Seamus?" he asked as he placed the tray on the table.

"Just fine," O'Quinn replied. "And yourself?"

Before Orion could answer, McTeague gestured toward the bottle and said, "We won't need that. We just want one drink apiece."

Orion nodded. "All right. I recall now tha' ye be in training, Seamus. Kinna be drinking too much, eh? And I'm doing just superlatively, to answer ye question."

Grinning, O'Quinn picked up the bottle and splashed generous amounts of the amber liquor into each of the glasses. McTeague had said one drink, but he had not mentioned anything about its size. O'Quinn set down the bottle, raised his glass, and said, "Here's to you, Mr. McCarthy . . . even if you are a bagpipe-player."

Orion threw back his head and laughed. "Remember, I've seen ye fight," he chortled. "I know ye be an Irisher 'cause I recall how many blows t'the head ye took. 'Tis easier when ye dinna have t'think t'start wi', ain't it?"

O'Quinn joined in the laughter. Despite the differences in their heritage, both men were a good deal alike and knew it.

As O'Quinn drank his whiskey, a speculative look came into Orion's eyes. He ventured, "I don't suppose ye'd care t'try ye luck this Saturday, would ye?"

"You mean in the arm-wrestling contest?"

McTeague shook his head. "Remember that bout you have scheduled back in Chicago, Seamus," he cautioned.

"That's true enough," O'Quinn agreed. "I'm sorry, Orion, but I don't want to risk getting hurt before I'm through with what I have to do."

"I understand," Orion replied. "Well, I hope ye enjoyed ye drinks, gentlemen." He took bottle, glasses, and tray back to the bar.

"Are you ready to head back to the rooming house now?" McTeague asked when Orion was gone.

"We just got here, Jack," O'Quinn protested. "Besides, I invited Leslie to join us after his meeting. I didn't get a chance to ask him about sparring."

McTeague looked as if he hoped O'Quinn had forgotten that invitation, but he said nothing. The two men stayed at the table, talking aimlessly and watching the other customers. A few townsmen came over and spoke to O'Quinn, having heard of his reputation as a prizefighter, but while he was polite to all of them, he did not ask anyone to join them.

An hour passed pleasantly, although McTeague was obviously impatient to get back to their rooms, and then Leslie Gibson strolled into the tavern. He spotted O'Quinn and McTeague at the table and came over to them. "Pull up a chair," O'Quinn said with a welcoming grin.

Signaling to Orion for a beer, Leslie sat down. The Scotsman brought it over, and the teacher sipped it gratefully. As he placed the mug on the table, he smiled and said, "Talking to the town council is a thirsty business."

"I'd think you would be used to talking, being a teacher," O'Quinn commented.

"Take my word for it, a roomful of kids and a town council full of businessmen are two entirely different things. But with Aileen's help, I think we convinced them to spend a little more on the school this year. We need more books."

"Aileen? That's the lady doctor, isn't it?"

Leslie nodded. "She's on the council. In fact, she's always been the best friend the school has in town government. As I understand it, she and Sister Laurel and Reverend Fisher were responsible for my being hired."

"Sister Laurel is that nun you mentioned, the one with the orphanage?"

"That's right. And Judah Fisher is Cody's brother. He's the pastor of the Calvary Methodist Church."

"You have influential friends," O'Quinn mused, "and it looks like you've made a good life for yourself here, Leslie."

"As I said, I'm happier than I've ever been." Leslie shrugged. "Are you thinking of getting out of the fight game, Seamus?"

The heavyweight laughed. "And do what? I'd never make a teacher like you, and I don't know what else I'm fit for but being a slugger."

"Well, if you ever decide to retire, Abilene would be a nice place to do it."

O'Quinn shook his head. "Too much country and not enough buildings. I'd go crazy here, Leslie."

The teacher grinned. "That's what I thought at first, too, but you'd be surprised how quickly you get used to it." Leslie finished his beer. "I have to get going. I still have to prepare tomorrow's lesson. Say, would you mind coming by the school tomorrow, Seamus?"

"Me come to the school? Why?"

"Some of the children want to meet you. They've

heard so much from their parents about you, and I think it would do them good to see that you're a normal man just like anyone else."

O'Quinn glanced at McTeague and saw that the detective was going to shake his head. The prizefighter bristled; he was tired of McTeague declining every invitation before he could answer for himself. "I'd be glad to," he said quickly, scowling at McTeague's sudden frown.

"Thanks." Leslie got to his feet. "Around lunchtime would be best, I think. That way we won't have to interrupt class; Mr. Simpson gets pretty upset if anything interferes with class."

"Around lunchtime, then," O'Quinn said, nodding. He waved off Leslie's offer to pay for the beer, insisting that it was on him, then said good night as the teacher left the saloon. O'Quinn turned to the glowering McTeague. "I know, you don't think it's a good idea for me to go over there. But what could happen at a school, for God's sake?"

"I don't know," McTeague said, shaking his head. "But I don't have a good feeling about this, O'Quinn. Somebody's going to get hurt."

O'Quinn tried to ignore McTeague's misgivings. It was the policeman's job to be cautious, but worrying about some sort of ambush at a school was taking things too far, O'Quinn thought.

A few minutes after noon the next day, the two men strolled west down Second Street toward the school. The large frame structure built of wide, whitewashed planks was a typical frontier schoolhouse. Set back from the street on a wide lawn, it was surrounded by several trees, and the slow-moving waters of Mud Creek angled across the lot behind it. The yard in front of the building was full of children as O'Quinn and McTeague approached. Some of the youngsters were still eating their lunch; others had already finished and were playing. Their laughter was a type of music O'Quinn had not heard often in his rather grim life.

Leslie must have been watching for them, because he came out of the building when O'Quinn and McTeague entered the school yard. A sturdy-looking, redheaded youth with freckles sprinkled over his impish face bounced at his side as he strode over to meet the two men.

"Hello, Seamus," Leslie said. "I'm glad you could come." Grinning broadly, he ruffled the boy's hair. "I think this is probably one of your biggest admirers. Meet Michael Hirsch. Michael, this is Seamus O'Quinn."

O'Quinn shook hands with the lad. "I'm glad to meet you, Michael," he said solemnly. "Hirsch, is it? Your sister must be the waitress at the Sunrise Café."

"Yes, sir," Michael answered breathlessly, clearly awed to be meeting Seamus. "That's Agnes, all right. She said you eat like a horse."

O'Quinn threw his head back and roared. "Aye, that I do," he agreed after a moment. "It takes a lot to keep a big fella like me going."

Other children began to crowd around now. O'Quinn greeted them, and several of the more daring boys shook hands with him. Michael said, "Orion's told us all about your fight with Kid Randisi, Mr. O'Quinn. Mr. Gibson here has fought him, too."

O'Quinn nodded. "I know. The Kid's a tough one, that's for sure. He hits hard, but he fights fair. I suppose that's what all of you try to do, too."

Leslie grasped the shoulder of a small boy who was standing timidly at the edge of the crowd and guided the youngster through the press of children, saying, "Here's another lad who wants to meet you, Seamus. This is Avery Burton."

Bending down, O'Quinn took Avery's hand. "Glad to meet you, son."

Avery nodded shyly, said nothing, and gazed at the ground. O'Quinn's eyes narrowed as he studied the boy. Something about Avery reminded him of a scared animal. The lad looked ready to bolt at the first sign of trouble or even disapproval.

O'Quinn glanced up at Leslie and saw the teacher shake his head ever so slightly. If Avery had problems, Leslie was already aware of them. Patting the boy lightly on the shoulder, O'Quinn straightened. "You be a good lad now," he said.

Looking over the heads of the children crowded around him, he saw that a few students had not joined the gathering. A half-dozen boys were grouped under a tree, watching out of the corners of their eyes and occasionally snickering. O'Quinn gave a mental shrug. He could not hope to impress everyone, he supposed.

"I've got an idea, Mr. Gibson!" Michael Hirsch exclaimed. "Why don't you and Mr. O'Quinn show us how you box?"

Leslie frowned at the redheaded boy. "You mean you want us to put on a match?"

"Sure!" Michael replied enthusiastically. "It'd be great!"

Leslie grimaced, and McTeague's expression was equally negative. The detective had stayed on the edge of the proceedings, watching the street. Before he could voice his disapproval, Leslie said, "I don't think we could do that, Michael. We wouldn't want to impose on Mr. O'Quinn."

Michael turned to O'Quinn. "You wouldn't mind, would you, Mr. O'Quinn? We'll probably never get a chance again to see two real prizefighters put on a match here in Abilene."

The boy could be persuasive, O'Quinn thought. And he *had* been planning to ask Leslie to spar with him. They would have to take it easy, since he was still recuperating from the bullet wounds, but O'Quinn could see nothing wrong with an informal exhibition for the children.

"I don't mind, Leslie," he said. "A little workout would probably do both of us some good."

McTeague stepped in. "I'm sorry, but I can't allow this," he countered. "Seamus has got to save himself for the fight back in Chicago."

"And I've given up fighting," Leslie added. "We just can't do it, Michael."

Michael sighed and nodded. "All right," he said. "I just thought it was a good idea. . . ."

O'Quinn caught Leslie's eye. "Could I talk to you in private for a minute?" he asked.

"All right," Leslie agreed. "You kids go back to what you were doing. I expect Mr. Simpson to return from town in a few minutes, and I know he'll want to get right back to work." As the children dispersed, Leslie and O'Quinn strolled toward one of the trees. McTeague, warily eyeing the prizefighter, followed.

O'Quinn turned to face Leslie and asked in a low voice, "Look, why can't we just put on a little show for the kids? Some footwork, a little sparring, things like that. We'll take it easy, and nobody will get hurt."

"Seamus . . ." McTeague warned.

"This is something I want to do, Jack." O'Quinn's voice was sharp as he spoke to his supposed manager. "These seem like nice youngsters, and I think they deserve a little excitement, don't you?"

McTeague made no reply, but his tightly-set features showed his displeasure. Leslie rubbed his bearded jaw in thought for a moment, then said, "I swore I wouldn't ever set foot in a boxing ring again, but I suppose this *would* be different. . . . If it's not too much trouble, Seamus, I guess we could show them a little of how it's done."

"Fine," O'Quinn agreed, starting to feel some of Michael Hirsch's boisterousness himself. "How about this afternoon, right after you're through with your classes?"

Leslie nodded. "That would be all right." He thrust out his hand, and he and O'Quinn shook on the deal. Then he turned to the students and raised his voice to announce, "Mr. O'Quinn and I have decided to put on a little boxing exhibition for you after all, children." He had to pause as shouts of excitement rang through the yard, led by Michael Hirsch's boisterous approval. "If you can stay after school for a few extra minutes this afternoon, we'll give you a demonstration of the art and science of pugilism."

"He means prizefighting," O'Quinn added with a grin.

Leslie lifted his arms to quiet the youngsters down. "Now, you'd better all go back inside. Mr. Simpson will be back from the general store any minute now with that new supply of chalk, and I'm sure he plans to use plenty of it this afternoon."

As the children trooped into the building, O'Quinn said, "I'll see you later, Leslie. I'm anxious to find out if you've lost any of your fighting skill, living this quiet life that you do."

The teacher's eyes sparkled as he replied, "It will be interesting, won't it?" Then with a wave he turned and went into the schoolhouse.

As O'Quinn and McTeague walked away, the detective said, "I don't like this, either, O'Quinn. You're only asking for trouble by calling so much attention to yourself."

"It's just an exhibition for some kiddies. Stop worrying about every little thing, Jack, or you'll wind up looking like that." O'Quinn nodded at the man hurrying down the street toward them. Thurman Simpson was carrying a box, no doubt that supply of new chalk Leslie had mentioned, and he sniffed and barely nodded when he passed the two men. As usual, Simpson looked sour, as if he had been eating something particularly distasteful.

McTeague glanced over his shoulder at the teacher. "Don't worry, I'll be able to smile again," he said. "I'll smile plenty when Darius Gold and that mad dog Rainey are both dangling from the end of a rope."

All afternoon long, Thurman Simpson thought that the children were unusually excited and happy. It was an attitude he attempted to repress as much as possible. Education was an arduous, trying process, and it was certainly no laughing matter. Simpson wondered if something was going on that he did not know about, but as usual, no one told him anything they did not have to.

In the second classroom, which had been built by putting up a partition to divide the old one-room schoolhouse, Leslie Gibson was also having problems, but his did not stem from the pupils who were looking up at him eagerly. Although he tried to concentrate on the lessons he had prepared, he kept remembering all the bouts he had fought, all the times fists crashed into his face and body, all the blood he had shed. And he recalled, too, the damage his own fists had inflicted on other men. He had vowed never to go back to that way of life.

He tried to convince himself that this simple sparring match with Seamus O'Quinn did not represent a return to anything. It would be a few moments' entertainment for the children, that was all. But he wondered if it was part of a trend, a course that had started with the boxing lessons he was giving to Avery Burton. Once violence had lived inside a man, did it always try to draw him back?

Jack McTeague was as disturbed as either of the two teachers, but for different reasons. Every time O'Quinn attracted attention to himself this way, he increased the risk that Gold's killers would be able to track him to Abilene. People passing through town might hear about the presence of a heavyweight boxer and unwittingly carry the word on to other cities. Sooner or later, McTeague thought pessimistically, the news would reach the wrong man. Then it would just be a matter of time until someone showed up with murder on his mind.

In fact, Seamus O'Quinn was the only one who was not concerned. He was looking forward to pitting his skills against Leslie's, even in an informal little affair like the one that would take place that afternoon.

When classes were dismissed for the day, he and McTeague were waiting in the yard outside the schoolhouse as the children burst through the doors with even more than their usual zest for freedom. Michael Hirsch and several other boys called greetings to O'Quinn, who acknowledged them with a grin.

By the time Leslie came out a moment later, the excited children had formed a large circle around O'Quinn, while McTeague stood off to one side. The group of students parted to let Leslie through. Smiling at O'Quinn, he shrugged out of his coat. "I suppose this will have to do for our ring," he commented.

"It'll be fine with me," O'Quinn replied, taking off his own coat. He unbuttoned his cuffs and rolled his sleeves up on his brawny forearms while Leslie did the same. Both men handed their coats over the heads of the children to McTeague.

"Shall we begin?" Leslie asked.

"Whenever you're ready," O'Quinn agreed. Positioning his feet, he brought his fists up and cocked them.

Inside the schoolhouse, Thurman Simpson was preparing to leave for the day. He heard the commotion outside, but thought nothing of it. Some of the children often stayed after school to play in the yard. That was fine with him as long as the town council and the parents of the children involved understood that he would take no responsibility for them after school hours.

But when Simpson stepped to the doorway and looked out into the school yard, he saw Leslie and O'Quinn standing in the middle of a group of children, obviously about to fight. Both of them had taken their coats off and were brandishing their fists.

Outrage shot through Simpson's slender frame. He had never liked the idea of hiring a man like Leslie to teach impressionable young children, and here was vivid proof that he had been right. The man was obviously a ruffian, and he was about to engage O'Quinn in a barbarous display of violence no doubt brought on by some loutish insult by one or the other of them.

For the sake of the children, Thurman Simpson had to stop this. He rushed forward just as Leslie Gibson swung.

O'Quinn heard the patter of rapid footsteps behind him and turned around, stepping aside quickly just in case McTeague had been right and some danger really was threatening. He was just in time to see Simpson push his way through the crowd of children and lunge toward the center of the impromptu prize ring. Leslie saw him coming, too, but could not stop the punch he had just thrown.

Simpson ran right into Leslie's fist. It was as if the teacher had plowed into a stone wall. His feet went out from under him, flying up into the air as his body was driven backwards. He landed heavily in the dirt while the children let out a huge roar of approval at the mishap. Lights pinwheeled in front of Simpson's eyes, lights that were abruptly replaced by utter blackness.

He came to a moment later with Leslie and O'Quinn and McTeague bending anxiously over him. One of the children had run to fetch some water from the creek, and Leslie splashed some of it in Simpson's face. The teacher came up off the ground, sputtering and blowing.

Leslie helped him to his feet, brushing off his clothes and asking, "Are you all right, Mr. Simpson?"

"All right?" Simpson squawked indignantly. "You just assaulted me, and you dare to ask me if I'm all right? I—I'll have you fired, you . . . you . . ."

"It was an accident, Mr. Simpson," Leslie assured

him. "Seamus and I were just putting on an exhibition for the children, so they could see what a boxing match is like. I guess we should have told you about it earlier." He paused, then asked, "You didn't think we were actually fighting, did you?"

"Well, what the devil was I supposed to think?" Simpson demanded. He winced and reached up to touch his aching jaw. "I think you broke something," he moaned.

"Let me see." Leslie prodded at the jaw while Simpson grimaced and groaned, then announced, "I don't think it's broken, Mr. Simpson, but if you want to go see Dr. Bloom, I'll be glad to pay her to take a look at it."

"I'll do that!" Simpson said thickly. He swung to face O'Quinn and pointed a quivering finger at him. "You! I'll wager this was all your idea, wasn't it?"

O'Quinn glanced at Michael Hirsch, who suddenly looked as if he wanted to be somewhere—anywhere —else. Then O'Quinn grinned and said, "It was my idea, all right. I thought the kids would enjoy it."

"Get out!" Simpson shrieked. "Get out of my school yard, do you understand? And don't come back!" He moaned again and clutched his jaw as his angry shouts made it hurt worse. Then he stalked away, bound for Aileen Bloom's office.

Leslie scanned the circle of now silent children, who were staring at him with awed expressions on their faces. They had expected something entertaining, but none of them dreamed they would see the schoolmaster knocked flat on his back. This day would become a legend.

Trying not to grin, Leslie said, "You kids go on home now. There won't be any more boxing today."

A few of them protested, but within minutes, they

were walking out of the yard, chattering animatedly among themselves about what they had just seen.

As the teacher watched the departing students, O'Quinn turned to him and said, "I suppose you'll be in a bit of trouble now."

Leslie shook his head. "It was an accident. Simpson may complain to the town council, but all of them know that, if I was going to haul off and punch the man, I would have done it a long time ago. He'll cool off sooner or later."

O'Quinn took his coat from McTeague. "Guess we'd better go," he said, "since we were ordered off the place. How about some supper at the café?"

"Sounds good." Leslie nodded.

As they walked away from the school, McTeague said gloomily, "I told you somebody would get hurt if you went through with that crazy idea."

O'Quinn's booming laugh shook his huge frame. "If getting thrown out of a school yard is the worst thing that happens to us while we're here, Jack, I'll be as pleased as I can be!"

# Chapter Five

❖

As Leslie Gibson had predicted, Thurman Simpson did calm down, although not until after he had gone to each member of the town council individually and demanded that Leslie be fired. Luckily, enough members of the council knew and liked the teacher and wanted to hear his side of the story rather than simply accepting Simpson's version. Leslie explained to them what really happened, and once he had, several council members chuckled at the thought of the pompous Simpson being knocked out cold. Of course, the teacher did not lose his job.

Several evenings later over beers at Orion's, Leslie told O'Quinn and McTeague what had happened. "The swelling on Mr. Simpson's jaw has just about gone down," he said, finishing his story. "He'll be angry with me for a while, but I think he realizes it was an accident."

"Too bad it was over so quickly you didn't get a chance to enjoy it," O'Quinn quipped.

Leslie shook his head. "I wouldn't have enjoyed it under any circumstances. I've had enough of fighting." He finished his beer and stood up. "Now, I'm paying for this round, and I don't want any argument from you."

"Wouldn't dream of it." O'Quinn grinned.

Leslie dropped some coins on the table. "I've got to be going," he said. "I'll see you later."

As the burly teacher strode toward the batwings, O'Quinn took another sip of beer, then glanced at McTeague. The detective had been especially tense ever since they had stopped at the telegraph office in the Kansas Pacific depot earlier that day.

"What's the matter, Jack?" O'Quinn asked. "Are you worried about that wire you sent to Chicago this afternoon?"

McTeague shrugged. "No need to worry about the one I sent. It was coded so that it just sounded like a question about that so-called upcoming boxing match. I'm worried about the answer. I should have heard from them by now."

"Maybe you will soon." O'Quinn knew that McTeague had sent the message to a trusted associate in the police department. The man was supposed to let them know if the date for Darius Gold's trial had been set, and if so when it was scheduled. McTeague had also asked if Mitch Rainey had been captured yet.

The detective shoved his chair back. "I think I'll go over to the telegraph office," he declared. "You were planning on staying here for a while longer, weren't you?"

"That's what I intended, but I can come with you if you'd like," O'Quinn offered.

"No, that's not necessary," McTeague said, after he had scanned the room. There were only a dozen men in Orion's, and during the last few days McTeague had become less nervous about O'Quinn visiting the tavern. He went on, "I'd rather have you in here than out on the street where somebody could take a potshot at you. I'll just run over and see if there's been a reply, then I'll come right back."

"Fine," O'Quinn agreed and inwardly heaved a sigh of relief. He much preferred to stay at Orion's rather than tag along with McTeague.

The detective pushed through the batwings, leaving O'Quinn sitting alone at the table. A few moments later Orion ambled over; the job of serving drinks to the few customers at the bar fell to his young assistant, Augie. The Scotsman pulled out a chair. "Ye mind if I sit down?"

"Not at all," O'Quinn replied. "It's your place, after all. And I'd be glad for the company."

"How's ye training coming along?"

O'Quinn shrugged. "All right, I suppose. A fellow gets a little bored just practicing, though." A light glittered in the prizefighter's eyes. "I want to get back to Chicago and start trading real punches."

"Aye, I kin understand tha' feeling—" Orion broke off suddenly and stared at the tavern entrance. O'Quinn followed his gaze and saw four men pushing through the batwings.

The one in the lead was tall, broad-shouldered, and brawny. A shock of red hair showed under his cuffed-back Stetson. He wore dusty range clothes, as did his companions, who were smaller but appeared to be equally rough. Besides his red hair, the leader was also distinguished by a black-and-white cowhide vest and wide leather cuffs on the sleeves of his shirt. He would have looked like a tough, competent cowboy were it not for the Colt riding in a low-hung holster on his hip. That said gunman.

Orion grimaced. "I hope there will no' be trouble," he muttered.

O'Quinn leaned over the tabletop and watched the four men stroll to the bar and order drinks from Augie. "You know them?" he asked.

"Aye." The saloonkeeper nodded. "The one in the vest is Willie Parker, and a bad 'un he be. 'Tis thought he's an outlaw, but Lucas has no' been able t'prove anything agin him. He and his friends have busted up more than one bar in this town. They dinna cause no trouble the last time they came in here, though."

Orion kept an eye on Willie Parker and his cronies as he talked to O'Quinn in a low voice. Parker and his friends downed the drinks that Augie brought them and seemed peaceful enough at the moment, but that abruptly changed when Parker idly glanced over his shoulder and spotted O'Quinn and Orion sitting at the table.

O'Quinn saw Parker's eyes narrow in recognition. The redhead nudged the man standing next to him and exchanged a few whispered words with him. That man spoke quietly to the other two. By the time Parker set his empty glass on the bar and turned to slouch toward the table, his companions had finished their drinks and fallen into step behind him.

O'Quinn watched them coming, and his hopes for a quiet evening evaporated when he saw the arrogant grin that twisted Parker's mouth. The man's face was slightly flushed as if he had been drinking heavily all evening, but he did not walk like a man who was drunk. In fact, Parker was light on his feet for a big man, O'Quinn realized.

The hardcase came to a stop beside the table and stared coldly at O'Quinn. After a moment, Orion asked impatiently, "Wha' is it ye be wanting, Parker?"

Ignoring Orion, Parker continued to glare at O'Quinn. "You're that prizefighter I've heard so much about, ain't you?" he demanded.

"I don't know, lad," O'Quinn said evenly. "I'm a prizefighter, all right, but I don't know that it's me you're talking about. What are folks saying?"

"That there's a fella in town from back East who can take on anybody and beat them," Parker snarled. "I ain't sure I like that. I've always been pretty damn good with my fists myself."

"I'm sure you are," O'Quinn replied, trying to keep his voice level and polite. He wanted to avoid a fight if he possibly could. Working out with the punching bag, even a little sparring, was quite different from a no-holds-barred saloon brawl with the likes of Willie Parker. Such a battle could rupture his healing wounds.

Pushing his hat farther back on his head, Parker hooked his thumbs in his gun belt and began rocking back and forth on his bootheels. "Maybe you'd like to fight me, mister. That way we can find out who's really better, you or me."

"I don't want to fight you, Parker," O'Quinn declared, shaking his head. "I've got a real fight waiting for me back home, so I can't be waltzing around with the likes of you."

Parker gave a short bark of humorless laughter. "So, you've heard of me, have you? I reckon most folks around here have. Ain't nobody I can't beat with gun or fist, prizefighter, and I ain't leavin' here until I hear you say the same thing."

Orion scraped back his chair and stood up. Parker's

friends closed ranks around the table as Orion snapped, "I've warned ye 'bout causing trouble in here, Parker. I'll thank ye t'leave me tavern right now."

"Not yet, old man," Parker snarled. "Now get the hell out of my way."

"Old man, is it?" Orion cried indignantly. "Why, ye bald-faced scut—"

Standing up, O'Quinn put a hand on the Scotsman's arm. "Take it easy, Orion," he cautioned. "This young fellow doesn't really want a fight with you. It's me he's trying to insult."

"That's right, O'Quinn. So how about it? We settle it once and for all?"

Again O'Quinn shook his head. "I'm not fighting you, and that's all there is to it. Now, if you won't leave and let folks enjoy their drinks in peace, I suppose I'll have to go." He nodded good night to Orion and started to move past Willie Parker.

The hardcase reached out quickly, grabbed O'Quinn's right shoulder, and shoved him back. The rough push jarred the half-healed bullet wound, and O'Quinn grimaced as pain shot through his shoulder. But, making an effort not to reveal his injury, he set his face in determined lines and tried once more to get around Parker.

Parker would not allow it. His face contorting in whiskey-fueled anger, he suddenly launched a fist at O'Quinn's head.

Instincts developed over years as a boxer warned O'Quinn that the punch was coming. The prizefighter reflexively moved his head out of the way. Parker's fist flew harmlessly by, and he stumbled as the momentum of the missed blow threw him off-balance. He staggered into O'Quinn but recovered quickly enough to drive a punch into the prizefighter's midsection.

As the breath was forced from O'Quinn's lungs, instinct took over again. The heavyweight's right hand balled into a fist and slammed into Parker's chin. The man's head jerked around, and the punch knocked him back a step. But he simply shook his head and charged again, his three friends right behind him. Roaring in anger, Parker swung wild, pile-driver punches at O'Quinn.

The first time McTeague left him alone since they had come to Abilene, O'Quinn thought fleetingly, and a brawl had to break out. The detective would never let him out of his sight again.

That thought was all O'Quinn had time for. He was too busy defending himself to worry about anything else. Parker and his friends swarmed over him, and he took several blows to the body before he could set his feet and start swinging. His first punch caught one of the other men, lifting him off his feet and dumping him atop one of the nearby tables. The table broke under the impact, and man and shattered table crashed to the sawdust-covered floor.

Curses shouted in a Scots accent told O'Quinn that Orion was joining the fight. The tavern owner grabbed the collar of one man, spun him around, and threw a right cross at his face.

At least none of them had gone for their guns, O'Quinn thought gratefully, while he tried to block Parker's punches and get in some of his own. Parker and his men could take punishment as well as deliver it, O'Quinn saw. They kept coming, throwing a flurry of blows that rocked him and Orion back. O'Quinn stumbled over a chair, kicked it aside, bobbed backwards momentarily out of the range of Parker's long arms. The man came after him without pausing.

While Parker and his friends knew little or nothing

about boxing, they outnumbered O'Quinn and Orion and packed plenty of power in their blows. The other customers in the tavern had scurried for cover when the fight broke out, and O'Quinn knew they could not count on any help from them. Young Augie emerged from behind the bar carrying a wooden mallet, but he was so nervous as he danced around looking for an opening that he would probably do more harm than good if he stepped in swinging the thing. O'Quinn tried to block a punch with his forearm, but it slipped past his guard and smacked into his right shoulder.

Fiery pain coursed through his arm and chest. He could already feel a hot wetness on his shirt and knew the wound in his side had opened up again. Now, as his shoulder throbbed agonizingly, he realized that it was bleeding, too. But there was nothing he could do at the moment except keep fighting. Parker and his men were bent on destroying him.

Orion lunged, wrapped his arms around one of the men, and pressed him in a crushing bear hug. As the man howled in pain, Orion spun around several times and then threw the man across the room. The hardcase smashed against the wall and slid to the floor heavily. The Scotsman shouted triumphantly, but before he could return to the fight, another man scooped up a chair and brought it crashing down on his head. Orion fell to one knee, and the man whipped the broken chair leg he still held across the back of the Scotsman's neck.

Another punch from Parker staggered O'Quinn, and he did not recover quickly enough to keep the fourth man from getting behind him. The man leapt on his back, wrapped his arms and legs around him, and immobilized him. "Get him, Willie!" the man bellowed in O'Quinn's ear.

Parker bore in, slamming punch after punch into O'Quinn while the other man held him. The blows battered O'Quinn's midsection, then Parker moved to his face. His head jerked from side to side as Parker alternated rights and lefts. His eyes swelled until he could barely see, but there was nothing to see except fists shooting toward his face.

He had lost too much of his edge during the long enforced inactivity, O'Quinn knew. He was being beaten by men who had no business getting the best of him. But he was too weary to break free of the iron grip of the man holding him, too tired to do anything but stand there and take the punishment.

"O'Quinn!" cried Jack McTeague from the tavern entrance. The detective hurtled across the room and threw himself into the fracas, lashing out at Willie Parker. But the detective had not reckoned on the man who had just downed Orion with the chair leg. The man slashed at McTeague's head with the makeshift weapon. McTeague's derby cushioned the blow somewhat, but the club thudded against his skull with enough force to send him staggering.

Parker had turned away from O'Quinn at the sound of McTeague's shout, and the prizefighter seized what he knew would be his last chance to turn the course of this battle. He threw himself backward, shoving off with all the strength remaining in his legs, and hoped that he was close enough to the wall for the maneuver to work. He was, he discovered an instant later. He crashed against the planks, pinning the man who had been holding him, and bouncing his head with a hollow thud off the wall. As O'Quinn straightened, the man slipped off his back, out cold. The prizefighter was still on his feet, swaying but upright.

He was facing Willie Parker and the man with the

chair leg. Orion was down, and so was McTeague. O'Quinn knew he could not hope to take on both men, but he still managed to clench his fists and raise one of them tauntingly. "Come on, you bastard!" he rasped hoarsely at Parker.

Parker snarled and started forward. He had taken one step when a gun blasted and a bullet kicked up splinters between his feet.

Everyone in the room froze. O'Quinn turned toward the doorway and squinted between his swollen eyelids. Through a bloody haze, he saw Luke Travis and Cody Fisher striding into the tavern. The marshal was holding a rifle, and smoke curled from the barrel of the Colt in Cody's hand.

Cody kept Parker and his remaining cohort covered. "You boys just stand still," he said grimly. "This isn't the first fight of yours we've broken up, Parker, and I wouldn't mind putting a bullet in you. Might slow you down for a while."

Travis came over to Orion, who had pushed himself onto his knees and was shaking his head groggily. The marshal slipped a hand under Orion's arm and helped him to his feet, supporting the burly saloonkeeper with surprising strength. "You all right, Orion?" Travis asked anxiously.

Orion reached up and rubbed the back of his neck. "Aye," he rumbled. "One o' the rapscallions clouted me from behind, Lucas. 'Twas a mean-spirited thing t'do!"

"About what I'd expect from Parker and his bunch," Travis grunted. He turned to O'Quinn. "What about you, O'Quinn?"

O'Quinn forced his bruised lips into a grin. "Bloody but unbowed, as they say. Still, I'm glad you showed up when you did, Marshal."

"Bloody is right," Travis muttered, nodding at O'Quinn's shirt. "We'd better get you to the doctor. Did Parker cut you?"

Before O'Quinn could answer, Parker said harshly, "I didn't have no knife, Travis! It was a fair fight."

Cody snorted. "Four against two is a fair fight?"

Parker turned toward him with a snarl on his battered face. "How about you and me then, Deputy? That fair enough for you?"

"I'll holster my gun right now," Cody threatened. "You're wearing one."

"Cody!" Travis's voice cut across the room. "I don't want any gunplay. Enough damage has been done in here tonight—Orion doesn't need bullet holes in the walls, too. Now get Parker and his friends over to the jail and lock them up. Orion, do you mind getting your shotgun and helping Cody keep an eye on them?"

"I'd be right happy t'do that, Lucas," Orion growled. He went behind the bar, spoke soothingly for a moment to the highly agitated Old Bailey, then drew out the sawed-off shotgun that he kept under the bar. Together, Cody and he covered Parker and his friend while they carried their unconscious cohorts out of the tavern.

Travis was helping McTeague get to his feet. "How are you feeling, Mr. McTeague?" the marshal asked. "We're about to take Mr. O'Quinn over to the doctor, and I think you'd better come along and let her take a look at you."

McTeague shook his head, jerked out of Travis's grip, and hurried over to O'Quinn. "Are you all right, Seamus?" he asked anxiously, eyeing the spreading bloodstains on O'Quinn's shirt. McTeague slipped an arm around O'Quinn's middle and said, "Never mind answering. Come on."

O'Quinn was not going to argue. With McTeague on one side and Travis on the other, he allowed himself to be led out of the tavern and steered toward the doctor's office next door.

As they walked down the boardwalk, O'Quinn unsteady on his feet, the prizefighter grinned crookedly and croaked, "You're acting like you care what happens to me, Jack."

"Why the hell shouldn't I care?" McTeague snapped in reply. "You know how much that fight back in Chicago means to me. You're not going to do any of us a damn bit of good if you die from loss of blood or some infection."

That was true, O'Quinn thought. McTeague wanted him alive long enough to testify against Darius Gold, and after that the detective did not care what happened. He had made that plain.

The three men turned at the walk that led to Aileen Bloom's office. O'Quinn noticed a light burning inside; evidently the doctor was still there. Frowning, he rumbled, "I'm not sure about letting a woman doctor poke around and examine me."

"You don't have anything to worry about, Mr. O'Quinn," Travis assured him. "Doctors don't come any better than Aileen Bloom. She can handle anything from gunshot wounds to major surgery."

In the shadows O'Quinn and McTeague exchanged a quick look. If the doctor had any training at all, she would instantly recognize O'Quinn's wounds as bullet holes, and that could lead to some awkward questions. But there was nothing they could do. The big man's shirt was already soaked, and more blood was flowing profusely from the angry wounds. O'Quinn was feeling light-headed, and he knew it was from loss of blood.

Travis and McTeague helped O'Quinn up the steps to the low porch. Then, leaving McTeague to support O'Quinn, the marshal went to the door and rapped sharply on it. A moment later the door opened, and the same attractive brunette O'Quinn had noticed a few days earlier peered out curiously. When she saw Travis standing there, she smiled brightly.

"Why, good evening, Luke," she said warmly. "What can I do for you?"

Travis half turned toward O'Quinn and McTeague. "We've got a hurt man here, Aileen," he declared. "Looks like he's bleeding pretty bad."

Aileen glanced over at them, the pleasant expression vanishing from her face to be replaced by one of concern. "He certainly is," she said crisply. "Hurry, bring him inside."

She stood back and held the door as Travis and McTeague assisted O'Quinn into the house. They went down a short hall and into one of the examining rooms. O'Quinn winced as he climbed onto the sheet-covered table, but then as the pain eased slightly, he was glad for the opportunity to sit down.

"Take his shirt off carefully, please," Aileen requested, her tone calm and professional, as she stepped into the room after them. McTeague quickly unfastened the buttons and peeled the garment off O'Quinn. Aileen paled slightly when she saw the wounds but made no comment. Taking a soft cloth and a basin of water, she began to wash the blood away from the injuries. As she worked, Travis introduced O'Quinn and McTeague without telling her why they were in Abilene.

O'Quinn felt himself flushing in embarrassment as Aileen swabbed his bloody torso. Up close like this, she was even more attractive than he had first thought. She could not be older than thirty, and her lovely, unlined face looked even younger than that. Her hair was a dark, rich brown, and even though it was pinned up in a bun at the moment, O'Quinn had a feeling that if it was undone and allowed to flow freely, it would be thick and luxurious.

He glanced over at McTeague and saw that he seemed to be equally aware of the doctor's charms. The detective had hardly taken his eyes off her since they had entered the office. As tired and beaten up as he was, O'Quinn had to smile slightly as he remembered McTeague's disparaging comments about frontier physicians, especially female ones. From the look in his eyes, McTeague might be changing his tune, O'Quinn thought wryly.

As Aileen swabbed the bullet wound in his shoulder, O'Quinn grimaced, and his breath hissed between clenched teeth. Aileen glanced at him and murmured, "Sorry." Her touch was as gentle as soft rain, but it was impossible to clean the wounds without causing some pain.

O'Quinn looked at Travis and saw that the marshal was watching intently, his eyes fixed on the wounds. The lawman had undoubtedly seen enough bullet holes to know them when he saw them. For the moment, though, Travis said nothing, evidently content to let the doctor concentrate on her work.

"Well, that should help," Aileen finally said, stepping back and dropping the cloth into the basin. The water in the vessel immediately turned pink. "At least we can see what we're doing now. I'd say these wounds look worse than they actually are, but we need to stop that bleeding." She turned and took bandages from a cabinet on one wall, then began to form some compresses to bind the wounds. As she worked, she asked, "How long ago did you receive these injuries, Mr. O'Quinn?"

"Nearly three weeks ago," O'Quinn answered. He glanced at McTeague and saw him shake his head slightly. Clearly the detective did not want him to say any more.

"They look as if they were healing very nicely until you tore them open again. How did you manage that?"

O'Quinn grinned, his expression considerably more cheerful than he felt at the moment. "There was a fight at Orion's."

"Oh, yes, I do seem to remember hearing a commotion a little while ago. And a shot."

"That was Cody breaking things up," Travis put in.

Aileen nodded. "I see. I want to disinfect those wounds, Mr. O'Quinn. It will hurt, but it needs to be done."

"Do whatever you need to, ma'am," O'Quinn told her.

Aileen poured carbolic acid from a bottle onto a sponge and placed it on the wounds, holding it there while O'Quinn gritted his teeth. That done, she covered the holes with the compresses and began wrapping the bandages around them.

"You'll have to be careful," she warned him. "You'll recover from the loss of blood fairly quickly and more scar tissue should form on the wounds, but there's a limit to the amount of damage you can do to them —not to mention the danger of infection. I want you to come back tomorrow so that I can change these dressings and check the wounds."

McTeague stepped in and nodded. "I'll see to it, ma'am. And I'll gladly pay you for your trouble tonight."

"No need for that," Travis said. "Aileen's fee will come out of the fine the judge is going to levy against Willie Parker and his friends for public brawling."

"I should have known Mr. Parker was involved in this," Aileen said tightly. "I seem to be spending more and more of my time lately patching up people who have made his acquaintance."

Travis nodded toward McTeague. "You'd better have a look at Mr. McTeague, too, Aileen. One of Parker's friends hit him on the top of his head with a busted chair leg during the fight."

"It's nothing," McTeague protested, trying to wave off Travis's suggestion. "I've been hit harder."

"Nonsense," Aileen replied. "It's only reasonable that you let me take a look at it, since you're already here."

O'Quinn watched with a grin as McTeague removed his rumpled hat and let Aileen probe the swelling on his head. She asked him how his vision was. "A little blurry," McTeague responded, shrugging, "but nothing to worry about."

"I suggest you take it easy for several days, too," Aileen said sternly. "You may well have a concussion, although I can't be sure. You'll have a headache, that's certain. If the blurred vision doesn't go away in a week or two, you may need more medical attention."

"I'll go to a doctor when we get back to Chicago," McTeague said. He was blushing furiously and seemed all too aware that Aileen was standing only inches away from him.

"Chicago!" Aileen said, smiling with delight. "Is that where you're from?"

McTeague nodded. "That's right."

"I always enjoyed visiting Chicago," Aileen went on, her soft brown eyes sparkling. "I haven't been there in several years, but I've never forgotten it. Such a bustling, metropolitan place. There's nothing more full of life than a big city."

For one of the few times since O'Quinn had known him, he saw a big smile on McTeague's face. "There's plenty of life in Chicago, that's for sure," the detective agreed warmly. "All kinds, in fact."

"I'd enjoy talking to you about it sometime, if you wouldn't mind," Aileen said. "I keep thinking that I'll make a trip east again, but there never seems to be time for it."

"I'd be glad to bring you up to date on the city," McTeague replied.

Travis had been paying close attention to this exchange, and now O'Quinn saw a frown creasing the marshal's brow. He wondered briefly if there was anything between the lawman and the physician, and then Travis said, "I'd like one of you to bring *me* up to date on why Mr. O'Quinn has a couple of bullet holes in him."

Aileen nodded, her smile fading as a look of professional concern replaced it. "I was wondering the same thing. I've heard some talk around town about you, Mr. O'Quinn. I understood that you were a pugilist, not a gunfighter."

O'Quinn was not smiling now. "I think these holes are my business, Marshal. No offense, but like I said, it happened three weeks ago, before I ever came to Abilene."

"It's my business if there's a chance somebody might try to put some more in you while you're in my town," Travis replied coolly.

"That won't happen, Marshal," McTeague assured him quickly. "It's true, we did have some trouble before we left Chicago, but that's all over. All we're interested in now is getting ready for Seamus's next fight."

"Not any time soon, I hope," Aileen advised. "Those wounds won't take too much abuse before they open up again, as you found out tonight."

McTeague nodded. "I know. And this may put us behind schedule. But I can promise you that Seamus will be fully healed in time for the bout."

"It's none of my business," Aileen said with a shake of her head. "But I don't like to see anyone hurt needlessly."

"Neither do I, Doctor," McTeague assured her. "I hope this won't have any effect on our plans to get together."

Aileen smiled. "Of course not. But please be careful, both of you."

"Don't worry about us, ma'am," O'Quinn grunted. "We can take care of ourselves."

"I'm sure," Aileen said dryly, picking his bloody shirt up off the floor.

Frowning, O'Quinn took it from her and eased into it with McTeague's assistance. McTeague said to Travis, "You're sure about taking Dr. Bloom's fee out of the fine?"

Travis nodded. "You two had best get back to your place and get some rest. And from now on, keep an eye out for Parker. I'll hold him tonight, but he'll be on the streets again soon, and he's the type who'll want to settle the score."

"I understand, Marshal," McTeague said grimly. "Come on, Seamus."

"Need any help?"

"We can make it," McTeague assured him.

With McTeague supporting him, O'Quinn walked stiffly out of the small house and turned at the boardwalk toward their rooming house. Once they were beyond earshot of the doctor's office, O'Quinn grinned through his pain and commented, "You seemed mighty impressed with that lady, Jack. I thought you said these frontier doctors weren't good for much, just like the lawmen."

"I could have been mistaken about Dr. Bloom," McTeague said archly. "She seemed very competent and professional."

O'Quinn chuckled. "And damned pretty, too."

"Come on," McTeague grated.

Travis and Aileen stood on the boardwalk in front of her office and watched the two figures move awkwardly away. "What did you really think about those bullet wounds, Luke?" Aileen asked.

"I think those two are lying about why they're here," Travis declared. "They're up to something besides getting ready for some prizefight. I'm going to keep a closer watch on them from now on."

Aileen shook her head. "They don't seem to be the type to cause trouble. Besides, Mr. O'Quinn is an old friend of Leslie Gibson's, isn't he?"

"That's right. But Leslie says he never heard of McTeague, knew nothing about him until he showed up here with O'Quinn. McTeague's the one who strikes me as fishy."

"I thought he was very nice," Aileen said. "He seemed genuinely concerned about his friend."

Travis glanced at Aileen. She had been so animated when she and McTeague talked about Chicago, he recalled. So big cities excited her, did they? Before tonight he had believed Abilene was big enough for her, had thought she was content to live here, happy with the people she knew.

*You're jealous, Luke,* Travis told himself. He might not want to admit it, but he knew it was true. And it was another good reason to keep an eye on Seamus O'Quinn and the smooth-talking Mr. Jack McTeague.

# Chapter Six

———◆———

SEAMUS O'QUINN WAS STIFF AND SORE THE NEXT MORNing from the blows he had taken in the fight with Willie Parker. But as Aileen Bloom had predicted, he recovered fairly rapidly. His iron constitution and the years he had spent learning to absorb punishment and shake it off made him a quick healer. When Aileen changed the dressings on his wounds that afternoon, she commented on how well they looked.

Jack McTeague had insisted on accompanying O'Quinn to the doctor's office, which came as no surprise to O'Quinn. Once again, the detective exchanged pleasantries with Aileen, and they spent several minutes talking about Chicago. McTeague told her about attending the opera there, which did surprise O'Quinn. McTeague had never struck him as the sort to enjoy three hours of caterwauling in some foreign language.

After several more days had passed, O'Quinn felt very much like himself again. He would take it easy, as Aileen had advised, but he was confident the wounds were going to heal just fine.

In the excitement of the saloon brawl, O'Quinn had had no opportunity to ask McTeague if there had been any reply to the wire he had sent to Chicago. Now when he asked he discovered that there had been —but the news was not good. Darius Gold's lawyers had tried every stalling tactic and had been successful in getting their client's trial date pushed back several more weeks. What was even worse, Mitch Rainey had not been captured. Speculation in underworld circles was that, knowing that a murder warrant had been issued for his arrest, he had fled Chicago.

"If he has left, you can bet that Gold got word to him first and ordered him to find you," McTeague said grimly. "Both of them know their only hope is to eliminate you."

"Well, he's not likely to find me out here in Abilene," O'Quinn replied.

McTeague did not look convinced of that.

The detective's headache had gone away after a couple of days, and his blurred vision had cleared. Aileen declared that he probably had only a minor concussion, but she advised him to continue being careful. McTeague promised faithfully he would.

They had not resumed the training sessions yet, since McTeague wanted to take no chances with O'Quinn's health, but the inactivity was making the big prizefighter nervous. On a bright November day the two men were in the cozy parlor of Hettie Wilburn's boardinghouse. O'Quinn, who was pacing the room like a caged animal, glanced at the grandfather's clock in the hall and said, "It's almost noon, Jack. I think I'll go down to the Sunrise Café and get something to eat. Want to come along?"

McTeague was sitting at a small writing desk; a piece of paper lay in front of him, and he held a pencil in his hand. He was frowning as he concentrated on writing another message to his associate back in Chicago. The telegram had to be carefully worded so that anyone reading it would not be suspicious, but at the same time, it had to contain the coded phrases that would convey the actual message to the man for whom it was intended. McTeague licked his pencil point and absently shook his head.

"I'm busy with this," he muttered. "Can I trust you not to get into any trouble if you go by yourself?"

"I'm not a little kid, Jack," O'Quinn protested. "I think I can walk a few blocks in broad daylight without anything happening to me."

McTeague sighed. "All right. It's against my better judgment, but I suppose I can't watch you twenty-four hours a day. Just keep a sharp eye out for anything suspicious."

Taking his hat from the hallstand, O'Quinn pushed it on his head and grinned. "Sure, Jack. I'll do that." He quickly left the house before McTeague could change his mind.

It was a beautiful autumn day. The sun was warm, and a crisp breeze rustled the dry brown leaves scattered on the ground. O'Quinn felt an exhilarating sense of freedom as he walked down Texas Street. It was good to be out from under McTeague's constant surveillance, even if the inspector did have his best interests at heart.

Quite a few people were on the street, but no one looked out of place. Cowboys, farmers, and businessmen moved among women who bustled about in sunbonnets and homespun dresses. In fact, O'Quinn thought, the only person on Texas Street who did not seem to belong there was himself.

He glanced across the street and noticed a familiar figure coming out of the Great Western Store. The boy was struggling with a keg of molasses that was too large and heavy for him. O'Quinn frowned as he tried to recall the boy's name. *Avery Burton, that's it.* Leslie had introduced him to O'Quinn during his first visit to the school. That was where Avery should have been at the moment, O'Quinn thought.

Behind the lad came a smaller child, a girl with long golden hair and the same delicate features as the boy. Avery's little sister, no doubt. O'Quinn paused on the boardwalk and wondered what they were doing out of school.

Someone else emerged from the doorway of the store, and at first O'Quinn could not see anything but a long skirt because the person's face was hidden behind the large sack of flour she was carrying. Struggling with it was more accurate; the bag was obviously heavy. It began to slip down as the woman neared a wagon parked at the raised boardwalk. Avery hurriedly placed the molasses keg on the seat of the wagon and sprang to help her.

The flour was still too heavy even for the two of them. The sack slipped from their hands and landed on the boardwalk with a thump, the impact raising a small white cloud that the woman fanned away. As her waving hands cleared the dust she turned, and O'Quinn saw her face for the first time.

*Why, she's just a girl,* he realized, a little surprised. Without thinking about what he was doing, he started across the street to help. As he approached, he could see the resemblance between Avery, his little sister, and the young woman. She was not old enough to be the children's mother—O'Quinn figured she was around twenty—so that meant she must be their sister. She was staring wearily at the bag of flour when O'Quinn stepped onto the boardwalk.

Tipping his derby gallantly, he asked, "Would you be needing some help, ma'am?"

"Mr. O'Quinn!" Avery exclaimed excitedly, glancing up and recognizing the prizefighter. "Emily, this is Mr. O'Quinn. I told you about the day he came to the school and Mr. Simpson got knocked out!"

"Yes, of course," Emily murmured. She looked up at O'Quinn and went on, "I hate to ask, but I suppose I could use some help. I'm Emily Burton." She extended her hand toward O'Quinn.

He took it, found her grip cool and firm despite the light dusting of flour on her skin. "Seamus O'Quinn, at your service, Miss Burton."

"You know Avery," Emily said, "and this is my sister, Nora." She indicated the little girl who smiled shyly at O'Quinn and slipped timidly behind Emily's skirt.

"Hello, darling." O'Quinn spoke gently to Nora. He guessed that the pretty child was around eight years old.

"Hello," Nora whispered.

As Emily tucked a strand of long brown hair that had fallen across her cheek under her bonnet, O'Quinn caught his breath. Her fine features, so like Avery's, were prettily arranged in a pale, oval face, and in her lovely brown eyes he saw an innocence he found refreshing.

"I ought to be able to handle something like this, but that bag is just too heavy," she said apologetically.

"Think nothing of it." O'Quinn bent and wrapped his arms around the sack of flour. He felt a slight twinge in his shoulder as he straightened but ignored it. Stepping over to the wagon bed, he carefully placed the bag just behind the seat. Then he lifted the keg of molasses and positioned it next to the flour. "I'd be glad to load the rest of your supplies."

"We don't have much more," Avery said, looking at O'Quinn with worshipful eyes. "The rest of the sacks are right inside. I'll show you." Obviously the boy was thrilled that O'Quinn had come to help them, and the prizefighter smiled warmly at him.

O'Quinn quickly loaded the rest of the supplies into the wagon. He knew that had McTeague been there he would have been angry that O'Quinn would risk reopening his wounds, but he did not care. He could not ignore someone who needed a hand—especially someone as pretty as Emily Burton.

"Thank you, Mr. O'Quinn," Emily said when he was finished. "I wish I could pay you for your trouble."

O'Quinn waved off the suggestion with both big hands. "Not at all, not at all. I was glad to help, Miss Burton. Do you live somewhere around here?"

"We have a small farm outside of town," she replied.

"Then I'd be glad to ride along and help you unload those goods."

Avery's face lit up, but Emily quickly shook her head. "That won't be necessary. Our father came into town with us, and we'll be picking him up as we leave. He can unload the supplies. I appreciate the offer, though, Mr. O'Quinn."

Avery looked disappointed, and O'Quinn thought

that little Nora did, too. But he shrugged and said, "Whatever you think best, ma'am. Any time I can give you a hand, just let me know."

"Thank you, Mr. O'Quinn." Emily smiled.

O'Quinn reached down to ruffle Avery's hair. "Say, why aren't you and your little sister in school today?"

The lad shifted his feet uncomfortably. "Aw, our pa said we didn't have to go. Said he wanted us to help pick up the supplies. Emily tried to talk him out of it—"

"That's enough, Avery," Emily interrupted him quickly. "We don't want to bore Mr. O'Quinn with our personal matters. Now come along. We have to get going."

She climbed onto the wagon, sat down on the wooden seat, and picked up the reins. Avery and Nora scrambled into the back and found places to sit among the supplies. Avery grinned and waved at O'Quinn as Emily urged the pair of mules that pulled the wagon into motion. Nora waved, too, and O'Quinn grinned as he returned the gesture.

Emily Burton did not wave, but she glanced over her shoulder as the wagon pulled away. O'Quinn was struck once again by her beauty—and by the sadness he saw in her deep brown eyes.

*That young woman's carrying quite a load,* O'Quinn thought. He was not thinking of the supplies packed in the back of the wagon.

He continued to watch Emily steer the wagon down Texas Street. As she brought it to a stop in front of a saloon a couple of blocks away, O'Quinn's eyes narrowed. Emily, Avery, and Nora sat quietly in the wagon for several minutes. Then the batwings of the saloon were pushed open, and a man appeared. Swaying slightly, he walked across the boardwalk to the wagon. *He's drunk,* O'Quinn decided.

Even at this distance, O'Quinn could make out quite a bit about the man. Dressed in work clothes, he wore a floppy-brimmed hat pushed back on his salt-and-pepper hair, and his bushy dark beard was streaked with white. Once he might have been muscular and powerful, but now his body had gone to fat. The man climbed awkwardly onto the wagon and sank down heavily next to Emily. He did not appear to say anything to any of the children. As his shoulders slumped and his head tipped forward on his chest, Emily flapped the reins and got the mules moving again.

"That's a shame, isn't it?" asked a voice nearby. O'Quinn turned to see Deputy Cody Fisher standing on the boardwalk a few feet away. He, too, was looking down the street after the Burton wagon.

"The man was drunk," O'Quinn snapped, not bothering to conceal his annoyance.

"Sure he was. Nobody's seen Charlie Burton anything but drunk for a long time now. From what I've heard, he used to be a good man, but his wife died a few years back, before I came to Abilene. According to folks who were around then, Charlie never was the same after that. Miss Emily's sort of had to hold things together."

"She has no help? She's raising those children by herself?" O'Quinn asked, appalled.

Cody shrugged. "I don't reckon Charlie is much help, if that's what you mean. He hides in a bottle most of the time. But Emily's been keeping things going. She's done a good job with those two kids, couldn't have done any better if they were her own."

The deputy grinned. "She's a good-looking woman, too."

"She certainly is," O'Quinn agreed.

"Most of the young bucks around here have been trying to court her for over a year now, but Miss Emily's not having any part of it. I reckon she feels she's got to worry about Avery and little Nora before she thinks about herself."

O'Quinn peered shrewdly at Cody. "You wouldn't be one of those would-be suitors, would you?"

Cody's grin widened. "I've always had an eye for a pretty gal, Mr. O'Quinn, and I wouldn't have been able to live with myself if I hadn't tried to get to know Emily Burton better. But I had about as much luck as everybody else—not a darned bit."

O'Quinn glanced toward the wagon. It had reached the edge of town and was just about out of sight. "Why are you telling me all this?" he asked.

"Well, . . . I figured from the look on your face you might be interested in Emily. Just thought I'd warn you not to get your hopes up too high."

O'Quinn laughed. "It's that obvious, is it?"

"I wouldn't worry about it. Like I said, you're not the first." Cody stopped smiling and went on, "Say, how are you doing? Seemed to me you took a pretty good beating the other night at Orion's."

"It looked worse than it really was." O'Quinn shrugged. "Dr. Bloom patched me up just fine. She seems like a good doctor."

"The best," Cody agreed. "Marshal Travis thinks so, too. He's fond of Aileen. Reckon all of us around here are. She's done a lot for the town."

Enough so that she was much more valuable staying here than she would be if she was in Chicago, where there were plenty of competent doctors, O'Quinn thought. McTeague had said nothing about wanting Aileen to return to Chicago with them, but O'Quinn would not have put it past the smitten detective.

Cody went on, "You haven't seen Willie Parker again, have you? We could only hold him for a night. When Willie paid his fine the next morning, the judge turned him loose. He just might come looking for you."

"Haven't seen him," O'Quinn replied, shaking his head. "And I hope I don't. I've had enough trouble here. I want the rest of my stay to be peaceful."

"When do you plan to start training again?"

"Soon, I hope. A boxer gets stale if he doesn't practice regularly."

Cody smiled again. "Why don't you put on another exhibition with Leslie Gibson? I heard that the first one didn't go very well." The deputy chuckled. "If you could arrange for Thurman Simpson to play the same part in it, you could invite the town and sell tickets. I would have paid money to see that!"

O'Quinn joined in Cody's laughter. "I'm afraid Leslie wouldn't go along. He came too close to losing his job to want to repeat it."

Cody shook his head. "If Simpson had gotten him fired, we would have done something about it. Folks out here stand behind their friends, Mr. O'Quinn."

O'Quinn nodded; he had already noticed that trait in Abilene.

"Well, I'd better be getting on about my business," Cody said. "Nice talking to you again, Mr. O'Quinn. I'm glad you're staying out of trouble."

"Of course. Trouble is the last thing I want, Deputy," O'Quinn assured him.

With a wave Cody strode down the boardwalk. O'Quinn watched him go, then crossed the street and resumed his journey to the Sunrise Café. As he walked, he mulled over what Cody had told him about Emily Burton and her family. The girl had obviously faced more than her share of hardships. O'Quinn's observation was laced with admiration for her, though, admiration for the way she had handled the problems and apparently conquered most of them.

But it had to be an added burden having a drunkard for a father. From the way Avery had spoken, Charlie Burton sounded like an obstinate, unreasonable man. Liquor probably just made him more so. O'Quinn wondered if he should have a talk with the man, try to straighten him out.

He gave a snort as he paused before the entrance to the café. He was a fine one to be thinking such things, he mused. Nothing but a struggling prizefighter to start with, and now he had hired killers after him. *Yes, I'm a fine one to butt into someone else's life and try to fix it,* he told himself sarcastically.

And given his circumstances, the last thing he needed to do was get involved with a woman, O'Quinn knew. He went into the café and tried to stop thinking about Emily Burton, concentrating instead on the huge platter of food that Agnes Hirsch brought to him. Roast beef, mashed potatoes, peas, corn bread, and gravy—that was all a man really needed.

Try as he might, however, O'Quinn found that he could not get Emily Burton out of his thoughts. She stayed with him all through his meal and during the walk back to the boardinghouse. He entered the house to find Jack McTeague seated in a chair just inside the front door, waiting for him.

"I was hoping you'd be back soon," McTeague said as he leapt to his feet. "Did you have any trouble?"

"Not a bit," O'Quinn told him. "I just had something to eat. And I talked to that deputy for a few minutes. He's a pretty friendly fellow, even if he does look like a gunslinger."

"Well, come along, I've got that telegram ready to send."

O'Quinn shook his head. "I'm sort of tired now, Jack. Why don't I go upstairs and rest for a little while?"

"You're all right, aren't you?" McTeague asked anxiously.

"I'm fine, just a little tuckered out, as they say around here. You go ahead. I'll be all right."

McTeague hesitated, then nodded. "If you're sure . . . but I'm worried I've already let you out of my sight too much today."

"Don't be," O'Quinn said with a laugh. "Nothing's going to happen here at Hettie's."

McTeague left reluctantly, and O'Quinn climbed the stairs to his room. It felt good to stretch out on his bed. He thought that he might doze off, especially after all the food he had eaten, but he found that his eyes would not stay closed. He kept staring up at the ceiling . . . and seeing Emily Burton's face.

When McTeague returned to the boardinghouse, he knocked on the door of O'Quinn's room, rapping softly in case the prizefighter was asleep. O'Quinn grunted, "Come in."

McTeague came into the room with a dark frown on his face. He glared at O'Quinn and snapped, "That door wasn't even locked, and you blithely told me to come in like you didn't have a care in the world, O'Quinn! What if I was Mitch Rainey, come to call with a gun in my hand?"

"You're not, though, are you?" O'Quinn replied,

rolling to the side of the bed and sitting up carefully. "Ease off, Jack. You ought to be able to see by now that nobody's going to bother us. You're worrying about nothing. And I've got other things on *my* mind."

The detective's face flushed with anger. "Oh? There's something more important than staying alive, I take it?"

"Damn right," O'Quinn growled. "I met a girl."

McTeague's mouth dropped open, and he stared at O'Quinn as if he could not believe what he had just heard. "You met a girl?" he repeated slowly. "One of the most vicious killers in the country is probably on your trail, and you're upset about some girl?" The detective's voice grew gradually louder. "Have you totally taken leave of your senses?"

O'Quinn glared at McTeague. "You're a fine one to talk, the way you've been mooning over that woman doctor!" he snapped. "I'm surprised you haven't claimed you're seeing double again, just so you could go back and have her feel your head some more!"

McTeague's hands knotted into fists. "Why, you . . . you damned lout!" he sputtered. "You don't have the brains to understand that a gentleman can have a perfectly harmless conversation with a lady without it meaning that he harbors any improper thoughts."

"Oh, you've been harboring them, all right, Jack. I saw the way you were looking at her the last time we went to her office." O'Quinn grinned mockingly. "And if you want to come take a swing at me because of it, you just go right ahead. I could use a little exercise."

McTeague took a deep breath and made a visible effort to relax. He slowly opened his fists and pressed fingers that were trembling with anger against his legs.

"This is ridiculous," he snapped. "We're on the same side, Seamus. We shouldn't be threatening each other."

"Maybe not," O'Quinn shot back. "I'm just getting tired of you pushing me around, mister. Just because you're a cop doesn't mean you can give me orders. Why, I could leave here and just forget about testifying against Gold and Rainey if I wanted to!"

"I suppose you could at that," McTeague replied in a hollow voice. "But that would be one sure way of getting yourself killed sooner or later. Gold would never rely on your silence unless you were dead. Besides, that would mean they would get away with killing Dooley Farnham."

O'Quinn's face fell. "You're right," he said. "I can't do that. But I can't stop thinking about that girl, either."

"You'll have plenty of time for her when this is over, O'Quinn," McTeague said more sympathetically now. "Just concentrate on staying alive. I know you think you're safe out here, but trust me. My instincts tell me we could still have trouble."

O'Quinn nodded. McTeague was right. Trouble could come at any time, in any shape or size—maybe even in the form of a beautiful young woman named Emily.

# *Chapter Seven*

◆━━◆━━◆

THERE WAS AN ACHE GNAWING AT WILLIE PARKER'S IN-
sides that hurt more than any of the cuts, scrapes, and
bruises he had picked up in the brawl with Seamus
O'Quinn. It was the pain of unfinished business. The
big Irishman probably still thought he could take
Parker in a fight. The issue had not been decided
because Marshal Luke Travis and Deputy Cody Fisher
had intervened, blast those meddling lawmen.

Laughing at him—that's probably what O'Quinn
was doing, Parker brooded darkly as he nursed a beer
in one of Abilene's smaller, more disreputable saloons
one evening, almost a week after the battle in Orion's.

Most of the bars in town would not serve him and
his friends anymore. There had been too many fights,
too much damage. Orion's had been one of the last
respectable places where he could buy a drink, and
now he knew better than to try to return. That crazy

Scotsman was liable to grab his shotgun and start blasting if Parker so much as showed his face over the batwings. So he was stuck drinking hot beer and watered-down rotgut in dives like this one.

And none of it was his fault, Parker told himself. It was all because folks thought they were better than he was, just because he was down on his luck and had to take on some shady jobs every now and then.

"Not fair," he muttered into his beer. "Dammit, just not fair."

"What'd you say, Willie?" asked one of his drinking companions. Several men were standing at the bar with him, not friends really, but as close to it as a man like Willie Parker was likely to get. They respected him—or at least they were afraid of him, and that was just as good.

"I said it was goddamned unfair," Parker growled. "We didn't start that fight in Orion's. It was that damned prizefighter."

Another man blinked owlishly at Parker. "I thought you told him you could whip him. I thought that was what started it."

Letting his rage boil over, Parker lashed out and backhanded the man, staggering him. "You stupid bastard!" he snarled. "I gave that Irishman a chance to back down. If he ain't got sense enough to do it, then the fight's his fault, understand?"

"Sure, sure," mumbled Parker's crony quickly, rubbing his sore jaw. "You're right, Willie, damned if you ain't!"

" 'Course I'm right," Parker grunted as he picked up his beer mug.

He was going to have to even the score with O'Quinn, but so far he had been unable to come up with a plan. Since the fight, he had spotted the prizefighter around town a few times, but O'Quinn had always been with that manager of his. Besides, the way Travis and Cody came running every time there was trouble, Parker knew he would wind up back in jail if he was not careful. This time the judge might not be so easy on him. He might have to serve a longer stretch. Parker knew he could not stand that, would never be able to bear being cooped up.

"Maybe I ought to just shoot the son of a bitch and be done with it," he muttered. None of the others paid any attention to him.

An ambush would not work, Parker decided. Travis would figure out who had done it and come looking for him. Besides, Parker wanted his revenge to be more satisfying than that. He wanted to be close enough to see pain on that black Irishman's face.

Other than Parker and his companions, there were three people in the saloon besides the bartender: a drunk who had passed out facedown on one of the tables, a young cowhand barely out of his teens whose face already showed the signs of dissipation, and a middle-aged prostitute who was trying to convince the cowboy that it was going to cost him more to get her to do what he had suggested. All of them ignored the man who came excitedly into the room and hurried over to Parker's side.

"I just saw him, Willie!" the newcomer babbled urgently to Parker. "I found out where he lives. Him and that manager of his just went into a boarding-house down on Second Street!"

Parker turned to peer at the man who was a minor member of the loose-knit gang. He had told all of his men to keep an eye out for O'Quinn in hopes of catching the prizefighter alone sometime. "What the hell good does that do?" Parker snarled. "He's still not where we can get at him, is he?"

"Maybe not," the man answered defensively. "But I thought maybe you could lay for him, now that you know where he's staying."

Parker nodded as he tried to force his brain to work. There might be something to what the man said. It might be even better if they could somehow draw O'Quinn's manager away from him.

A plan suddenly suggested itself to him. He drained the last of his beer and then grunted, "Come on." The other men trooped out of the saloon behind him.

They walked the few blocks to Second Street, then allowed the other man to direct them to the boarding-house where O'Quinn and McTeague were staying. Several lamps were lit inside the house, and Parker and his men crouched in the deep shadows of the yard. Clutching the arm of the man who had brought the information, Parker demanded, "Do you know which rooms they're in?"

The man shook his head. "Sorry, Willie, I don't. But I swear I saw 'em go into that house."

"All right." Parker nodded, releasing the man. The desire for revenge had burned away some of the drunken stupor that had gripped him earlier. Fumbling in his vest pocket, he pulled out the packet of matches he used to light cigars—whenever he could cadge one from somebody—and pressed it into the hand of another man. "There's an empty house just down the block," he ordered. "I want you to go down there and set it on fire."

"On fire?" the man echoed. "Willie, I can't do that—"

"The hell you can't," Parker cut in, his voice

grating. "You get a good blaze going and yell fire. It'll bring everybody in that boardinghouse out to see what's going on. We'll grab O'Quinn then."

"I don't know," the man said dubiously.

Parker's hand closed over his arm. "Do what I told you, dammit! Get moving!" He shoved the man away. "Get moving!"

"All right, all right," the flunky muttered thickly. He turned and disappeared into the night.

Parker hoped the man would do as he was told and not just keep going. But all of his companions knew what would happen if they riled him; none of them would want him coming after them.

"Come on," Parker whispered, jerking his head to indicate that the others should follow him. Quietly and carefully, they slipped into an even darker patch of shadows near the porch of the boardinghouse.

A few minutes crawled past, and Parker grew more nervous. He wondered if he should have set fire to the vacant house himself, rather than trusting someone else to do the job. But if he had done that, he would not be on hand here to capture the boxer.

Suddenly, he saw a flame flickering in the darkness up the street. It grew rapidly, throwing a harsh red glow into the yard around the house. "Fire! Help, somebody! Fire!" shouted Parker's man.

Inside the boardinghouse Parker heard the pounding of footsteps. A moment later, the front door burst open, as did several other doors along Second Street. Men ran onto the porch, looking around to try to locate the source of the commotion. The fire in the empty house was blazing on the second floor now. Through its windows Parker could see flames licking the inside walls and climbing steadily toward the roof.

Parker put out a hand to warn his companions to be

quiet. More tenants of the boardinghouse, accompanied by Hettie Wilburn herself, came outside and stared at the fire. One of them said sharply, "Come on, men! They'll be forming a bucket brigade!" Several men vaulted off the porch and raced toward the burning house. The others, including Hettie, followed behind them.

As the crowd on the porch cleared, Parker suddenly spotted O'Quinn and McTeague standing there, obviously uncertain about what to do. O'Quinn took a step forward, but McTeague stopped him with a hand on his arm. "What do you think you're doing?" McTeague demanded.

"We've got to help, Jack," O'Quinn answered as he turned to the other man. "That fire could spread!"

"I know all about fires spreading," McTeague replied grimly. "I was there when half of Chicago burned a few years ago. But this is none of our business, O'Quinn."

"Dammit, I can't just stand by and not help!"

Crouched in the shadows next to the porch, Parker sneered as he listened to the boxer's self-righteous words. O'Quinn was acting as if he really cared.

"All right," McTeague snapped. "I'll go down there and see if there's anything I can do to help. You stay here until I get back."

"But Jack—"

"I mean it, O'Quinn! I'm tired of you plunging into things without thinking."

O'Quinn looked angry, but he stayed on the porch while McTeague hurried away. A big crowd had gathered around the burning house, as people from all over town came to fight the fire. Hiding in the shadows, Parker heard the clanging of a bell and knew that Abilene's fire department, such as it was, was on its way to the scene. The horse-drawn water wagon could cut down the length of the line required for a bucket brigade, but that was about all it could accomplish.

Parker felt excitement coursing through him. He had certainly stirred up the town. That had not been his main goal, but it still felt good. At the moment, though, he had more important concerns.

Seamus O'Quinn was standing alone at the railing around the porch. No one was paying any attention to what was happening at the boardinghouse.

Parker hissed, "Now!" He reached up, grasped the railing, and pulled himself over it. The thud of his boots on the planks of the porch made O'Quinn whirl around. Parker threw himself forward, swinging a fist with all of his weight behind it.

The blow smashed into O'Quinn's jaw and drove him back against the porch railing. As he crashed into it, the wood splintered and cracked, then gave way completely, dumping him into Hettie Wilburn's flower bed. Parker staggered and had to grab what was left of the rail to keep from falling himself. He had not expected this. One of his men bumped into him from behind, and he suddenly felt himself falling toward O'Quinn.

The prizefighter caught his breath and rolled out of the way. Parker landed heavily in the dirt, the impact knocking the air out of his lungs. O'Quinn came up on his knees and shouted, "Jack!" just as one of Parker's men dove off the porch and tackled him.

Parker pushed himself up on his hands and knees and started to shake his head. He lifted it just in time to see a fist coming at him. O'Quinn had punched the other man, knocking him out, and thrown him aside.

128

Parker did not have a chance to get out of the heavyweight's way. The blow cracked into his jaw and sent him sprawling.

Everything was going wrong, Parker thought groggily. It had been such a good plan; it should have worked. But now when he looked up he saw McTeague running toward the knot of struggling men. In the garish firelight the barrel of the gun in McTeague's hand glinted dully.

For a second, Parker thought about reaching for his own gun, but he quickly discarded that idea. He did not want bullets flying around until he was more in control of the situation. Throwing lead wildly was a good way to get yourself shot. He pulled himself to his feet and yelled to his men, "Come on! Let's get out of here!"

O'Quinn was holding one of the men and was shaking him like a rat. Drawing on the strength of desperation, the man tore himself free and dropped to the ground, falling into a staggering run after his cronies. Parker was leading the group, and when he glanced back over his shoulder, he saw McTeague hurry up to O'Quinn. For a moment, McTeague leveled his gun at the fleeing men, but then O'Quinn caught his arm and pushed it down. Parker gulped a deep breath and ran harder, wanting to vanish into the shadows before McTeague got any more ideas about shooting.

Parker gasped curses as he ran. Everything had gone wrong, and he had been humiliated even worse than before. Now there was also the chance that someone might decide he and his friends had been responsible for the fire. That could bring the law down on his head for sure.

"I'll just . . . shoot the son of a bitch . . . next time!" Parker vowed as he ran. "Damned if I won't!"

Mitch Rainey lifted a hand to his face and wearily rubbed his eyes. He was tired, and it was hard to sleep in the smoky, noisy railroad car. Rainey was starting to feel the effects of a couple of weeks of living like a hunted animal pursuing his quarry. Always on the move, always searching . . . But he had a feeling his search was almost over. And when it was, Seamus O'Quinn would die.

Rainey was riding on a westbound train from Kansas City; a place called Abilene was one of the stops. Rainey had heard of the town before but knew nothing about it except that it had once been a wild, booming cattle town several years earlier when the railhead was located there. Over time the Kansas Pacific had been extended west, but Abilene was still a center for cattle shipping, although a succession of tough frontier lawmen had tamed it. Various people had told Rainey these things, but they did not prepare him for the veritable wilderness he was encountering now. In his entire life, he had not traveled any farther than twenty miles from downtown Chicago.

Had he been in Chicago right now, though, he might well be in jail—or dead. He knew a detective named McTeague had an eyewitness who would testify against them in the murders of Mel Rutherford and Dooley Farnham. Like Darius Gold, he had received a tip from one of their informers within the police force that the cops were closing in on him. However, Rainey had moved faster than Gold—and had been luckier, too. He did not mind admitting that.

Knowing where to run had not been a problem. A man named Dunleavy ran a tavern in a town on the outskirts of Chicago, but the place was actually owned by Darius Gold. Dunleavy had hidden wanted men in the tavern more than once, and the police had no clue as to its real purpose. Rainey knew he would be safe there, at least for a while.

He had been staying in a room above the tavern for two days when a visitor arrived. The man was a clerk in the Chicago prosecutor's office but had actually been working for Darius Gold for years, accepting payments for tidbits of interesting information that he could pass along. The news he brought to Rainey was considerably more than a tidbit. The clerk had gathered the information from several sources within the police force, and it told the whole story of how Seamus O'Quinn had survived the attempt to kill him. Inspector McTeague had left the city, according to the clerk, along with O'Quinn, in an effort to hide the prizefighter until it was time for him to testify in court.

Rainey digested this and then asked, "Does Mr. Gold know about this?"

The clerk nodded. "I gave the information to one of the officers who works as a guard in the city jail. He saw to it that Mr. Gold heard the news. He sent a message back out, too."

"And what was that?"

"Mr. Gold says for you to find McTeague and this boxer O'Quinn," the clerk told him. "He wants you to kill both of them."

Rainey nodded. The orders were certainly not unexpected. Getting rid of O'Quinn and McTeague —but especially the prizefighter—was the only way to be sure that the prosecutor would have no case against them. Rainey looked around the squalid room where he had been hiding and thought that it would be a relief to get out of there, even on such a desperate mission.

He did not think he would have any trouble tracing O'Quinn and McTeague. Darius Gold had contacts all over, people who would be anxious to provide assistance in hopes of putting a powerful man like Gold in their debt. Despite that, for several days Rainey found the trail cold. He knew that his quarry had left Chicago and was even able to learn they had boarded an eastbound train. But he could trace them no farther.

Then a break had come his way. A railroad porter in Indiana who was burdened with heavy gambling debts had reported seeing two men traveling together who answered the descriptions of O'Quinn and McTeague. They had been heading west this time, no doubt changing their direction in an attempt to throw off any pursuers. Rainey followed them, and in every town along the rail line, he stopped to ask questions. Usually there was someone who remembered seeing a big Irishman.

The trail continued to lead west, and then in Kansas City, Rainey encountered a gambler whom he had known briefly in Chicago several years earlier. The man remembered Rainey and was only too happy to tell him that he had heard stories about some prizefighter who was training in the town of Abilene. The gambler had been thinking about taking a trip out there himself, in hopes of getting a line on some upcoming bout. Rainey persuaded him not to. If the man in Abilene was Seamus O'Quinn, as seemed likely, Rainey did not want to do anything to scare him into running again.

Now, as Rainey sat in one of the passenger cars of the westbound train, he thought back over the long days that had led him here and hoped that his journey to Abilene would pay off.

If O'Quinn and McTeague were really there, it would be a payoff in blood, Rainey thought, smiling in anticipation.

Marshal Luke Travis did not regularly meet all the trains that came into Abilene, but if he happened to be near the depot when one was scheduled to arrive, he would walk onto the platform to take a look at the passengers who got off. He believed that keeping track of such comings and goings was part of his job.

Travis strolled through the station a few minutes before a westbound train was due to arrive. One of the porters was standing beside the door to the platform. "Hello, Marshal," the middle-aged black man said with a friendly smile.

"Morning, John," Travis replied. He glanced at the big clock on the wall. "Or rather, I should say afternoon."

"That's right, Marshal. Say, I heard there was some trouble last night. Something about a fire?"

Travis nodded. He was tired today, and part of the reason was the events of the night before. "The old Trimble house on South Second burned down," he said. "We were able to keep the fire from spreading to any of the other houses, but we couldn't save the one where it started."

The porter shook his head. "That's a shame. Anybody hurt?"

"No, that was lucky. The house was vacant, but it looked as though somebody had decided to camp there and their cooking fire got out of hand."

That was the theory advanced by the chief of Abilene's volunteer fire department, but Travis was not so sure it was correct. While he certainly could not prove it, he would have bet there was some connection between the fire and Willie Parker.

Seamus O'Quinn had told him that Parker and his men jumped him while everyone in the neighborhood was fighting the fire. McTeague had confirmed O'Quinn's story. Both men had gotten a good look at the man and were sure it was Parker. Travis wondered if Parker had purposely started the fire to create an opportunity to ambush O'Quinn. If not, it had certainly been a lucky coincidence.

Since he could not prove his speculation at the moment, he shared his thoughts only with Cody Fisher. The deputy had agreed that it was a possibility, given Parker's history of violence.

"I wouldn't mind having a little talk with Parker," Cody had said.

"Neither would I," Travis agreed grimly. "Keep an eye open for him."

So far this morning, though, no one had seen Parker around town. He had probably gone into hiding, afraid that he would be arrested for the attack on O'Quinn. He might have even lit out of the area, and if that was the case, it would be all right with Luke Travis.

As the sound of a train whistle floated through the autumn air, John, the porter, straightened. "That's the westbound," he said to Travis. "Right on time." He went out onto the platform to wait for the train to pull in, and Travis followed him. Several passengers were already there waiting to board, their baggage stacked beside them.

Travis leaned against one of the pillars that supported the roof over the long platform and looked to the east, where the tracks cut through the stockyards of the Great Western Cattle Company on the edge of town. This train would not stop at the stockyards, since it was heading west. Spewing smoke and steam, the locomotive pulled into the station a few moments later, accompanied by the hissing and squealing of brakes. As the engine slowed to a stop the conductor leapt from the caboose and hurried up the platform. "Aaaabileeeene!" he bawled at the top of his lungs.

Quite a few people got off the train. Businessmen and salesmen mingled with several families, some of whom came to visit relatives, others immigrants who planned to make Abilene their home. Travis watched as they stepped down from the train and decided that all of them looked fairly innocuous. He was glad to see the immigrant families. Abilene was a growing town, and he liked to think that new folks were always welcome.

Among the last passengers to disembark was a tall blond man who was wearing a city suit that was a bit rumpled from long travel. However, there was no mistaking the fine cut or the expensive fabric of the clothes. The man was handsome and in his twenties, Travis estimated. As he got off the train, he nearly bumped into a young woman who had just left one of the other cars with her family. He stepped back lithely and flashed a gracious smile at the young woman as he reached up to tip his soft felt hat. She blushed, smiled nervously, and hurried on.

Travis's eyes narrowed as he watched the incident. The newcomer was probably a ladies' man, accustomed to charming all the females he met with his good looks and that quick smile. There was nothing wrong with that. But something about the man alerted the instincts that Travis had developed in his years as a lawman. Something said that here was trouble.

But he could not arrest a man just because he did not like his looks, Travis thought. Still, he kept an eye on the blond newcomer as he claimed his bag from the baggage car and then strolled through the station and out into Railroad Street. The man headed for one of the saloons across the way, obviously intending to slake his thirst after a long train ride.

Travis let him go. There was nothing else he could do.

It did not take long for Mitch Rainey to discover that his search was indeed at an end. At the first bar he stopped in that afternoon Rainey learned that Seamus O'Quinn was in Abilene. Posing as a friendly, talkative stranger, Rainey bought drinks for several townsmen, and in return they told him all about the famous prizefighter who had chosen Abilene as the place where he would train for an important fight.

Rainey saw through that ruse immediately. He knew that his gunshots had hit O'Quinn, and the boxer could not have recuperated from his wounds by now to be planning a prizefight. That was just the story he and McTeague were using to cover the fact that they were hiding out. Now all Rainey had to do was make sure O'Quinn and McTeague never left Abilene alive.

After renting a room at the Grand Palace Hotel, Rainey spent the afternoon sizing up the town. There were plenty of saloons and taverns in Abilene, and he visited most of them during the rest of the day. In each place, he would nurse a beer, buying drinks for the men he subtly pumped for information. He heard about the boxing exhibition between O'Quinn and a local schoolteacher that had not quite come off. Several men also mentioned the brawl at Orion's that had involved O'Quinn and someone named Parker. Rainey got the impression that O'Quinn had become a fairly popular man in Abilene; his presence had livened things up and given people something to talk about.

His death would cause even more of a stir, Rainey was willing to wager. But he would be gone by then, on his way back to Chicago to resume the life he had been forced to abandon.

Early that evening as Rainey was leaving the Bull's Head Saloon, he spotted a tall man standing on the boardwalk across the street. Instinct told Rainey that he was being watched. He glanced over at the man and saw lantern light reflecting on the badge pinned to his vest.

A grin tugged at Rainey's mouth. The local lawman, obviously keeping an eye on the stranger in town. Rainey was not worried about that. No small-town badge-toter was going to cause him trouble. He remembered seeing the man watching him as he got off the train that afternoon. Rainey had paid little attention to him then, and he gave him not much more notice now. Cheerfully, Rainey turned and strolled down the boardwalk, ignoring the marshal.

Later that evening, Rainey found himself in a small saloon on Cottage Street near the stockyards. The lingering, pungent odor was familiar to him, growing up as he had in Chicago. However, this smell lacked the bloody undertones that hung in the air around the slaughterhouses.

Out of habit, Rainey kept one eye on his back, and he knew that the lawman who had been watching him earlier had gone on about his business. Rainey had no idea why the man seemed to be suspicious of him. He had done nothing to attract the attention of the authorities since arriving, and he intended to keep it that way. It would be best for him to remain behind the scenes until the time came to strike at O'Quinn and McTeague. Then he would hit hard and fast and be gone before anyone knew what had happened.

He leaned on the bar in the narrow, low-ceilinged tavern and ordered a whiskey from the bartender who was wearing a filthy apron. The building was constructed of weathered, unpainted planks that had warped from exposure to the elements. Night breezes whistled through large cracks in the walls, but the extra ventilation helped disperse the thick smoke in the air, so the cracks were not all bad.

Rainey had been sipping beer all day long, and he needed a real drink now. He picked up the glass the bartender set in front of him, frowning at the grimy smears on it, then tossed back the whiskey anyway. As the raw, potent stuff burned all the way down his throat, he grimaced but began to smile when a welcome fire started in his belly.

Someone pushed up to the bar beside him, jostling him a little. Rainey felt a sudden surge of anger and turned to see who had bumped him. The newcomer was a tall, broad-shouldered man with red hair who looked like a down-on-his-luck cowboy. "Whiskey," he growled to the bartender.

The man behind the bar picked up another glass and splashed rotgut into it. "Here you go, Parker," he said as he shoved it across the scarred hardwood. "You better be able to pay this time."

"I can pay, I can pay," the redheaded man grumbled. He pulled a coin from the pocket of his greasy jeans and slid it across the bar. As he picked up the glass, his hand trembled a bit. His face was flushed, and Rainey figured that he had probably been drinking most of the day.

The man swallowed the liquor in one gulp and then dragged the back of his hand across his mouth. He glanced at Rainey, saw that the blond man was watching him, and snapped, "What the hell's the matter with you?"

At first Rainey intended to make the man see the error of jostling him, by force if necessary, but then he decided to control his anger. He did not want to attract any more attention to himself than was necessary. When he heard the bartender speak the man's name, he was doubly glad of that decision, because he remembered what he had heard earlier in the day about a man called Parker. From the looks of things, this could be the same man.

Rainey ignored the redhead's question and said, "You wouldn't be the same Parker who just had a run-in with Seamus O'Quinn, would you?"

Parker's fingers tightened around his glass, and for a moment Rainey thought he was going to shatter it. "You ain't a friend of that son of a bitch, are you?" he demanded thickly.

Rainey shook his head. "Not at all. But I've heard of him. He's supposed to be quite a fighter."

"I would have taken him if folks hadn't kept buttin' in," Parker replied with a contemptuous snort.

Rainey nodded, trying to convey sympathy and understanding. "I've heard that O'Quinn can't fight his own battles," he said. "Surely you're going to even the score with him."

"Already tried," Parker grunted. "It didn't work out too good, though. I been lyin' low all day, 'til I couldn't stand it no more." He clenched one big fist and smacked it into his other palm. "That big Irishman's goin' to regret the day he met me, you mark my words."

Rainey tried not to grin too broadly. If he could get this simpleton Parker to do some of the dirty work for him, his job would be that much easier. "Oh, I believe you, my friend," he said. "And maybe you and I can help each other out."

Parker stared at him in puzzlement. "How's that?"

"You see, I have good reason to hate Seamus O'Quinn, too."

# Chapter Eight

O'QUINN MOVED A LITTLE AWKWARDLY AROUND THE sandbag hanging inside the stable. While his footwork was slightly off because he had spent too much time away from these workouts, the bag still shivered and swayed at the flurry of hard shots he peppered into it.

"Take it easy," McTeague advised. He was sitting on a chair several feet away from the perspiring heavyweight. "You know what the doctor said about putting a strain on those wounds."

"I'm being careful, Jack," O'Quinn puffed breathlessly. He shook his head in disgust. He had neglected his training for too long and let himself get into terrible shape. That was going to have to change from now on.

O'Quinn had talked McTeague into starting these mock training sessions again, but for the prizefighter the hours spent in the livery barn were more than a ploy. Sooner or later, this whole business with Darius Gold would be over. The trial would be concluded, and Gold and Rainey would either be in jail or hanged, just as they should be. Then O'Quinn would have to get on with his life. That meant going back into the prize ring. He vowed he would be ready—for his own sake, and for Dooley Farnham's.

It was going to be more difficult now that Dooley was gone. He would have to find a real manager again, instead of a fake like McTeague. But O'Quinn was confident that the right man would come along.

He suddenly wondered if Leslie Gibson had ever given any thought to a career as a manager. Leslie certainly knew the ropes and probably still had contacts in the business.

O'Quinn shook his head and pounded a blow into the sandbag. No point in even asking Leslie, he decided. He had never seen a man so content with his lot in life. Nothing was going to pry Leslie Gibson away from his schoolteaching.

For almost an hour, O'Quinn pummeled the bag. From time to time, when he wanted to put a little extra force into a blow, he imagined that he was trading punches with Willie Parker. O'Quinn's jaw hurt for days after he had taken that sucker punch on Hettie's front porch. He would have welcomed another shot at Parker, but the man seemed to have dropped from sight. According to Luke Travis, Parker had been seen around town a few times since the night of the fire, but he was keeping a low profile. The marshal had not been able to locate him to question him about the conflagration that destroyed the empty house.

By the time he finished the session, O'Quinn's face glistened with a fine sheen of sweat. He took the towel that McTeague handed him, wiped away the moisture, then draped the cloth around his neck. McTeague unlocked the stable, and they started back toward the boardinghouse.

As they passed Northcraft's apothecary, O'Quinn stopped abruptly. "I'm going to be sore in the morning," he said. "I think I'll step in here and see if they've got any liniment."

"All right." McTeague nodded and began to move toward the doorway.

"No, that's all right, Jack," O'Quinn said quickly. "I've got a few coins in my pocket. I can get it." He placed a hand on McTeague's arm to stop him from entering the store.

McTeague frowned, then shrugged. "All right. I'll wait out here for you."

"I'll just be a minute," O'Quinn said, grinning as he ducked through the doorway.

Inside the apothecary shop he saw that the two side walls were lined with shelves filled with sparkling, colorful jars and bottles. Across the rear wall was one of the new-fangled soda fountains. O'Quinn had seen a few of them in Chicago, but he was surprised to find one in Abilene.

Standing at the glass-fronted counter on the left side of the room was the reason O'Quinn had abruptly decided he needed some liniment. Emily Burton was studying the contents of several large jars that sat on top of the counter. O'Quinn had spotted her through the drugstore's large front window.

The jars Emily was looking at contained ribbons of licorice, peppermints, and horehound candies. O'Quinn suspected she was choosing a treat for Avery and Nora. With a broad grin on his face, he pulled a coin from his pocket and placed it on top of the counter. "Why not get the little ones some of each?" he asked.

Startled, Emily gasped and spun around to look up at him. "Why, Mr. O'Quinn!" she exclaimed. "I knew someone had come into the shop, but I had no idea it was you. You're certainly light on your feet for . . . for . . ." She paused, suddenly embarrassed.

"For someone as big as I am?" O'Quinn finished her sentence for her. "That's part of my training, Miss Burton. And I seem pretty lead-footed to myself at the moment." He gestured at the candy jars. "Buying a little something for the children, are you?"

Emily smiled. "Actually, I was trying to decide which one *I* wanted. I'll get some for Avery and Nora, too, of course."

O'Quinn threw back his head and laughed. "Then by all means get some of each," he told her. "We can't have you worrying over such a decision."

Emily looked down at the coin on the countertop and shook her head. "Oh, no, I couldn't—" she began.

"You can, and you will," O'Quinn insisted. "Otherwise my feelings will be hurt."

Emily shrugged and smiled again. "Well, in that case I suppose I will try all three of them."

She turned and caught the eye of the clerk who was standing behind the soda fountain. He came up the narrow aisle behind the counter, and Emily asked him to put several pieces of candy from each jar into a sack for her. As the clerk filled the bag, O'Quinn walked to the other side of the pharmacy and reached across the counter to pluck a bottle of liniment from one of the shelves. Returning to Emily's side, he told the clerk, "I want to buy this, too."

"Yes, sir," the young man replied. "You're Mr. O'Quinn, the boxer, aren't you?"

O'Quinn glanced down at his clothes and wondered who else the boy might take him for in this get-up. But he just grinned and nodded. "That's right."

"You'll find that liniment is just the thing to take care of sore muscles and bruises, sir," the clerk began, but O'Quinn cut him off with a wave of a big hand.

"I know all about it, son," he said. "Now, if you don't mind, I was talking to the young lady . . . ?"

"Oh." The clerk grinned and scooped up the coin from the counter. "Of course, sir." He went to resume his position behind the soda fountain.

Emily picked up the sack of candy. "I appreciate this, Mr. O'Quinn, and I know Avery and Nora will, too. Sweets are a rare treat for the children. I happened to have a little extra money I made doing some sewing, so I thought I would buy a little surprise to give them when they got home from school."

"You save that money," O'Quinn told her. "I'm sure there are plenty of ways you can put it to good use."

"Yes, indeed." Emily sighed, and the happy glow on her face faded a bit. "There seem to be more expenses than ever these days."

O'Quinn understood what she meant. With her father's drinking, it was doubtful that he earned much from the family farm. And from what O'Quinn had heard, raising children was an expensive proposition.

"Well, I'd better be getting back," Emily went on. "Thank you again, Mr. O'Quinn."

"Call me Seamus."

"All right. Thank you, Seamus," she said and started toward the doorway.

O'Quinn snatched up his bottle of liniment and fell

in step beside her. "I didn't see your wagon outside," he commented.

"I'm riding one of our mules today," Emily said. "I'm afraid it's not very dignified or ladylike, but it's easier than hitching up the wagon."

*That explains her outfit,* O'Quinn thought. She was wearing denim pants, a man's shirt, and scuffed work shoes. The garments would be appropriate for riding a mule, even if they were not very glamorous. Nevertheless, O'Quinn thought Emily looked just fine in them.

"Perhaps I should rent a horse and ride out to the farm with you to make sure you get home all right," O'Quinn suggested.

Pausing at the doorway, Emily laughed, then said quickly, "I'm sorry, Mr. O'Quinn—"

"Seamus," he reminded her.

"I'm sorry, Seamus, but you're the visitor in these parts, not me. I've ridden the trail from our farm into town and back hundreds of times. I'm perfectly capable of getting home. But I appreciate the offer."

O'Quinn had to grin. She was right. He was letting gallantry—and the desire to remain in her company for a while longer—overcome logic. He said, "Be that as it may, I would like to see your farm sometime."

"There's really not much to see. Some fields that don't grow as much as we'd like, a few chickens and milk cows and goats."

"Ah, but to a city boy like myself, I'm sure it would be fascinating," O'Quinn assured her.

Emily looked thoughtful for a moment, then peered at him with the prettiest brown eyes he thought he had ever seen. "Why don't you come out and have Sunday dinner with us?" she asked.

As anticipation and delight surged through him, O'Quinn nodded. "I'd like that," he said. Sensing someone watching him, he glanced up and saw McTeague glaring through the window of the drugstore. O'Quinn grinned and went on, "I'd like that very much."

"Good. I know Avery and Nora will, too. The place is easy to find. You just follow the main road south out of town for about a mile, and then you'll come upon a trail turning to the east. We're two miles down that trail."

"I'll find it," he assured her.

A soft smile curved Emily's lips. "We'll be looking forward to your visit."

"Not as much as I will be," O'Quinn promised.

Emily said good-bye and stepped onto the boardwalk. O'Quinn followed, standing and watching as she climbed onto the mule that was tied at the hitchrack. With a cheerful wave she turned the animal and rode off, and O'Quinn returned the gesture with a broad grin on his face.

"You look utterly ridiculous," McTeague snapped. He was leaning against the building wall a few feet away.

O'Quinn snorted. "No more than you when you were talking to Dr. Bloom," he declared.

McTeague shook his head. "You don't know what you're talking about. My admiration for Dr. Bloom is strictly professional." Changing the subject, he went on quickly, "I suppose that was the woman you mentioned the other day."

"Emily Burton is her name. Did you ever see such a lovely thing, Jack?"

"As a matter of fact, I have. I suppose she's the reason you suddenly had to go in there?"

O'Quinn held up the bottle he had purchased. "I went in to get some liniment, just like I told you."

McTeague nodded, but his expression made it clear that he did not believe O'Quinn for a second. He turned and started on toward the boardinghouse, and O'Quinn fell in beside him.

*Sunday dinner.* That was two days away, O'Quinn thought. Two long days for him to wait before he saw Emily again. He told himself to be patient, but he knew it was going to be difficult.

One thing was certain. He would not tell McTeague about it until the last minute; otherwise, the detective would try to forbid him to leave. And O'Quinn did not intend to let anything stand in the way of his visit to the Burton farm.

Luke Travis shook hands with the tall, brown-haired man in a sober dark suit. "Good sermon today, Judah," Travis told him.

"Thank you, Luke," Reverend Judah Fisher replied with a smile. "Do you think that next week we could convince Cody to stop by and offer his opinion on my preaching?"

Travis chuckled. "You know your brother better than I do. What do you think?"

Judah smiled ruefully and shook his head.

The two men were standing in the vestibule of the Calvary Methodist Church following Sunday morning services. The congregation was filing out, and Travis moved on so that other people could shake hands with Judah. As he stepped into the bright sunshine, the marshal put his hat on. In the yard in front of the church a large group of youngsters raced about, laughing and letting off steam after sitting quietly for an hour in church. Many of them were orphans who lived in the large parsonage next door. The building had been converted into an orphanage by Judah Fisher and Sister Laurel, the Dominican nun who had brought the homeless children to Abilene. There were also quite a few other children belonging to the families that came not only from Abilene but also from many of the surrounding farms and ranches. The youngsters ran around the buggies and wagons, their laughter filling the air and giving Luke Travis a feeling of contentment.

From the little knoll on which the church sat, he could see Abilene spread out before him to the southeast. It was a growing town, a good town, and Travis knew that he had helped make it so, along with a lot of other people. It was a feeling of satisfaction, of working for the common good and getting things accomplished.

Travis untied his horse and swung into the saddle. He rode down Elm Street, crossing the Kansas Pacific tracks, and turned east on Texas Street. As he pulled his mount to a stop in front of the marshal's office, the sound of angry voices coming from across the street caught his attention. He turned to see Seamus O'Quinn and Jack McTeague walking down the boardwalk past the Sunrise Café.

"I don't care what you say, Jack, I'm going," O'Quinn declared in a voice loud enough for Travis to hear clearly. The prizefighter stopped walking and glared angrily at McTeague. "She invited me, and I intend to be there."

"The hell you will!" McTeague snapped. "I've told you and told you about things like this—" He broke off his protest and grabbed O'Quinn's arm. "Come on."

Frowning, Travis dismounted slowly and continued to watch the two men over the back of his horse. From the look on O'Quinn's face, he expected to see the big prizefighter take a poke at his manager. But O'Quinn took a deep breath, jerked his arm out of McTeague's grip, and stalked away. McTeague hurried after him, talking in lower tones now, but Travis could see the urgent, anxious look on his face.

As O'Quinn and McTeague turned a corner and disappeared, Travis shook his head and stepped onto the boardwalk. He could not help but wonder what the men had been arguing about. In the time they had been in Abilene he had learned very little about them, and he was still suspicious of them, especially McTeague. Travis's instincts told him there was more to the man than he was revealing.

Shrugging, he went into the office. Sooner or later, he thought, he was going to find out what those two were up to.

McTeague had reacted just as O'Quinn had expected him to—like a bullheaded fool. As he stalked toward the boardinghouse, McTeague hurried along beside him, telling him all the reasons why he could not keep his appointment with Emily Burton and her family.

O'Quinn did not care about any of the reasons McTeague was spouting. The only thing that mattered to him was that he did not intend to let Emily down.

"Look, just forget it!" O'Quinn snapped, cutting off the detective's angry speech. "I'm sorry I ever brought it up. I thought it would be safe to take a ride in the country, but I guess I was wrong."

"You certainly were," McTeague said stiffly. "You've wandered off entirely too much since we've been here."

"We haven't had any trouble, have we?" O'Quinn asked.

"What do you call that brawl in Orion's Tavern?" McTeague demanded. "And that night when Parker jumped you at the boardinghouse?"

O'Quinn poked a blunt finger into McTeague's chest. "And neither one of those ruckuses had one damned thing to do with Gold and Rainey and the real reason we came out here," he pointed out. "They were just pure bad luck."

McTeague pushed O'Quinn's finger aside. "There's no such thing as bad luck, only bad planning," he snorted.

There was no arguing with such reasoning, O'Quinn thought. He turned and started toward the boardinghouse again.

McTeague thought he had won, O'Quinn mused grimly. But the detective would soon find out just how wrong he was.

When the two men entered the boardinghouse, they discovered that Sunday dinner was on the table and that the other tenants had gathered in the dining room and were just sitting down.

"Well, we were about to decide you two weren't going to make it today," Hettie called from her seat at the head of the table. "Have a seat, gentlemen."

McTeague sat down in the vacant chair where he had been taking his meals. The chair next to it was empty also, since O'Quinn usually claimed it.

O'Quinn hesitated, waiting until McTeague was seated to say to Hettie, "I'll be right back, ma'am. The rest of you go ahead and start without me."

McTeague started to slide his chair back and stand up, but O'Quinn's hand came down hard on his shoulder. "No need to get up, Jack," the prizefighter went on. "I'll just be out back for a few minutes."

McTeague and Hettie Wilburn both flushed, the

detective from anger, the landlady embarrassed that O'Quinn had made it so clear he was going to visit the outhouse. The other boarders paid no attention to the exchange; they were busy passing around the platters of food Hettie had prepared. McTeague glared at O'Quinn for a second, then settled back down in his chair and reached for a plate of biscuits. There was no way he could insist on accompanying O'Quinn without looking utterly foolish.

O'Quinn nodded to Hettie and ducked out of the dining room, going down the hall to the rear door of the house and stepping outside. He was grinning as he skirted the outhouse and walked briskly toward Texas Street.

He had not known if his ploy would work, but luckily McTeague's sense of decorum had prevented him from following O'Quinn. The inspector had to be sitting at that table in a rage, knowing that O'Quinn had given him the slip.

When O'Quinn reached Abilene's business district, he headed for the livery stable where he worked out. He knew most of the men who worked there, and when he got to the barn he saw that an older fellow named Wiley was sitting in the office today.

"Hello, Mr. Wiley," O'Quinn nodded to the man. "Not very busy today, is it?"

Wiley shook his head. "Not right now. Might be some folks wantin' to rent buggies later for Sunday afternoon drives. You come to punch that sandbag some?"

"Not today," O'Quinn told him. "I want to rent a horse."

The older man frowned. "I didn't know you could even ride, Mr. O'Quinn."

"Well, maybe now would be a good time to learn," O'Quinn said with a grin. "Have you got a nice gentle mount that I could ride out into the country?"

"Reckon I do. You headed any place in particular?"

"Just out for some fresh air," O'Quinn told him. "Thought I'd ride into the country south of town."

Wiley nodded and stood up. "Come on. I'll show you a couple of mares I've got that are good riding horses. You'll need a saddle, too, won't you?"

"The whole outfit," O'Quinn agreed.

He left the livery stable a few minutes later, mounted on the horse that he had selected with Wiley's assistance. It was a five-year-old mare, sturdy enough to carry his large frame without any trouble yet easygoing enough for a novice to manage. Awkwardly he pointed the animal's nose south and managed to get her moving. As he rode out of town, he hoped that Emily did not think he had forgotten about her dinner invitation. He was going to be a little late, but he was sure now that he was going to get there.

And there was not one thing Jack McTeague could do about it.


Luke Travis had been taking a leisurely turn around the town prior to eating his dinner when he saw O'Quinn riding out of the livery stable. The big man looked pretty uncomfortable on horseback, but he seemed to be managing to make the animal go where he wanted it to go. Seeing O'Quinn on a horse was one of the last things Travis would have expected. He strolled over to the stable to satisfy his curiosity.

Wiley confirmed that O'Quinn had rented the horse. "Said he was just going for a ride south of town to get some fresh air," Wiley told the marshal. "Reckon he must've been tellin' the truth. Don't know why else a greenhorn like that would want to get on a horse."

Travis nodded thoughtfully, then thanked Wiley for the information and headed toward his office, forgetting for the moment his plan to visit the Sunrise Café for his Sunday dinner. As he strode along the boardwalk, he thought about the angry conversation between O'Quinn and McTeague he had overheard earlier. O'Quinn had mentioned an invitation of some sort from a woman.

Cody was in the marshal's office cleaning the rifles from the wall rack when Travis came in. He looked up and nodded a greeting, then peered at the marshal more closely as he noticed the puzzled expression on Travis's face. "Something bothering you, Marshal?" he asked.

"I just saw Seamus O'Quinn riding out of town on a horse," Travis said.

"Was that McTeague fella with him? He's been sticking to O'Quinn like a grass burr."

Travis shook his head. "O'Quinn was alone, as far as I could tell. He rode south out of town. Wiley over at the livery stable rented him the horse, said O'Quinn told him he was going for a ride."

"A ride out to the Burton place, most likely." Cody grinned.

Travis's interest quickened. "What's that about the Burtons?"

"I saw O'Quinn talking to Emily Burton a few days ago. He asked me a few questions about her afterwards, seemed pretty taken with her." Cody's grin widened. "I warned him he probably wouldn't get very far."

Remembering O'Quinn's statement about an invitation, Travis was not so sure about that. Given the day and the time, Sunday dinner was pretty likely to figure in any invitation.

"The Burton farm is south of here, isn't it?"

"Southeast," Cody replied. "Over past the Mahaffey place."

Travis nodded, again deep in thought. "Maybe I'll ride out there a little later and make sure O'Quinn got there all right. He looked like he might get thrown off that horse if he wasn't careful."

"Probably never been on one before," Cody commented. "You think he was going to see Emily Burton?"

"Reckon we'll find out. Now, why don't we go get some dinner ourselves?"

Cody quickly finished cleaning the rifle he was working on and replaced it on the rack. "Sounds good to me," he said.


Seamus O'Quinn was not the only man traveling south out of Abilene on this sunny autumn Sunday. Riding far enough behind him so that they would not be seen were two men, who were keeping an eye on the distant figure of their quarry.

Mitch Rainey reached down and stroked the stock of the Winchester sheathed in the saddle boot. The smooth wood was reassuring. He felt slightly uneasy sitting on the back of a horse, but with Willie Parker along, he expected no trouble.

Enlisting Parker as an ally had been simplicity itself. The man was not overly intelligent, but he knew this area and, as far as Rainey could tell, had no scruples. He also possessed a grudge against O'Quinn that demanded vengeance. Parker had been only too happy to keep an eye on O'Quinn and report his movements to Rainey, allowing the man from Chicago to remain in the background. For several days, Parker had watched O'Quinn, but until today the big prizefighter had always been with a man Rainey recognized as Inspector Jack McTeague of the Chicago police force.

Now O'Quinn was alone, and Rainey was not going to miss this opportunity to kill him. As the only eyewitness against Rainey and Darius Gold, O'Quinn was the more important target. McTeague could be disposed of later. Once Parker had brought him the news that O'Quinn was riding out of town by himself, Rainey had quickly gotten horses and guns ready. All that remained was finding the right spot.

Today, Rainey thought as he patted the stock of the rifle again, Seamus O'Quinn was going to die.

# *Chapter Nine*

———◆———

As Seamus O'Quinn followed the broad, well-beaten trail south from Abilene onto the rolling prairie, it occurred to him that he had always judged distances in city blocks. Emily had told him to take this route for a mile, but he had no idea how far that was. There were few landmarks on the vast, open landscape, and O'Quinn quickly saw that he had no way of knowing how far he had come from town.

After he had been riding on the road for what seemed to be a long time, he came upon a smaller track that veered off to his left. That should be east, he supposed. Pulling back on the reins, he brought his horse to a halt and studied the trail for a moment before making up his mind.

*Might as well follow it for a while and see what I find,* he decided. Turning the horse's head, he gently urged it down the narrow track.

When he had traveled on the smaller trail for what he figured was as far as he had come from Abilene, he noticed a cluster of buildings nestled in a copse of trees up ahead. The house was a dirt structure that Leslie Gibson had told him was called a soddy. At one point, the teacher mentioned that it was expensive to build frame houses in Kansas because timber was scarce and that settlers often lived in soddys for quite a while. Near the house stood a barn with a corral next to it. The small farm looked well-cared for and fairly prosperous.

In front of the sod house a man was lounging in a chair, whittling while several small children played on the ground around him. Suddenly spotting O'Quinn, the man straightened, reached behind him, and plucked a rifle from the ground. Resting the weapon lightly on his lap, he stared at O'Quinn and waited for him to ride up to the house.

Feeling the cautious settler's eyes upon him, O'Quinn realized that, while the area seemed pretty civilized, danger from outlaws and possibly even Indians was a persistent threat to what he assumed was an easygoing, perhaps monotonous life. He wondered how Emily felt about living so far from town when a situation could become precarious with very little warning.

O'Quinn reined in, pulling too hard on the lines and making his horse dance around nervously. When the mare quieted down, O'Quinn grinned and pushed his derby back on his head. "Hello," he said to the vigilant settler. "I'm looking for the Burton place. Am I going in the right direction?"

The farmer spat on the ground. "You got business with the Burtons?" he asked warily. As the man spoke, O'Quinn noticed a woman standing half-hidden in the shadows of the doorway, peering at him. She motioned abruptly with her fingers, and the children scurried inside the house.

"Miss Emily Burton invited me to take Sunday dinner with them," O'Quinn replied in a soothing tone. "Don't worry, mister. I didn't ride out here to cause any trouble."

The man seemed to relax. "It don't pay to take chances this far out. Yeah, you're on the right trail, friend. My name's Mahaffey; my place borders the Burton farm." He nodded toward the east. "You just keep on followin' this trail. You'll see their place in about another mile."

"Thanks," O'Quinn answered and glanced around again at the farm. "Looks like you've got a pretty nice place."

"We've worked hard enough for it," Mahaffey observed dryly, but he nodded and smiled slightly at the compliment.

His wife reappeared in the doorway. "Not like that shiftless Charlie Burton," she snapped. Obviously the lean, sour-faced woman had been listening to their conversation.

Mahaffey glanced up at her. "Now, Frieda, you got no call to talk like that," he chided. "I reckon Charlie does the best he can—"

"No, he don't, and you know it, Daniel Mahaffey. When I think about those poor children having to do without so Charlie can keep drinkin' up every cent he makes . . ." She shook her head and clucked her tongue.

"Mind what you say now, woman. It ain't none of our business." Mahaffey scowled and shook his head. Evidently he had been fighting this battle with his acid-tongued spouse for quite some time.

O'Quinn tipped his hat to the lady and said to Mahaffey, "Thanks again for the help. I'd better be going." Turning the horse's head back toward the trail, he bumped his heels gently against its flanks and nudged it into a walk.

The exchange between the settler and his wife confirmed O'Quinn's suspicions about Charlie Burton. After Burton's wife died, he must have retreated into the bottle in an attempt to ease his pain. O'Quinn had watched several boxers do the same thing, only they were trying to forget physical rather than emotional aches. Early in his career he himself had gone on an occasional binge, but then Dooley had come along and turned his career—and him—around.

Dooley had probably saved his life, O'Quinn reflected. Maybe all Charlie Burton needed was someone to take him in hand and straighten out his thinking.

He mulled that over as he followed the trail. After he had ridden for what he guessed to be a mile, he began to look around for signs of the Burton farm. As he topped a rise and started down into the shallow valley below, he saw the house near a line of brush and small trees that indicated the presence of a stream. Pleased with himself, O'Quinn smiled. Mahaffey had told him it was about a mile farther on; he was getting better at judging distances.

As he drew closer, O'Quinn could see that at one time the Burton house must have been considerably nicer than Mahaffey's soddy. Now it really needed work. The two-story structure was built of planks that had once been whitewashed, although it had obviously been a long time since a new coat had been applied. There were a couple of broken posts in the front porch railing. Several shingles had blown off the roof sometime in the past and had never been replaced. The barn behind the house was in no better shape. O'Quinn shook his head sadly. What had once been a fine little farm was falling apart.

Suddenly O'Quinn was angry. Charlie Burton had stopped caring. How could a man—even one who had suffered the loss of his wife—neglect his responsibilities like this when he had such a fine family in Emily, Avery, and little Nora?

Then he reined in his roiling emotions and told himself not to voice those thoughts once he got in the house. As an itinerant boxer, a slugger who made his living by being able to take more punishment and dish out more pain than the other man in the ring, he had no right to judge anyone. He was no example.

But that did not change the way he was starting to feel about Emily. It did not matter that he had only seen her and talked with her a couple of times. O'Quinn knew his feelings were genuine.

The front door of the house burst open, and Avery ran out on the porch. "Mr. O'Quinn!" he cried gleefully. "Mr. O'Quinn's here!"

O'Quinn wondered if the boy had been sitting inside watching through the window, waiting for him. He rode into the yard in front of the house and slid out of the saddle, glad to feel the solid ground beneath his feet again. Avery, a broad smile on his pale face, rushed down the steps to meet him.

"Hello, Avery," O'Quinn greeted him. "I hope I'm not too late for dinner."

"Oh, no, Emily wouldn't let us eat until you got here," Avery blurted. "She said nobody was touching a bite until then."

"Avery!" Emily cried from the doorway. O'Quinn glanced up and saw she was blushing. Nora pushed past Emily and came onto the porch, beaming at O'Quinn.

O'Quinn extended the mare's reins toward Avery. "Do you think you could do something with this horse, lad?" he asked.

"Oh, sure. I'll put her in the barn and give her some grain," the boy replied happily. He took the reins and started leading the animal toward the barn. Over his shoulder, he called, "Don't start without me!"

"We won't," Emily assured him. Suddenly she blushed again and reached quickly behind her to untie the apron she was wearing. O'Quinn stepped onto the porch.

He rested a hand on Nora's blond head for a moment, then looked at Emily and smiled. "You're looking as lovely as ever," he told her.

"Thank you," she murmured, her blush deepening as she met his gaze.

O'Quinn had never seen a more beautiful woman. Her dress was made of simple homespun calico, like Nora's, but on her slim figure it was attractive, almost elegant. She had brushed her clean, long hair until it shone, and her eyes were warm and soft.

"Goddamn it, he's here, ain't he? Get inside and let's eat! A man could damn well starve to death around here."

Emily flinched at the harsh words bellowed from inside the house. Little Nora suddenly looked frightened and cowered against her sister's skirts. Emily squeezed her shoulder and said softly, "It's all right, Nora. It's not your fault. I'm the one he's mad at."

O'Quinn frowned. "I made trouble for you by being late, didn't I?"

"Not at all," Emily said, shaking her head quickly. "My father's just not feeling very well today."

O'Quinn nodded, willing to accept the fiction rather than cause her any more embarrassment. At that moment Avery came running back from the barn, and the four of them went into the house, the two children leading the way.

They entered a large room that served as the parlor, dining room, and kitchen, and O'Quinn glanced around. The disrepair he had noticed outside continued inside the house as well. At one time the walls had been plastered, but large cracks had developed that badly needed attention. Moisture from a leak in the roof had warped the floor boards. The upholstered furniture, which was arranged in one corner of the room, was heavily patched, and the sofa's stuffing threatened to cascade onto the floor in a few places. Despite these problems, the place was clean and neat, and O'Quinn knew that Emily was doing her very best with little or no help.

In the center of the room stood a long table, and a man was slumped in a chair at its head. O'Quinn recognized Charlie Burton from the brief glimpse he had had of him in Abilene. Now that O'Quinn was in the same room with him, he could see the dull yet haunted expression in Burton's eyes and the silver streaks in his hair and beard. His lined face, which once had been handsome, was set in what seemed to be a perpetual scowl.

Burton looked O'Quinn up and down and said, "So you're the one these whelps have been talkin' about for a week. Big bastard, ain't you?"

"Pa, this is Seamus O'Quinn," Emily said in a tightly controlled voice. "He's our friend, so please be nice to him."

"Are you sayin' I ain't always nice?" Burton snapped. "What the hell kind of a way is that to talk?

Do you know how hard I work for you and those brats? Ain't that nice?"

O'Quinn felt his hands slowly bunching into fists. He saw the way Emily stoically withstood her father's unpleasantness. Avery and Nora, however, did not take it quite as well. Both children looked ashamed and frightened at the same time, as if they wished they could run away and hide.

For a moment O'Quinn thought how satisfying it would be to grab Charlie Burton's shirtfront, drag him to his feet, and backhand him a few times. But with great effort he controlled that impulse. Taking a deep breath, he forced himself to say calmly, "There's no need to get upset, Mr. Burton. I'm sure Emily and the kids know what you've done for them." He stepped forward and extended his hand. "I'm glad to meet you."

Burton grunted and said nothing, but after a moment he half rose and grudgingly shook his hand. O'Quinn could smell the liquor on his breath as he sank back in his chair. Burton had probably been drinking since he got up that morning.

Emily hurried to the stove that stood against one wall of the big room. "We don't have anything fancy," she said apologetically to O'Quinn as she started carrying the food to the table.

"I came for some good home-cooked food," he assured her, waving off her comment. "And I'm sure everything will be just fine."

Smiling at his compliment, Emily nodded to the children to help as she put down a large pot of stew that smelled wonderful to O'Quinn. She instructed Nora to bring a dish of buttered greens, while Avery carried two pans of cornbread. Returning to the stove, she picked up a pot of coffee and brought it to the table.

While they worked, O'Quinn had remained standing. Now Emily stood at her chair with a puzzled frown creasing her brow until she realized that he was waiting for her to sit down. She smiled and blushed again, then sat down after seeing that Avery and Nora were both settled in their seats.

As O'Quinn took his own seat across the table from the two children, he realized he must seem like quite a gentleman to Emily after what she was used to. The idea surprised him because he had never thought of himself that way. Where he had grown up, the fight game had been the only thing to aspire to. While it had been good to him, it had not taught him manners or turned him into a gentleman. There were usually gentlemen around, gamblers and swells like Mel Rutherford, but the boxers were a pretty rough lot.

Evidently Emily had a higher opinion of him than he had of himself. The smile she gave him as she held out a bowl of stew warmed him more than the hot food ever would.

Gradually the atmosphere around the table became more relaxed. Charlie Burton busied himself with eating and did not speak. But Avery, emboldened by O'Quinn's friendly demeanor, asked him a multitude of questions about prizefighting. Then Emily wanted to know about Chicago and Philadelphia and New York. O'Quinn tried his best to answer all their questions and enjoyed himself hugely in the process. The food was excellent, and with the exception of the surly, silent figure at the head of the table, he could not have asked for better company.

Time seemed to fly. Before O'Quinn knew it, the

meal was over, but everyone except Nora was content to remain at the table. The little girl slipped into one of the other rooms and came back with a doll that she showed to O'Quinn with quiet pride. He took the small stuffed figure in his large, calloused hands and examined it with great care. "Why, that's just about the finest doll I've ever seen," he proclaimed.

"Emily made her for me," Nora said, beaming. "Her name is Abigail Elizabeth."

"That's a very pretty name." O'Quinn glanced at Emily. "And she's a pretty little doll, just like you, Nora."

"Thank you." Nora took the doll back and scampered away to play.

"Why'd you come here, mister?" Charlie Burton demanded suddenly, speaking for the first time since the meal began.

"Pa!" Emily cried before O'Quinn could answer. "I told you I *invited* Mr. O'Quinn."

"Shut up," Burton growled. "I didn't ask you. I asked *you*, mister. Why are you prowlin' around here? You hear in town that my little girl's a whore?"

"Pa . . ." Emily moaned.

O'Quinn had never heard more pain in a voice than there was in Emily's at that moment.

"Well, that's what folks say, ain't it, gal?" Burton snarled. "For all I know it's true. You may be a whore, but you couldn't prove it by the money you bring in."

O'Quinn felt the blood pounding in his head. He was as angry as he had ever been in his life, but he was trying very hard not to give in to that emotion. If he did, he knew he would beat Charlie Burton to within an inch of his life.

Avery did not have that much self-control. He rose from his chair and turned toward his father, shouting,

"Shut up! Don't say that about Emily, you drunken old man! Just shut u—"

The boy, shaking with fury as he spoke, had unwittingly edged closer to Burton. Moving with surprising speed, Burton lashed out and cracked the flat of his hand across Avery's cheek. The boy cried out in pain and caught himself on the table as he started to fall.

Fists clenched, O'Quinn was out of his chair in an instant, but before he could reach Burton, Emily grabbed his arm and hung on tightly. "No, Seamus!" she begged. "Don't! Please . . ."

Scraping his chair back, Burton stood up. His hand slid to his belt and drew a knife that was sheathed on his hip. O'Quinn had not seen the weapon, since Burton had been sitting ever since he arrived. Waving the blade menacingly, he bellowed, "Come on, you damned fancy prizefighter. I'll carve you into little pieces!" Curses poured from his mouth as he continued to taunt O'Quinn.

"You'd better go," Emily said in a wounded voice. "We're all right, Seamus, we really are. We can handle him."

O'Quinn glanced at Avery. The boy had straightened, and although a bright red imprint from his father's blow marked his pale cheek, he seemed all right. In one corner of the room, Nora sat on the floor, clutching the doll called Abigail Elizabeth and sobbing softly to herself.

Taking a deep breath, O'Quinn shrugged off Emily's hand. He pointed a finger at Burton and said, "If I get word that you've hurt any of these children, I'm going to come out here and kill you. You understand, mister?"

Burton laughed, the sound a cackle edged with hysteria, and uttered more abuse, but he made no move to attack any of them with the knife. Emily grasped Avery's shoulder and gently steered him toward the doorway. O'Quinn stepped between the children and Burton as Emily pulled Nora to her feet to bring her along.

A moment later they had all moved onto the porch, and O'Quinn shut the door firmly. Turning to Emily, he cried, "You and the kids can't stay here. That man's crazy!"

Emily shook her head wearily. "He's just drunk. Now he'll get one of his bottles and finish it, then he'll go to sleep. When he wakes up, he'll be sorry about all of this . . . if he remembers it. But he won't hurt us. He's our father, I know he wouldn't hurt us."

O'Quinn turned to Avery. The boy was staring down at the planks of the porch, clearly more ashamed than frightened. "What about that?" O'Quinn demanded, gesturing at the mark on Avery's face.

"He might slap us around a little," Emily agreed, then she went on, her tone pleading, "but he doesn't mean to hurt anybody. He just . . . drinks too much. And he remembers our mother too much. . . . I'm so sorry this happened, Seamus. He's been doing a little better lately. I thought when I asked you to come for dinner that he might not cause any trouble. I thought it would be good for him to see someone besides us and the men he drinks with in town."

As Emily spoke, she dropped her head, ashamed at having to explain her father's behavior. O'Quinn placed one hand on her shoulder and cupped her chin with the other, gently lifting her face so he could look at her. "Why don't you hitch the wagon and come back to Abilene with me?" he urged. "Nobody should have to put up with this."

"I'm sorry," Emily whispered sadly. "We can't. He's our father, and this is our home."

Frustrated, O'Quinn sighed. Talking was not going to do any good; he would not be able to convince Emily to come with him. "I'm sorry, too," he said. "If I can help, any time, just get word to me. I'll do anything I can."

"Thank you," she said softly.

He took a deep breath. He wanted to tilt her head back again and kiss her, even with the two children right there on the porch with them. But he could not bring himself to do it. He had known women in the past, but they had always been bar girls. Never before had he been involved with someone as fresh and beautiful as Emily. Despite what Burton had said about her, O'Quinn knew there was no truth in the man's drunken accusations.

He squeezed her shoulder and said, "I'd better be going. I hope I'll see you in town again."

Emily smiled bravely. "I'm sure you will."

O'Quinn ruffled Avery's hair. "So long, son," he said.

"Good-bye, Mr. O'Quinn." Avery did not raise his head, and his voice sounded defeated. O'Quinn frowned, not liking that a bit.

Nora was a bit more animated in her farewell, throwing her arms around his neck and giving him a hug when he bent down to tell her good-bye. Awkwardly, O'Quinn patted the little girl on the back, then stood up and strode quickly to the barn to reclaim his horse. He did not look back until he was mounted and riding away, and then the three figures standing on the porch of the ramshackle house seemed so small and helpless that he wished he had not.

When he got back to Abilene, he decided, he was going to have a talk with Marshal Travis about the Burton family. McTeague would not like that, but the detective would already be angry with him for coming out here. Going to see Travis would not make things any worse. Surely something could be done about Charlie Burton, O'Quinn thought. There had to be some way to rescue the three children from their horrible situation.

Furious and deep in thought, O'Quinn rode toward Abilene, never noticing the sudden flash of light from the top of a knoll several hundred feet away. And even if he had seen it, he probably would not have recognized it as the glinting of sunlight on the barrel of a gun.

Jack McTeague had told himself that O'Quinn would be back any minute, that he had just gone to visit the outhouse as he had intimated. He doubted that the big prizefighter was devious enough to use that as a ploy to go visit that girl.

However, when O'Quinn had not returned by the time the meal was almost over, McTeague knew that O'Quinn had tricked him. He remembered how obstinate O'Quinn had been about the invitation to have dinner with the girl's family. He was going to have to start giving O'Quinn some credit for his intelligence and determination. After he tracked him down and got him back safely to Abilene, that is.

Heedless of how it might look to the other boarders, McTeague pushed back his chair and stood up. "Excuse me," he muttered to Hettie. Mentally cursing O'Quinn for ruining his meal, he left the room quickly, stepped out the back door of the boardinghouse, and went straight to the small frame structure with the half-moon cut in the door. Even before he jerked it open, he knew he would find the outhouse empty.

There was no sign of O'Quinn, just as McTeague had figured. He slammed the door and stood for a moment with his hands on his hips, trying to decide what his next move should be.

*Burton, that was her name. Emily Burton,* McTeague recalled now. He would have to find out where she and her family lived. He was confident he would find O'Quinn there.

The logical person to ask for help was Luke Travis. McTeague grimaced as that thought went through his head. If he went to the marshal to inquire where the Burton farm was located, Travis would almost certainly want to know why he was interested. McTeague had already sensed more than once that the lawman was suspicious of them. After the fight at Orion's, Travis had seen O'Quinn's bullet wounds, and although he had not pressed them for an explanation, his curiosity had to have been aroused.

He could go to Travis and reveal their true identities, McTeague thought; he could tell the lawman why they had really come to Abilene. Then the marshal would be duty-bound to help McTeague track down O'Quinn and make sure that he was safe. After all, Travis was a fellow officer of the law.

But here in the West that might not mean much. At least that had always been McTeague's opinion. Abruptly he shook his head. He would not go to Travis for help, he decided. There had to be some other way.

Another name suggested itself to him—Leslie Gibson. Gibson was O'Quinn's friend, and while he was a relative newcomer to the area, the Burton lad was a student of his. There was a chance Leslie would know how to find the Burton farm. And McTeague was confident he could allay any suspicions Leslie might have. He headed for the teacher's house at a fast walk, worry eating at him every step of the way.

Luckily, Leslie Gibson was at home, and he was obviously surprised when he answered the urgent knock on his door and found McTeague standing there. "Hello, Mr. McTeague," he said, frowning. "Where's Seamus?"

"That's what I want to know," McTeague answered. "Have you seen him today?"

The teacher shook his head. "I haven't seen him in a couple of days. Did he slip away from you? I thought the two of you were inseparable."

Ignoring Leslie's comment, McTeague asked, "Do you know where a family named Burton lives? I think they have a farm somewhere around here."

Leslie looked thoughtful. "Avery Burton's family? I've never been there, but I suppose I could find the place. I know roughly where it is."

"Can you take me there? I think Seamus has gone out to see some girl."

Leslie paused before answering, taking in McTeague's agitated state. "That would be Emily Burton," he said at last. "What's wrong with Seamus going to visit her? You can't believe the stories you hear around town about her. I think that's just jealous talk started by fellows who didn't have any luck courting her."

"I don't care about that," McTeague snapped impatiently. "I'm just afraid something might happen to Seamus."

Understanding dawned on Leslie's face. "You think Willie Parker might make another try for him, is that it?"

"That's right," McTeague said quickly, seizing on that idea. Even though he was far more worried about one of Gold's men tracking them down than he was about some local bully, Parker's grudge against them was a good excuse for his concern. He went on, "I don't want Parker catching Seamus by himself. Now, will you come out there with me or not?"

"You're right about Parker," Leslie said, a worried scowl on his face. "Let me get my hat and coat. I keep my horse at the livery stable, and I'm sure we can rent one for you there."

McTeague nodded impatiently. Leslie hurried into the house and emerged a moment later wearing his coat and Stetson and carrying a Winchester. The former big-city prizefighter looked for all the world like a westerner. Glancing at the rifle, McTeague asked, "What's that for?"

"If we run into Parker and his friends, we don't want to be unarmed," Leslie said grimly. "Come on." Turning on his heels, he headed for Texas Street, his long strides moving him along quickly. McTeague had to run to keep up.

The detective had been afraid that Leslie would suggest going to Marshal Travis with their problem, but Leslie never mentioned it during their brisk walk to the stable. Maybe Leslie was adapting to western ways and wanted to handle his own problems, McTeague speculated. Whatever the reason, he was grateful that the teacher did not turn to Travis.

When they arrived at the livery stable, they rented a mount for McTeague. Leslie saddled his own horse while Wiley put the rig on McTeague's animal. The old man said, "You're the second city feller to rent a horse today. That friend of yours was here earlier."

"I'm not surprised," McTeague muttered. "Which way was he going when he left?"

"Headed south out of town," Wiley said laconically. "Was going for a ride to get some fresh air."

McTeague nodded and clumsily hauled himself up into the saddle. Leslie mounted much more smoothly and, placing his rifle across the pommel of his saddle, led the way out of the stable.

"I hope we don't run into any trouble," he said as the two men turned their horses south.

"So do I," McTeague agreed fervently.

"Of course, Seamus isn't going to like us sticking our noses into his business this way, especially if he's as fond of Emily Burton as you seem to think he is," Leslie said.

"We'll worry about that when we find him," McTeague replied, bouncing awkwardly in the saddle. He could already tell this was going to be a painful, unpleasant journey. And when he found Seamus O'Quinn, the prizefighter would have a lot to answer for. Blast his black Irish soul!

# Chapter Ten

Mᴵᴛᴄʜ Rᴀɪɴᴇʏ ᴀɴᴅ Wɪʟʟɪᴇ Pᴀʀᴋᴇʀ ʟᴀʏ ᴏɴ ᴛʜᴇ
ground at the top of the knoll. Only their heads and
the barrels of their rifles peeked over the crest of the
rise. Winding like a ribbon below them was the trail
that led from the Burton farm to Abilene. The afternoon had grown very warm. Rainey lifted a hand to
wipe away the sweat beading on his forehead before it
trickled into his eyes. He could not afford to have
sweat blurring his vision at a crucial moment.

The two men had followed Seamus O'Quinn all the
way to the farmhouse where the prizefighter dismounted and went inside. "That's the Burton place,"
Parker told Rainey. "I reckon O'Quinn must've come
out here to court the gal who lives there. Can't think of
another reason why he'd be here."

Rainey laughed coldly. "Let him enjoy his visit,

then," he sneered. "He won't be making another one."

They had ridden back along the trail to choose a spot for their ambush, then returned to watch the farmhouse from their hiding place among the trees. As soon as they saw O'Quinn walk toward the barn and lead his horse into the yard, they galloped back to their ambush point.

Now it was just a matter of letting O'Quinn get within rifle range. They had spotted him a few minutes earlier, approaching from the east along the trail.

"Wait until there's no chance of missing," Rainey cautioned Parker. "I don't want anything going wrong. O'Quinn has to die."

Parker turned and squinted at the man from Chicago. "You ain't never told me exactly why you've got it in for O'Quinn," he said. "Not that it's any of my business—"

"That's right," Rainey snapped. "It's none of your business. All you need to think about is the five hundred dollars you'll get when both O'Quinn and McTeague are dead."

Parker licked his dry lips and grinned slowly. "I reckon five hunnerd bucks is enough explanation for me, Mr. Rainey."

Rainey laid his cheek against the smooth wooden stock of the rifle and peered over the barrel, lining the sights on the trail. To his left, Seamus O'Quinn was riding closer and closer. "Come on, come on," Rainey breathed, feeling the tingle of anticipation he always experienced before a kill.

Beside him, Parker abruptly raised up slightly. "I can get him for you," he growled as he lifted his rifle to his shoulder.

Rainey twisted, saying, "No! Not yet!" and tried to

get his hand on the barrel of Parker's Winchester to force it down. He was too late. In his impatience, Parker had jerked the trigger.

The rifle blasted, sending a slug screaming at Seamus O'Quinn.

O'Quinn heard something that sounded like a large bee buzz close by his right ear. A split second later came the sharp crack of a rifle. He frowned for a moment, then realized that someone was shooting at him. With a yell, he leaned against his horse's neck and banged his heels into its flanks. The animal surged forward into a gallop.

O'Quinn grabbed the saddlehorn and held on for dear life; with every lunging stride, the horse threatened to unseat him. Over the pounding of the hooves, he heard more shots. He glanced in the direction they came from and saw puffs of gunsmoke coming from a small rise. That was where the ambushers were, he thought, but there was no way he could fight back. All he could do now was hang on and pray that the bullets missed him.

He hoped, too, that the madly running mare would not throw him from the saddle. The prairie sped by him at a dizzying speed.

"You idiot!" Rainey shouted at Parker as he scrambled onto his knees to get a better shot at the fleeing O'Quinn. "You should have let me take him!" Rainey flung the Winchester to his shoulder and fired.

Parker levered another shell into the chamber and triggered again. "I thought I could cut him down!" he replied angrily. "I can still get him!" He fired as fast as he could.

Rainey worked the action of his rifle and cursed his

unfamiliarity with the weapon. Back in Chicago he was accustomed to using handguns, and no one was better with a derringer at close range. There did not seem to be such a thing as close range out here in the West, however. He took a deep breath, trained his sights on O'Quinn's back, and pressed the trigger again.

Through the haze of gunsmoke, Rainey suddenly saw the horse stumble as one of the bullets struck it. Its legs tangled, and it tumbled to the ground hard. O'Quinn flew out of the saddle and through the air, landed heavily, and rolled for several feet, sending up a cloud of dust. As the dust blew away, revealing the motionless body sprawled on the ground, a thrill coursed through Rainey.

The gambler had no time to congratulate himself, however. There were farms in the area, and the residents might well have heard the gunfire. He had better hurry and make sure O'Quinn was dead, then get back to Abilene as quickly as possible before someone came to investigate the shooting.

But this was still the Wild West, after all, Rainey thought. Maybe gunshots were such a commonplace sound that no one would get excited about them. Nevertheless, he still had to make certain O'Quinn was dead.

"Get the horses," he ordered Parker. "We're going down there."

"That fall had to have killed him, even if we didn't hit him with any of those shots," Parker argued. "We'd better get out of here."

"After I'm sure he's dead. Now get the horses." Rainey's tone contained an unmistakable edge of menace.

Parker got to his feet and gave a surly nod. He went

quickly to the clump of brush where their horses were tied and brought them back to the top of the knoll. Both men mounted up and started toward the trail. Rainey kept the muzzle of his rifle pointed toward the motionless body.

When they reached O'Quinn, he intended to pump several more bullets into him just to make sure. A savage grin tugged at his mouth. It had taken him a while, but he was finally going to finish the job he had started on that dark, wind-swept Chicago pier.

Leslie Gibson and Jack McTeague had just passed a farm that the teacher identified as the Mahaffey place when they heard the piercing crack of gunfire somewhere up ahead. "Dammit!" McTeague exclaimed. "That's got to be where Seamus is!"

"Come on," Leslie cried, urging his horse into a run.

McTeague struggled to get his own mount to gallop, wincing every time he landed on the sore spots where the saddle had rubbed him. Clutching the reins and the saddlehorn with his left hand, he reached under his coat with his right hand for his pistol and yanked the Remington Number Four from his pocket. It was not very accurate at distances over ten or fifteen feet, but at least he could make some noise with it.

As more gunshots rang out, the two men rode hard over the rolling prairie, making good time for men who were not accustomed to riding galloping horses. McTeague's pulse was racing not only from the exertion of this desperate dash but also because he was worried about O'Quinn. He could almost see the case against Darius Gold and Mitch Rainey going up in smoke.

Suddenly the firing stopped, and the only sounds

Leslie and McTeague could hear were the hoofbeats of their animals. Leslie was in the lead, and he glanced anxiously over his shoulder at McTeague. Both men knew what the abrupt silence might mean.

The trail dipped through a shallow depression and curved around a hill, then opened into a long straight stretch. North of it rose a small knoll. Coming down that slope were two figures on horseback. Up ahead, on the trail itself, lay a fallen horse, and beyond that a man was sprawled in the dirt.

"Seamus!" McTeague yelled. He felt as if someone had plunged an icy blade into his belly. The body on the ground was still and lifeless.

The two men riding down the knoll stopped short at the sight of Leslie and McTeague. One of the riders jerked a rifle to his shoulder and blasted a shot at them. The slug whined past, high overhead, but close enough for them to hear the eerie sound of its passage. Leslie hauled back on the reins, bringing his horse to a halt. He lifted his Winchester and pressed the trigger.

McTeague, desperate to stop his horse, tugged frantically on the reins. Nervous from the shooting and the inexperience of its rider, the horse skittered to a stop and reared up on its hind legs. McTeague almost fell from the saddle. He grabbed at the saddlehorn and wrapped his scrabbling fingers around it. The horse came down on all four hooves with a bone-jarring thud. McTeague started to slip again, but he caught himself and lifted the revolver.

The Remington's blasts were a counterpoint to the cracking of the Winchester. Leslie glanced over in surprise, unaware until this moment that McTeague had been armed. It was a good thing he was. Now the odds were even.

Leslie hated having to resort to violence, but there was nothing else they could do. He recognized the fallen man as O'Quinn and knew that the other two had probably been on their way down the hill to finish him off. If O'Quinn was even still alive, Leslie thought grimly. From the looks of the horse, it had been shot out from under him. O'Quinn had to have taken a bad fall.

The two ambushers altered their course, spurring their horses forward and angling toward Leslie and McTeague. Leslie fired again but was unsure where his bullet went. Given time to aim, he was not a bad shot when his only goal was to hit a target. But this was the first time he had ever traded lead with anyone who was also trying to kill him. Fear was a sharp, acrid taste in his mouth.

McTeague was calmer, but he was plagued by a nervous mount, and his gun was ineffective at this range. He emptied the Remington and then coolly took more shells from his pocket and began reloading. As he glanced up at the two riders charging toward them, he saw that he would not have the little pistol ready in time to meet their attack.

Leslie levered the Winchester and fired again. Looking over at McTeague, he cried, "We've got to get out of here!"

McTeague shook his head. "Not without Seamus," he snapped as he thumbed fresh cartridges into his revolver.

Suddenly Leslie felt ashamed. He had wanted to run when O'Quinn was up there maybe badly injured, maybe already dead. But regardless of his condition, he was Leslie's friend, and the teacher knew now that he could not leave without trying to help him. Arranging his features into a stony expression to conceal his fear, Leslie jacked another shell into the rifle and raised it to fire.

More shots rang out, this time coming from behind Leslie and McTeague. The detective jerked his head around, expecting to meet a new threat, but instead he saw Luke Travis galloping toward them, firing a Winchester from the back of his speeding horse. As Travis swept past them, the marshal shouted, "See to O'Quinn!"

McTeague urged his mount forward. With the fire from Travis and Leslie covering him, he hurried up the trail toward the fallen figure of his friend.

The two ambushers pulled up when they saw that the odds had turned against them. They wheeled their horses and started back up the slope. As they did, Leslie Gibson kicked his horse into a gallop and raced to catch up to Travis. The two men from Abilene fired their rifles together, the slugs kicking up dust just behind the fleeing duo. The ambushers reached the top of the hill and vanished over it.

Reining in, Travis called, "Hold on, Leslie!" When Leslie had halted his own horse, the marshal went on, "We might be riding into a trap if we go over that hill after them. Better to let them go right now and try to catch up to them later."

Leslie nodded. His heart was pounding heavily in his chest, and he could not seem to catch his breath. "Could you tell who they were?" he asked Travis in a hoarse voice.

Travis shook his head. "Not for sure. One of them might have been Willie Parker. I thought I caught a glimpse of that cowhide vest he wears all the time. The other fellow I didn't know at all." He slid his Winchester back into the saddle boot. "Are you all right?"

Leslie looked down at himself as if to check for blood or bullet holes. He grinned sheepishly. "I wasn't sure for a minute there. But I don't seem to be hit anywhere. I don't think Mr. McTeague was, either."

"I'm not surprised," Travis grunted. "Even with all that lead flying around, it's mighty hard to hit anything from horseback. Come on, we'd better check on O'Quinn."

The two men trotted their horses toward the sprawled figure, their faces bleak at the prospect of what they might find.

By the time McTeague reached O'Quinn, he was convinced that the big prizefighter was dead. O'Quinn had not moved during the chaotic gun battle. His horse was also motionless, and as McTeague passed the animal, he saw the bloody wound in its side, just behind the forelegs. A lucky shot, but one that had probably found the heart. The horse was dead.

He slid out of the saddle as soon as he reached O'Quinn's still form, lying facedown in the dust. He dropped to one knee and grasped the prizefighter's shoulders. Dreading what he was going to see, McTeague turned him over as gently as possible.

To his surprise, he saw no blood on O'Quinn's clothes, only the dirt of the trail. And with a mixed feeling of relief and excitement, he saw the boxer's chest rising and falling rhythmically. O'Quinn was alive! Not only alive, McTeague decided, but not too badly hurt.

Travis and Leslie rode up then. McTeague had seen their fight with the ambushers out of the corner of his eye, had seen the two men fleeing over the rise. Now, as Leslie hurriedly dismounted and joined McTeague beside O'Quinn, Travis watched the knoll in case the two men tried to attack again.

"How is he?" Leslie asked anxiously.

"I think he may be all right," McTeague replied. "I can't find any bullet wounds, and the fall doesn't seem to have opened his old injuries."

"Give him some of this," Travis said. He pulled a canteen from his saddle and tossed it to Leslie. The teacher uncapped it and knelt beside O'Quinn's head, lifting it to let some of the water trickle into his mouth. O'Quinn choked, then swallowed and began moving his head from side to side. He let out a moan.

A moment later, he was sitting up, still shaking his head from side to side and grunting occasionally in pain. McTeague asked, "Are you all right?"

"Ohhh . . ." O'Quinn lifted a hand and rubbed a swollen knot on the side of his head. "I think so. But what happened?"

"A couple of men shot your horse out from under you," said Travis, still astride his mount. "We came along and stopped them from finishing you off."

O'Quinn looked around at the three of them. "But who would want to . . . ?"

"That low-life bully Parker," McTeague grated. "It had to be him and one of his friends."

"I thought I saw him, all right," Travis agreed. "And the other man could have been one of his pards. Is there any other reason why somebody would be trying to kill you, O'Quinn?"

O'Quinn quickly glanced at McTeague, trying to discern what the detective wanted him to say. Before he could answer, McTeague said, "Of course there isn't. It was Parker, I tell you. He's been trying to settle his grudge against Seamus ever since that brawl in Orion's."

O'Quinn nodded. "Makes sense to me, Marshal. I

don't know why anybody else would want to shoot me."

"All right," Travis said, accepting the explanation. "You reckon you can get on your feet?"

"I can try," O'Quinn said. With Leslie's help, he pulled himself upright. He was a little shaky for a moment, but then the feeling passed. He went on, "I think I'll be fine once I—oh, no!"

Travis followed his gaze and saw that O'Quinn had noticed the horse. O'Quinn walked unsteadily over to the animal and looked down at it sadly. When he raised his eyes he murmured, "That was a good horse. They had no right to do that."

"No, they didn't," Travis agreed, his voice hard with anger. "You and Mr. McTeague will have to ride back to town together. When we get there, we'll let the folks at the livery stable know what happened. They'll want to come out to get the saddle."

"Come on, Seamus," McTeague said, steering him toward the other rented animal. "We'll get you back to Abilene and have the doctor take a look at you, just to make sure you're not hurt badly."

O'Quinn angrily shook off McTeague's hand. "All right," he said. "But somebody's going to pay for this."

"Damn right they will," Travis agreed in a deceptively quiet voice.

McTeague and O'Quinn mounted up, O'Quinn taking the saddle at McTeague's insistence and the detective climbing on behind him. They started down the trail at a slow pace. Travis rode even more slowly, keeping an eye on the knoll and falling several yards behind. Leslie Gibson let his mount drop back until he was riding beside Travis.

"What were you doing out here, Luke?" Leslie asked. "Was it just luck that you happened to be around when we needed you?"

Travis shrugged and nodded toward the horse moving ahead of them with its double load. "I rode out to make sure that nothing happened to O'Quinn while he was visiting the Burtons, but I guess you could say it was luck that made me curious in the first place." Quickly and in a voice low enough that the other two men could not hear him, he told Leslie about the angry conversation between O'Quinn and McTeague he had overheard earlier in the day. "And Cody had talked to O'Quinn and seemed to think that he might be interested in the Burton girl," Travis went on, "so I figured it might be a good idea to keep an eye on him. He's a greenhorn out here."

"Like me," Leslie commented.

Travis shook his head. "You and McTeague were holding your own." A thoughtful expression appeared on the lawman's lean face. "Did you happen to notice that gun McTeague carries?"

"I noticed it, all right. I was surprised when he started firing it earlier."

"Why would a fight manager be carrying a gun?" Travis mused.

Leslie gave a short laugh. "Why do men out here always carry guns, Luke?"

"Out here you never know when you'll need one," Travis replied. "Even if there weren't plenty of two-legged skunks around to give trouble, there are snakes and all kinds of other varmints."

"It's the same in the big cities back East," Leslie told him earnestly. "Especially in the areas where prizefights take place. The matches are illegal in most states, but they go on anyway with the police usually looking the other way. That means the people attracted to the bouts aren't the most law-abiding citizens in the world. A lot of the fight managers I've known carry guns just as a matter of course, Luke, like the men out here."

Travis nodded in understanding. What Leslie said made sense. But Travis still thought there was something that O'Quinn and McTeague were not telling him. As quick as it had been, he had still seen the look that passed between the two men when he asked who else besides Parker might have been responsible for the ambush. There was some sort of secret between them.

And he was going to find out what it was before somebody in his town got killed because of it, Luke Travis told himself.

The group returned to Abilene without further trouble. There was no sign of the men who had ambushed O'Quinn, and Travis figured that they might be miles away by this time. "If it was Parker, he may not try again," the lawman speculated as he and the others paused in front of the boardinghouse where O'Quinn and McTeague were staying. "This would be the second time he's tried to even the score since the fight, and he's failed both times."

"From what I've seen of him, Parker's got a head like a rock," Leslie commented. "He's not the kind to give up easily."

"Well, we can hope," O'Quinn replied. He extended his hand to Travis. "Thanks for the help, Marshal."

"I'm just glad I happened to be there," Travis said as he shook the prizefighter's hand.

O'Quinn turned to Leslie. "And you, Slugger—I guess I'd be dead now if it wasn't for you."

Leslie clapped him on the shoulder. "Don't worry about that," he assured him. "Just get some rest. I think Aileen is getting a little tired of you having a new bump or bruise every time she sees you."

O'Quinn laughed. "Could be, but at least that way Jack here gets to see her again."

"That's enough of that, Seamus," McTeague snapped. "Come on. I want you to take it easy for the rest of the day."

O'Quinn nodded and let McTeague lead him into the boardinghouse. He waved to Travis and Leslie as he climbed onto the porch with McTeague.

They had stopped at Aileen Bloom's office first. Even though it was a Sunday afternoon, she was there, reading the medical journals that she had shipped out to her from the East. Travis was not surprised by her presence; he knew how dedicated she was to her practice, how little time she spent in the room she rented. She quickly examined O'Quinn and pronounced him very lucky. He had the bump on his head, a result of the impact that had knocked him out when he was thrown from the horse, and several other bruises, but that was the extent of his injuries. The weeks-old bullet wounds had not been torn open by the fall.

From there they had gone to the livery stable to tell Wiley about the shooting of the rented horse. The old man was upset, as could be expected, but he calmed down when McTeague handed over enough cash to cover the cost of the animal. Wiley promised to have some of the hostlers go out and retrieve the gear from the animal and tend to the body, unpleasant though the chore might be. Then Travis and Leslie accompanied O'Quinn and McTeague to the boardinghouse.

Now, as they walked away from the place, the

teacher asked Travis, "What do you think of that fellow McTeague?"

Travis glanced over at him, thinking about McTeague's mysterious behavior and the interest he had shown in Aileen Bloom. "I'm not very fond of him," the marshal said bluntly. "Why do you ask?"

"I've been thinking about what you asked me, about him carrying a gun," Leslie replied. "The fact that he was armed doesn't surprise me, but until I thought about it I didn't realize how he acted when those two bushwhackers started shooting at us. He was mighty cool, Luke, a lot calmer than I was. Like he was used to being shot at or something."

Travis nodded, deep in thought. After a moment, he said, "You think there's something strange about this situation, too, don't you?"

"Something sure doesn't seem right," Leslie agreed. "I don't think either McTeague or Seamus is telling the whole truth about why they're here."

"That's what I've thought ever since I saw those bullet holes in O'Quinn. Somebody tried to kill him not too long ago, and I'd like to know why."

Leslie paused and met Travis's level gaze. "If there's anything I can do to help, Luke, I'd be glad to."

"I thought O'Quinn was your friend. He might not want us poking around in his business."

"He *is* my friend," Leslie said solemnly. "That's why I don't want somebody trying to kill him."

Travis nodded. "Thanks, Leslie. If I need any help, I'll let you know. Right now it seems to me McTeague is the key to this puzzle. I think I'll pay him a visit later and see if I can convince him to open up."

Leslie looked doubtful. "He strikes me as a pretty hard nut, Luke. Good luck on getting him to talk."

They parted company then, Leslie heading toward

his house, Travis returning to the marshal's office on Texas Street. It was empty when he got there, and he assumed that Cody was out somewhere keeping an eye on the town.

Not that Abilene needed much watching on a Sunday afternoon. Everything seemed fairly quiet, and Travis took advantage of the lull to catch up on some of his paperwork. After an hour or so, he straightened his desk and retrieved his hat from the peg next to the door. If Seamus O'Quinn had followed Aileen's advice to rest, he would probably be napping by now. Travis hoped so; he wanted a chance to talk to McTeague alone.

He opened the door of the office just as Cody was about to walk in. The young deputy nodded and said, "Howdy, Marshal. Did O'Quinn get back from the Burton place all right?"

"Eventually," Travis said dryly. Quickly, he filled Cody in on what had happened between Abilene and the Burton farm. Cody let out a whistle as Travis described the ambush.

"Somebody really wants O'Quinn planted," Cody commented when Travis had finished. "You think it was Willie Parker again?"

"That's what McTeague claims, and I thought I spotted him, too. But something tells me there's more to it than that. I thought I'd go over and have a talk with McTeague."

Cody nodded. "Sounds like a good idea. Want some company?"

"No, you stay here at the office in case somebody comes looking for us. I'll be back in a little while."

Cody took off his black hat and skillfully tossed it onto one of the pegs. "I'll be here."

Travis walked to South Second Street, nodding greetings to the few pedestrians he passed. When he reached the boardinghouse, he knocked on the door. A moment later, Hettie Wilburn answered. "Hello, Marshal," the middle-aged widow said with a smile. "What can I do for you?"

"Do you know if your two new boarders are here, Mrs. Wilburn?" Travis asked.

"You mean Mr. O'Quinn and Mr. McTeague? I believe they are. Mr. O'Quinn said he wasn't feeling very well when they came in earlier. He said he was going upstairs to lie down."

"Which rooms are they in?"

"The third and fourth doors on the left in the upstairs hall. Mr. O'Quinn is in the third room, Mr. McTeague in the one just past it." Hettie frowned. "Is there some sort of trouble, Marshal?"

"No, I just want to talk to Mr. McTeague for a few minutes. I won't disturb Mr. O'Quinn."

"I'd appreciate that. The poor man looked absolutely exhausted when they came in. If you ask me, he's been training too hard for that fight he's supposed to have." Hettie shook her head. "If I didn't know better, I wouldn't have believed that Mr. O'Quinn is a boxer. He seems so nice and polite."

"I guess he is," Travis grunted. "But I still wouldn't want to step into a prize ring with him."

He went up the stairs, thinking about Hettie's comment. The way he felt at the moment, he doubted there was even going to be a boxing match. That was just another of the lies the two visitors had been telling, Travis thought.

He went past O'Quinn's door and knocked lightly on McTeague's. There was no answer. Travis frowned and rapped again, a little louder this time. When there was still no response, he tried the doorknob. It turned under his fingers.

Travis opened the door and stuck his head inside the room. "McTeague?" he called. The place was empty, which was a surprise. He had expected McTeague to stick close to O'Quinn after what had happened today. Moving to the wall that separated the rooms, Travis put his ear to it and heard the rumbling growl of O'Quinn's snoring. Knowing that his companion was sleeping, McTeague must have stepped out for a moment, Travis speculated, maybe to pay a visit to the outhouse.

The marshal glanced around the room. There was not much to show that it was occupied. A few shirts hung on a nail, some coins were scattered on the dresser top, and the corner of a carpetbag peeked out from under the bed—these were the only signs of McTeague's presence.

Travis rubbed his jaw thoughtfully. Snooping around someone else's room was not something he enjoyed doing, but ever since O'Quinn and McTeague had arrived in Abilene, a threat seemed to hang in the air. It had exploded into actual violence on several occasions, and Travis decided abruptly that the time had come to find out why.

He pulled the carpetbag from under the bed, opened it, and quickly pawed through the contents. At first he thought it contained only clothes, but then his fingers touched a sheaf of papers. He pulled them out of the bag and frowned when he saw they were wanted posters. He flipped through them quickly, then put them down on the bed and delved deeper into the valise. A moment later, he found a box of ammunition for the Remington that McTeague carried. No surprise there.

Travis grimaced; something was tugging at his memory. Picking up the stack of wanted posters again, he began looking through them. He paused to study the third one from the top, and suddenly he knew where he had seen the man pictured there.

Several days earlier, at the train station, Travis's instincts had warned him about one of the disembarking passengers. And now here was the man, staring at him from a wanted poster.

Mitch Rainey, that was the man's name. Travis scanned the information underneath the picture and saw that Rainey was wanted for murder in Chicago —the same town that O'Quinn and McTeague were from.

Travis tossed the reward dodger back onto the bed with the others. There had to be a connection between this Rainey and the two visitors from Chicago. He stuck his hand back into the carpetbag. On the very bottom of it, his fingers touched a small leather folder of some sort. He was about to draw it out when the door of the room was shoved open roughly. Travis looked up to see McTeague standing in the doorway, the little pistol leveled at him. He stayed very still, not wanting to spook the man.

"Dammit, Marshal," McTeague said bitterly, "I almost shot you. A man can't even answer the call of nature around here without something happening. What the hell are you doing in here poking around in my things? How dare you?" His voice quivered with indignation.

Regarding McTeague with a cool stare, Travis said, "The same way you dared to come into my town and lie to me, mister. Somebody is after you and O'Quinn, has been all along. And now I know why." Moving slowly, he drew out the folder he had found in the valise. McTeague's jaw tightened, and a small muscle there began to jump slightly. Travis flipped open the folder, saw the badge and identification papers. He read aloud, "Inspector Jack McTeague, Chicago Police Department. I had you figured for a liar, McTeague, but not a policeman."

McTeague grimaced and took a deep breath. He carefully let down the hammer of the Remington and stowed it under his coat. "Well, now you know," he said harshly. "What are you going to do about it?"

Travis tossed the identification folder to the detective, who caught it deftly. "I'm going to tell you something that maybe you don't know," Travis said as he turned to pick up the wanted poster from the bed. He thrust it toward McTeague. "This fellow's in town, or at least somewhere close by. I saw him getting off the train the other day. I reckon he's the one you're trying to keep from killing O'Quinn."

McTeague stared at the poster for a moment before taking it from Travis. "Rainey is here?" he asked.

Travis nodded. "He was probably the man who ambushed O'Quinn along with Parker this afternoon. I don't know how those two got to know each other, but I'd be willing to bet they're working together now."

Abruptly McTeague's fingers tightened around the poster of Mitch Rainey and savagely crumpled it into a ball. "I'd say there's a good chance you're right, Marshal," he snarled.

Travis nodded, trying to put together the facts he had discovered in the last few minutes. "So Seamus is on the run for some reason, and you came along to try to keep him alive. Don't you think it's time you told me what this is all about, McTeague?"

"What business is it of yours?" McTeague demanded.

"You picked my town to hide out in," Travis told him quietly, keeping his own anger in check. "That makes it my business. Besides, maybe I can help."

McTeague sighed. He looked down at the crumpled reward poster in his hand and then tossed it into a corner. "Maybe you're right, Travis," he said. "Anyway, it's not a very long story . . . or a pretty one. It begins with a man named Darius Gold."

# Chapter Eleven

THE FACES OF THE FOUR MEN WHO ATTENDED THE MEETING that evening in Luke Travis's office were grim. The marshal sat behind the scarred desk. Cody Fisher lounged beside it, his hip resting on one corner. Seamus O'Quinn and Jack McTeague sat side by side in the old wooden chairs in front of the desk. To bring Cody up to date, Travis repeated what McTeague had told him that afternoon.

"So that's why this Rainey fellow came here," Travis explained, as he finished the story. "He was tracking O'Quinn and McTeague."

Cody nodded. "And now he's caught up to them." The deputy turned to O'Quinn. "If your testimony can do what you say it can, I can see why Rainey wants to get rid of you."

"I saw Rainey and those other men kill Dooley," O'Quinn rumbled. "That's just about as damning as you can get. Not to mention the death of that gambler. Rainey and Gold had a hand in that, too."

"Rainey's trying to keep both himself and his boss out of jail," Cody concluded. "Or away from the gallows, maybe. He's not going to give up easily."

"He's not going to give up at all," McTeague declared. "The police have had dealings with Rainey before. Even though we haven't been able to prove anything, we all know he's one of the most ruthless bastards you'd ever want to meet. He won't stop at anything."

Travis nodded and clasped his hands together on the desktop. "That's why I want the two of you to stay close to your room at the boardinghouse. Eat as many meals there as you can, and I want you to stay together. Rainey's been around for several days, but he waited until today, until O'Quinn was out in the open by himself, before he made his move. Chances are he won't try anything in town unless he gets desperate."

"That's exactly what I'm concerned about, Marshal," McTeague said anxiously. "Gold's lawyers will stall and pull all the tricks they know, but sooner or later the case will go to trial. By that time, it will be too late to silence Seamus. Rainey has to do it now, before the trial."

"How would he know what date the trial is set for, or if it's even on the docket yet?" Travis asked.

McTeague laughed curtly. "Rainey can contact any number of people back in Chicago, both in the police department and in the underworld. I have no doubt that he could send a wire and know the status of the case within an hour. He may be doing just that from one of the smaller towns around here that have telegraph offices."

"Most of them do," Cody informed him, "at least the ones where the trains stop. But the marshal is right. The only thing you can do now is lie low."

Travis shoved his chair back. "We'll try to locate Willie Parker. From what we saw today, he's working with Rainey. I'll tell all the bartenders in town I'm looking for him." The lawman stood up, leaned over the desk, and placed his palms on its scarred surface. Looking directly at McTeague, he went on, "Now, I want to know why you didn't come to us and ask for our help as soon as you got here."

"I didn't think I needed it," McTeague replied, bristling. "This matter is the responsibility of the Chicago police."

"More folks have a stake in this than just the ones in Chicago, Mr. McTeague," Travis argued. "You and O'Quinn may have brought most of the trouble with you, but now it's affecting Abilene." He paused, eyes narrowing. "Maybe you just thought that you couldn't trust us."

McTeague flushed. "I didn't know how close behind us Rainey or some of Gold's other men might be," he snapped angrily. "And I didn't know one damn thing about you, Travis. From what I had heard of Western lawmen, I thought those killers might be able to buy your assistance for a few dollars."

Travis straightened, his face tightening at the harsh words, his eyes blazing with anger. Cody watched him for a moment, then said softly, "Take it easy, Marshal. That's what you always tell me, isn't it?"

Travis stared at McTeague for a few seconds longer, then drew a deep breath. "Thanks, Cody," he said.

"You're right. Look, McTeague, we've got to work together from here on out, so I'm going to forget you just said that. Why don't you and O'Quinn head on back to the boardinghouse? Cody, go with them."

"Look here, we don't need a bodyguard—" McTeague began to protest.

"Speak for yourself, Jack," O'Quinn cut in. "I've been lucky once today. Any boxer can tell you that you don't rely on lucky punches."

"All right," McTeague grudgingly agreed. "But I don't like it."

Grinning, Cody stood up and went to get his hat from the peg. "Nobody asked you to like it, Mr. McTeague," he remarked. "We just want to keep you and O'Quinn alive."

O'Quinn gave a hollow laugh. "That sounds like a fine idea to me. I don't like being shot at. Or being tossed off a running horse." He put his derby on, adjusting it carefully so that it would not press on the lump on his head.

The three men left the office. Travis stepped onto the boardwalk to watch them go. Cody was a good man; he would see to it that nothing happened on the short walk between the office and Hettie Wilburn's place. Travis would start passing the word that he was looking for Willie Parker. He reached into the office to get his own hat.

Abilene on a Sunday night was relatively quiet, but the saloons were still open for business and doing a leisurely trade. During the next hour Travis dropped in on as many of the taverns as he could and quietly let the owners and the bartenders know why he was there. In most of the saloons he met with a friendly reception, even some of the rougher establishments along

Railroad Street. The saloonkeepers knew that, while Travis did everything in his power to enforce law and order, he had never tried to close them down or interfere with their normal business. In fact, the only tavern Travis had ever closed was the Salty Dog Saloon, and that was because its owner had been the head of a criminal network that threatened to take over Abilene. So in most cases the marshal received quiet promises of assistance.

Travis's final stop on his tour of the town was Orion's. As he pushed through the batwings he noticed there were only a few customers in the place, and Orion was behind the bar by himself. Old Bailey, the parrot, was half-heartedly squawking out the lyrics of a bawdy song. Travis approached the bar, and a grinning Orion said, "Good evening, Lucas. What'll ye be having?"

"Just a beer, Orion," replied Travis, pushing back his hat. "I've been doing some talking, and I'm thirsty."

"Talking 'bout what?" Orion asked as he drew the beer and slid it across the hardwood.

Travis explained the situation in a low voice, eliciting a frown of concern from Orion. He knew the burly Scotsman liked Seamus O'Quinn and would not want to see anything happen to him.

"I'll be keeping me eyes open f'tha' scoundrel Parker," Orion promised. "Though I dinna believe he would come back in here after last time."

"I don't, either," Travis agreed. He sipped the cold beer. "But if you hear anything about him, you let me know."

"I certainly will. You think he and tha' Rainey fella will try again t'kill Seamus?"

Travis nodded grimly. "I'm sure of it." Placing the mug on the bar, he lifted his hand to rub his eyes. He was tired, but there seemed to be something else he should be doing. It nagged at him but stayed elusively beyond recall. He hoped it was not so important that it might get O'Quinn and McTeague killed.

Hours after the ambush that failed to dispose of Seamus O'Quinn, Mitch Rainey was still seething with anger. He glared at Willie Parker across the table, and the big redheaded roughneck looked uncomfortable as he picked up a bottle of whiskey and took a long slug from it.

The two men were sitting in a cabin that was little more than a shack, west of Abilene on the banks of the Smoky Hill River. It had once belonged to a farmer who struggled for years to scratch a living from the earth. Eventually the man gave up and moved on, abandoning the cabin. Parker had chanced upon it a few months earlier and moved in. He usually did not have enough money to rent a room in town, so finding this place had been a stroke of luck.

For the last few days, it had served as the headquarters for Rainey and Parker as they schemed to kill O'Quinn. Rainey had hated every moment of his stay in the squalid cottage, but he had to admit that it was so isolated that no one was likely to notice them there. If everything had gone right this afternoon, he would have been in Abilene tonight, waiting for the opportunity to kill Jack McTeague. McTeague might even have been dead already, and Rainey might have been on a train at this very moment, heading back to Chicago and the life he enjoyed.

But O'Quinn was still alive, and that ruined everything. Rainey and Parker had circled back after trading shots with Travis and Leslie Gibson, being careful not to be spotted but getting close enough to see that O'Quinn was up and walking around under his own power. Obviously, none of the shots had hit him, and he had not been seriously injured in the fall from the horse.

As if reading Rainey's mind, Parker stared down at the table and muttered, "He's a lucky son of a bitch."

"And you're a trigger-happy fool," Rainey said coldly. "If you had waited a few moments longer, we both would have had a sure, easy shot at O'Quinn. But you had to try to show off."

Parker clenched a fist and slammed it on the table, making the bottle of whiskey jump slightly. "Dammit, I told you I make that shot nine times out of ten! I should have had him."

"That's not good enough," Rainey snapped. "Now O'Quinn is still alive, and I'm stuck in this godforsaken wilderness. Well, it won't be for much longer, I promise you that." He pushed back his chair and stood up, stalking over to the cabin's single window. Flicking aside the piece of oilcloth that covered it, he peered out into the night, his brain rapidly turning over all the possibilities.

Parker took another drink, then growled, "We'll have another chance at O'Quinn. He can't hide out forever."

Abruptly Rainey turned away from the window and shook his head. "We're not going to wait for O'Quinn to come out in the open again. We're going to force him out."

Parker stared muddily at him. "How are we goin' to do that?"

"Didn't you say that a girl lives at that farm where O'Quinn went today?"

A smile slowly stretched across Parker's craggy face. "That's right," he said. "Emily Burton's her name. Can't think of any other reason O'Quinn would've gone out there unless it was to court her."

"Who else lives there?"

"Don't know for sure," Parker replied. "There's the gal's pa, Charlie Burton. He's drunk most of the time, from what I've seen of him around town. I think he's got a couple more whelps 'sides Emily, too, younger ones. Burton's wife died a while back, at least it seems like I heard that."

Rainey nodded, smiling now himself. "This Emily Burton, is she attractive?"

"Reckon most folks would say so." Parker's smile became a leer. "I'd damn sure say so. Too good for a bastard like O'Quinn."

Rainey sat down at the table. "O'Quinn is bound to care for the girl, and that's going to be his undoing. We might be able to take a little pleasure ourselves along the way, besides disposing of O'Quinn." Rainey reached for the bottle of whiskey, in a much more expansive frame of mind now. "Do you think you could round up a few of your friends who'd be willing to help us out?"

Parker chuckled. "If you're willin' to pay, I know I can come up with a couple of boys who'd be glad to go along with us. Especially when they hear what you're plannin'."

"Excellent." Rainey gave Parker a stern look. "But this time all of you will do as you're told, or I'll kill you myself."

Parker flushed angrily for a moment, but then he

laughed harshly and nodded his head. "Sure. You're the boss, Mr. Rainey."

"Don't forget it." Rainey tilted the bottle to his lips and took a long swallow. He grinned wolfishly as he lowered the whiskey. "Tomorrow, then, we'll pay a little visit to the Burton farm."

Charlie Burton rolled over, the sheets rough against his skin, and squinted at the light that hit his eyes. Even though the day was a bit overcast, the sunlight was still bright enough to be painful to him.

He forced himself to sit up in bed, not because it was nearly noon and long past the hour when any normal farmer would have been out working his land, but because his head was pounding and his throat was as scratchy as sandpaper. He desperately needed a drink, and the bottle on the floor beside the bed was empty.

Standing up shakily, Burton turned toward the open door of his room. He made his feet work and shuffled into the large room that was the parlor, kitchen, and dining room. His footsteps echoed hollowly in the silent house. He was the only one here, he knew. The children would be out working if they knew what was good for them.

Burton went to a cabinet near the stove. One of the hinges on the cabinet had broken sometime in the past and never been repaired, so the door hung crookedly. Burton pulled it open, reached inside, and drew out a bottle that gurgled satisfactorily when he shook it. A grin pulled at his mouth. He lifted the bottle and yanked the cork from its neck, then took a long drink from it. The liquor seared his throat as he swallowed it, and he could feel the warmth immediately calming his frenzied nerves. The stuff dribbled from his mouth into his thick, bushy beard. When he finally lowered the bottle, he wiped the back of his hand across his mouth. "Damn, that's good," he murmured.

Carrying the whiskey with him, he walked over to one of the windows and looked out, narrowing his eyes against the still-painful brightness. From the window, he could see one of his fields, and in the field his three children were working to harvest the last of a late corn crop. Avery and Nora had expected to go to school today, but Burton told them the night before that they had to work instead.

"You don't want your big sis to have to do it all herself, do you?" he had asked. The question seemed reasonable enough to him. Avery just bit his lip and then agreed to stay home from school. Nora said nothing, but Burton was used to that. Seemed like none of the kids talked to him as much as they once did.

That was all right with him. They were all ungrateful little brats, anyway. It was better for them to keep their traps shut than pester him all the time with stupid questions like why was the sky blue and why did it rain and what was that over there and do you love me, Papa? Mollie had been alive when they asked him questions like that and then threw their arms around his neck when he answered them. *Mollie* . . .

Burton put his free hand against the wall to steady himself. He blinked, shook his head, and raised the bottle to his mouth again. Mollie was gone and the children did not ask him anything now, but he still had the raw bite of whiskey to take away the memories and the pain.

He peered through the window and tried to focus on

the work his children were doing. The cornfield was only about fifty yards from the house, and he could see Emily moving along the rows picking the higher ears, leaving the lower ones for Avery and Nora, who dragged the bushel baskets in which the corn was placed. They were working hard, as they always did. Burton supposed they were not such bad kids after all.

Looking past the three youngsters toward the edge of the cornfield, he blinked again and frowned. Four men on horseback had suddenly appeared there, and with no warning they charged through the rows, trampling the stalks heedlessly. Burton heard Emily scream; the sound seemed to come from a long way off.

"What the hell!" Burton exclaimed. For an instant, he thought he was imagining things, that the liquor that had befogged his brain for so long was making him see phantoms. But then he realized the sight was all too real. In a matter of seconds, the strange riders would gallop right over his three children.

Emily dropped the corn she was holding and spun around to grab Avery and Nora. She tried to push and pull them into a run, but their feet sank in the soft, wet ground, and they could not pull them out quickly enough. They would never be able to elude their pursuers, Burton knew.

He snapped out of the trance that held him and lunged toward the doorway of the house. There were pegs above the door, and on them was hung an old Winchester. Burton reached up and yanked the rifle down. He had no idea who the men attacking his children were, but he was not going to stand by and let them get away with it.

Staggering onto the porch, Burton worked the lever

of the rifle to see if it was loaded. It was. Somehow he caught the ejected cartridge in midair and thumbed it back into the magazine. Then he hurried to the end of the porch where he would be able to see the cornfield.

He got there in time to see the riders veering around the fleeing youngsters. One of the men leaned over and tried to grab the collar of Emily's dress. Shrieking, she twisted away from him. Burton raised the Winchester to his shoulder and took a deep breath as he tried to steady it. The barrel seemed to dance around by itself. When the sights settled for an instant on one of the strangers, Burton pressed the trigger.

The blast of the rifle hurt his ears, and the butt thumped back painfully against his shoulder. He jacked another shell into the chamber without waiting to see if his first shot had hit anything. As he squinted over the wavering barrel, he saw that one of the men had wheeled his horse around and was now galloping toward him. Burton tried desperately to line up the sights on the man.

The raider lifted his hand. Just as Burton touched off another shot, he saw the pistol that the man was brandishing. Burton had no idea where his slug went, but the man kept coming and now noise and flame spurted from the barrel of his weapon. The sharp crack of a gunshot assaulted Burton's already aching head.

What felt like a fist thumped hard in his chest, throwing him back a couple of steps. He tried to work the lever on the Winchester again, but he suddenly discovered he did not have the strength. The rifle slipped from his fingers and thudded to the planks of the porch.

Reeling forward, Burton heard the thunder of hoofbeats close by and then another gunshot. Again something hit him in the chest. He grunted and sank to his knees, feeling how wet the front of his shirt was. He must have spilled some whiskey on it, he thought fuzzily. Waste of good liquor, that was what it was.

The sun did not seem nearly as bright now, but there was enough light for Charlie Burton to see his children, smiling and laughing and happy as they came toward him. They were happier than he had seen them in years, he thought, and that was because he suddenly realized that Mollie was with them again. He held out his arms to them. Little Nora ran into his embrace and hugged his neck, her soft hair tickling his cheek. Then the others were with him, and Mollie put out a hand and took his, her fingers cool and soft just as he remembered them. . . .

There was one more shot, but Charlie Burton never heard it.

The men were all strangers to Emily—evil, laughing strangers who lunged toward her and tried to grab her. She ducked away from them as best she could and urged her brother and sister to keep running, even though she knew it was hopeless. There was no way they could get away from three men on horseback.

One of the raiders had galloped toward the house, and a minute later Emily heard the shots. She knew what had happened. More grief than she would have thought possible tore at her for a few seconds. Then she was overwhelmed by fear—for herself and for Avery and Nora. When the men had first ridden into the cornfield, Emily thought that they intended to trample the three of them. Now she knew they had something even worse in mind.

"Run, Avery! Run, Nora!" she cried.

One of the men, a burly redhead in a calfskin vest, leaned over in his saddle and lashed out at her. She tried to dodge, but his fingers grasped her dress and clamped down. The fabric gave for a moment with a ripping sound, then held. Emily was jerked around as the man pulled his horse to a halt. She screamed again.

Avery stumbled along behind Nora, but he stopped short when he heard Emily's terrified cry. Turning around, he shouted, "Let her go!"

"Avery, no!" Emily called to him, her voice breaking in a sob. "K-keep going!"

Avery ignored her. He flung himself at the man who held Emily, but before he could reach him, one of the others nudged his horse forward. The animal's broad chest banged into Avery's shoulder, knocking him down. The horse danced around nervously, its hooves coming perilously close to the fallen boy.

The man who was holding Emily laughed, and she felt a powerful anger surge through her. Then she noticed the pistol holstered on the man's hip. She twisted in his grasp, bringing her head closer to his arm, and before he knew what she was doing, she sank her teeth into his forearm, biting right through his filthy shirt. At the same time, she reached blindly for the gun, trying to get her fingers around it.

Her captor shouted in pain and tried to dislodge her teeth from his arm. Suddenly the weapon was free of its holster and in Emily's hand. Her arm sagged at the gun's weight, but she managed to slip her finger around the trigger. She yanked on it as hard as she could, although she had no idea where the pistol was pointing.

It blasted, the report thunderous and deafening, and the recoil almost tore it out of her hand. But she forced herself to fire it again and again.

Now the cornfield was a dusty, nightmarish place, filled with a whirlwind of desperate activity. The man who had caught her smashed his balled fist at her head, knocking her away from his other arm. As Emily reeled she caught a glimpse of his sleeve and noted with fleeting satisfaction that it was bloody. But then she saw Avery struggle to his feet only to be struck down again by one of the other men. This time he fell limply, unconscious—or worse. That was all Emily had time to see before someone grabbed her wrist, wrenched it savagely, and forced her to drop the pistol. Her jaw ached where the man had struck her, and now that pain was joined by another as a fist rammed into her stomach. A voice yelled, "Don't kill her, goddammit!"

Strong hands grasped her shoulders and flung her face down to the ground. She tasted the dirt of the cornfield in her mouth and jerked her head up, spitting. Someone came down on her back, a knee driving painfully into her spine and pinning her there.

"That other kid's getting away!" one of the men yelled.

Emily lifted her head. Her hair had fallen over her eyes, but through the strands she could see Nora still running, her figure small and distant as she vanished into a stand of trees a hundred yards away.

"Let her run," a voice replied, the same voice that had warned them not to kill her. "We don't need all of them. These two will do just as well. And the little girl will probably save us the trouble of getting in touch with O'Quinn. She's liable to go right to him."

The man was right, Emily knew. Nora had idolized

O'Quinn. There was every chance that she would try to reach him now that she was alone and scared.

They hauled her to her feet. All of them were on foot now except for one man. He was much better dressed than the others and looked out of place on the frontier. He peered at her with the coldest eyes she had ever seen and said, "Don't worry, Miss Burton. You won't be hurt if you cooperate with us."

Emily saw Avery lying a few feet away. She ran to him, dropped to her knees beside him, and lifted his head to cradle it in her lap. With a surge of relief she saw that he was breathing and, other than being unconscious, seemed to be all right.

Emily glanced toward the house. "My father . . . ?" she whispered.

The man with the cold eyes said, "He was shooting at us. I'm sorry, Miss Burton. There was nothing else we could do."

But to Emily he did not sound sorry at all. She stared up at him, at the little half-smile that would have been charming and handsome under different circumstances, and saw the utter evil in his gaze. Horror suddenly chilled her to the core of her being, a greater horror than she had ever known before.


"Marshal! Marshal!"

Luke Travis heard the urgent cries, pushed back his chair, and hurried from behind his desk. Cody, who was dozing on one of the bunks in the empty cellblock, leapt to his feet. He appeared in the doorway seconds after Travis started for the door of the office.

Both lawmen burst onto the boardwalk and saw a wagon careening down Texas Street toward the marshal's office. The driver was whipping his team, urging more speed from the lathered animals. Beside him, holding on tightly, was a woman with a little girl in her arms. More children were huddled in the back of the wagon.

"That's Dan Mahaffey!" Cody exclaimed. "Looks like he's got his whole family with him!"

The farmer suddenly stopped whipping his mules and began hauling back on the reins instead, trying to bring the plunging animals to a halt. As the team slowed, Cody ran into the street, grabbed the harness of one of the leaders, and pulled hard to make the animal stop. The wagon shuddered to a halt in front of the office.

Mahaffey jumped down from the box, breathing heavily. The dust that coated his face was streaked with sweat. "There's bad trouble at the Burton place, Marshal!" he cried. "You'd better get out there!"

Travis caught the man's arm as he frantically waved his hands around. "Hold on there!" Travis said sharply. "Now slow down and tell me what's going on."

"There was a bunch of shootin' over at the Burton farm, Marshal," Mahaffey gasped as he gulped air. "I don't know what happened, but it was bad!"

"Nora came to our soddy," Mahaffey's wife put in as she stroked the trembling little child in her arms.

Travis recognized Nora Burton now. He nodded toward her and said softly, "Cody."

The deputy moved forward and reached up to take Nora from Mrs. Mahaffey. At first she did not want to go to the young man, but she seemed to relax as he spoke to her in a surprisingly gentle, soothing voice. Cody nestled her head against his shoulder and carried her to Travis.

Glancing around at the crowd drawn by the commotion, Travis ordered, "You people go on about your business." He was worried that a mob, even just a curious one, would frighten the terrified Nora even more. While Cody still held her, Travis asked, "Can you tell me what happened, Nora?"

"I don't think she can, Marshal," Mahaffey said before Nora could answer. "She was bawlin' and scared out of her wits when she got to our place. Mighty tired, too. Reckon she ran all the way from her house."

Travis glared at the distraught farmer, making him fall silent, then turned back to Nora. "What about it, darling?" he asked. "You know Cody and me. We just want to help you. Why don't you tell us what happened?"

"Th-they chased us," Nora said in a voice so small that Travis had to lean closer to make out the words.

"Chased you? Who'd do a thing like that?" Cody asked as he patted her back.

"Some men . . . I think they . . . they hurt Emily and Avery . . . and maybe Papa. They yelled at us, and they shot their guns. . . . " Suddenly the little girl wailed, "I want Abigail Elizabeth!"

Travis and Cody exchanged a puzzled glance, unsure whom Nora was referring to. One of the Mahaffey children piped up from the back of the wagon, "That's her dolly."

"Oh," Travis said. "Well, we'll see that you get Abigail Elizabeth back, Nora. Did you know any of the men who hurt your family?"

Nora shook her head and sniffled.

Travis heard footsteps behind him and turned to see Aileen Bloom hurrying up to him. "My God, Luke," she said. "What happened?"

"We're not sure yet, Aileen, but I'm glad to see you. Can you take care of this little girl for us?"

"Of course." Aileen reached out to take Nora from

Cody. The youngster went eagerly to her, still muttering about her doll.

"Come on, Cody," Travis continued. "I reckon there's a lot more to the story, but we'd better get out there in case anybody needs help."

"You want me to get some of the boys together?" Cody asked.

Travis shook his head. "I don't want to take the time to raise a posse right now. Aileen, we may have some more work for you in a little while." His grim expression made it plain what he meant.

The doctor nodded as she comforted Nora.

"You want me to come along, Marshal?" Mahaffey asked, sounding distinctly nervous.

"You and your family had better stay here," Travis told him. "I don't know what we're heading into out there."

The farmer looked visibly relieved.

Less than two minutes later, Travis and Cody were riding hard out of Abilene, heading for the Burton farm. Calling over the pounding of hoofbeats, Cody asked, "You think this has something to do with O'Quinn and McTeague?"

"That's what I'm afraid of," Travis replied, raising his own voice. That was the first possibility that had occurred to him. For the life of him, he could not think of any other reason why someone would want to hurt the Burtons. Except for Charlie's drinking, they were about as harmless a family as any in the area.

But now there was a connection between them and Seamus O'Quinn, and the big prizefighter seemed to attract violence wherever he went.

At first glance, everything looked normal as Travis and Cody rode up to the Burton farm. But then they saw the trampled stalks in the cornfield and the dark shape sprawled on the porch of the house. Travis reined in and slipped his Colt from its holster. Cody did the same.

"There was trouble here all right," Travis said quietly as he sat in the saddle and studied the scene for a moment. There was no sign of anyone around now, and his instincts told him that whatever had happened was over. He walked his horse slowly toward the house.

Cody followed until Travis gestured silently for him to circle the house. The deputy steered his horse to the right to loop around the building as Travis rode up to the porch.

Charlie Burton lay motionless on the rough planks, stretched out on his back with his arms and legs splayed to the sides. His shirtfront was soaked with blood, drying now to a dark rust-brown. There was a black-rimmed hole in his forehead, just above his sightlessly staring eyes, and an ugly stain on the wall behind him told where the bullet had exited. Travis grimaced.

Aileen Bloom could do nothing for Burton; no one could help him now but the undertaker. Travis swung down off his horse and climbed onto the porch, still holding his gun ready. He moved into the house to see if anyone else was there.

When he emerged a few minutes later, he found Cody sitting on his horse in front of the porch. The deputy shook his head. "Nobody else around," he told Travis. "I didn't see hide nor hair of the other two. What about inside?"

"It's empty," Travis said flatly. "Whoever was here took Emily and the boy with them. This will tell you why." He thrust a piece of paper at Cody.

Cody took it and scanned the precise writing. A low

whistle escaped from his lips. "You were right," he said. "They want O'Quinn and McTeague."

The note was simple. It stated that Emily and Avery Burton were prisoners and they would be killed unless the kidnappers' orders were followed to the letter. The note contained directions to a shack west of Abilene on the Smoky Hill River and instructed O'Quinn and McTeague to come to that cabin—alone and unarmed. If they did not, no one would ever see the two captives alive again.

"What are you going to do?" Cody asked grimly.

Travis squinted into the distance, his expression bleak. "There's only one thing we can do," he replied. "We have to let O'Quinn and McTeague decide how they want to play this."

"They could be riding into a trap," Cody pointed out.

Travis nodded. "They'll know that as well as we do."

"We could get a posse and hit the place. Wouldn't even have to trail those bastards. They've told us where to find them."

Travis glanced at Charlie Burton's body. "That might just get those youngsters killed." He mounted up. "Come on. Let's get back to town."

"What about him?" Cody nodded toward the corpse.

"We'll send somebody out to get him later. He's not hurting anymore." That was the first time anyone had been able to say that about Charlie Burton in a long while, Travis thought ruefully.

# Chapter Twelve

───※───

WHEN LUKE TRAVIS AND CODY FISHER RODE INTO ABI-
lene a little later, they found a crowd of anxious
people waiting in front of Dr. Aileen Bloom's office.
As they reined in their horses at the hitchrack, they
saw Aileen and Nora Burton standing on the front
porch with Orion, O'Quinn, and McTeague. A doz-
en citizens had gathered in the small, tidy yard and
were peering with puzzled expressions at the marshal.

As the two lawmen dismounted, O'Quinn charged
off the porch, pushed through the crowd, and hurried
to the marshal. "Is it true, Travis?" he asked anxiously. "What did you find out?"

Travis flipped his reins around the rail. "Charlie
Burton is dead," he said grimly, shaking his head.
"There's no sign of Emily or Avery." He reached
inside his coat and drew out the piece of paper on

which the note was written. "But the men who took them left this."

O'Quinn snatched the paper from Travis's outstretched hand and scanned it. McTeague came up beside him and read the note over his shoulder.

"It's a trap," the detective snapped angrily. "This is just the kind of thing that Mitch Rainey would do. He doesn't care who he hurts as long as he gets what he wants."

O'Quinn looked up from the note and met Travis's gaze. "Can you tell me how to get to this place?" he asked.

Before Travis could answer, McTeague cried, "No, dammit! I can't let you do this, Seamus. They'll kill you for sure."

O'Quinn turned and stared at him coldly. "You don't have to go, Jack. I know they asked for you, but I think they'll settle for me. *I'm* the eyewitness, after all."

"But—"

"Forget it, Jack. They've got Emily and Avery. I've got to go."

McTeague looked at Travis. "Marshal, can't you talk some sense into him?"

"Seems to me it's his decision," Travis said with a shrug. "But it would be foolish just to waltz in there like Rainey says. And I don't think that would save the lives of those two youngsters, either. Rainey would just kill all three of you, O'Quinn."

O'Quinn shook his head. "I've got to go," he muttered.

McTeague suddenly took a step back, his hand darting under his coat. He drew out the derringer and lined it up on O'Quinn. "You're not going anywhere," he rasped. "I'll keep you here at gunpoint if I have to!"

Travis saw his deputy reaching for his own gun and snapped, "Cody! Hold it!" As the deputy froze, Travis went on, "I don't want any shooting here in town, McTeague. Why don't you put that gun down?"

O'Quinn grimaced. "That's right, Jack. Anyway, you can't shoot me without doing Rainey's job for him. That would sort of defeat your purpose, wouldn't it?"

"I can put a bullet in your leg so that you can't ride or walk," McTeague said coldly. "But you'd still be able to testify against Gold and Rainey. Dammit, Seamus, don't you realize there's more at stake here than just a couple of lives, no matter how precious they are to you? Darius Gold has been ruthlessly killing people for years. There's no telling how many deaths he's responsible for. Now that we have a case against him at last, we can't let it be destroyed."

The group of bystanders watching from the yard gaped at the gun McTeague was pointing at the man they all believed was his friend. Orion, who had remained on the porch with Aileen and Nora, hurried to the marshal with a shocked look on his face. "Wha' is this, Lucas?" he cried. "Has McTeague gone daft?"

Travis shook his head. He had been afraid the two visitors from Chicago would react like this, bitterly split in the course of action they each wanted to follow. He said to O'Quinn, "Maybe McTeague's right. You know Rainey won't hesitate to kill all of you once you're in his hands. Emily and Avery will stand a better chance if we try to get them out of there ourselves."

"With a posse, you mean." O'Quinn laughed humorlessly. "He'll kill Emily and Avery as soon as he sees you coming."

"He won't see us coming until it's too late," Travis said pointedly.

Cody looked at him. "You sound like you've got a plan, Marshal."

"Maybe. I need to take a look at the lay of the land first. I think I've been to that old cabin where they're holed up, but I don't remember exactly what the terrain around it is like. We might just be able to take them by surprise."

"How about it, Seamus?" McTeague asked the prizefighter. "Are you willing to give the marshal a chance to rescue them?"

O'Quinn drew a deep breath. "What else can I do?" he asked bleakly. "You've got a gun on me, and I believe you'll shoot if you think you have to."

"Damn right I will," McTeague growled.

O'Quinn reached out and grasped Travis's arm. "Get them out of there, Marshal," he said fervently. "For God's sake, get them out."

"We'll do our best, Seamus," Travis promised, calling the desperate prizefighter by his first name for the first time. He turned to Cody. "Now you'd better round up that posse."

Cody nodded and hurried off, Orion at his side. The Scotsman would be riding with them, Travis knew, and there were plenty of other good men in town who would be willing to join the rescue effort.

Travis just hoped the attempt would not end in more deaths. On the ride back to Abilene from the Burton farm, he had realized that this whole thing was his fault. O'Quinn's friendship with the Burtons was the connection he had overlooked, the nagging detail that he had failed to cover.

He was going to get Emily Burton and her brother back safely, Travis vowed to himself, or die trying.

O'Quinn let McTeague talk him into returning to the boardinghouse while Travis and Cody gathered their posse. McTeague holstered his gun and said, "I'm glad you decided to be reasonable about this, O'Quinn. I really didn't want to shoot you."

"But you would have," O'Quinn accused bitterly.

"Of course."

O'Quinn snorted. He had never doubted that for a moment.

It had been sheer coincidence that they were at Aileen's office when she came in with Nora Burton. They had gone to the office to have her check the bump on O'Quinn's head. Finding it empty when they arrived, they waited on the porch, and within a few minutes Aileen came up the walk carrying Nora. The little girl immediately threw herself into O'Quinn's arms and wailed as she told the horrible story of the raid on the farm. The commotion brought Orion from the tavern next door.

Waiting for Travis and Cody to return from the farm had been one of the most harrowing experiences of O'Quinn's life. For all he knew, the entire family might be dead except for Nora.

Now he knew they were alive, but the situation was still horrible. Emily and Avery were the captives of two ruthless men.

"I'm sure Travis knows what he's doing," McTeague went on. "He'll bring them back all right, you'll see."

"I thought you didn't have a high opinion of frontier lawmen," O'Quinn retorted.

McTeague shrugged. "Let's just hope I've been wrong all along, shall we? In the meantime—"

"In the meantime, we wait," O'Quinn cut in.

"That's right. That's all we can do."

The two men plodded toward the boardinghouse in silence. There was nothing else to say, and both of them knew it. When they reached the house and entered it, Hettie Wilburn appeared from her kitchen and wanted to know all about the commotion downtown. McTeague quickly gave her a modified version of the story, leaving out the connection O'Quinn and he had with the bloody events at the Burton farm. While McTeague was talking to the landlady, O'Quinn went upstairs to his room.

He hung his hat on a hook, sat on the bed, and stared down at his hands. The knuckles were knobby, the palms calloused. He made a living with those fists, shaped his own destiny, such as it was, with them. But now, when the people he cared most about in the world were in danger, there was nothing he could do for them. He had to sit by helplessly and wait for someone else to save Emily and Avery—or bring him the news that they had been too late.

He had never planned beyond the next prizefight, sometimes not even beyond the next round in a match. But now he suddenly realized that he had started to make plans for his future, and those plans included Emily Burton.

He was in love with her. Even though he had not known her for long, he had no doubt about his feelings. And there was no way he could sit idly by while her life was in danger.

O'Quinn heard footsteps in the hall outside. The door opened, and McTeague entered without knocking. The detective said, "There you are. I was hoping you hadn't tried to slip out again."

Moving with the speed that had saved him from more than one defeat in the prize ring, O'Quinn came up off the bed, his fists bunched. He lashed out, his right hand slamming into McTeague's jaw before the shocked detective had a chance to move. The blow jerked McTeague's head around, and he dropped to the floor. He never had a chance.

O'Quinn knelt beside him and checked to make sure that McTeague was only unconscious. Even in his desperate state of mind, he had tried to pull his punch, aware of how easy it was to kill a man by hitting him too hard. He nodded in satisfaction when he saw the steady rise and fall of McTeague's chest. The inspector was out cold, but he seemed to be all right otherwise.

O'Quinn stood up. The posse would be gone by now, riding hard out of Abilene on their rescue mission. That was all right; O'Quinn doubted that Travis would have let him accompany them anyway. He had to find someone else who could show him the way to the cabin where the prisoners were being held.

Leaving McTeague where he lay, O'Quinn clattered down the stairs and out of the house, ignoring the questions that a surprised Hettie called after him. He turned west on Second Street, heading for the schoolhouse at a fast walk that was almost a run.

When O'Quinn opened the door of the school and strode into the classroom, a startled Thurman Simpson turned from the figures he had just chalked onto the blackboard. When he saw who the visitor was, he paled and cried, "You! What are you doing here, you barbarian?"

O'Quinn snatched off his hat, not wanting to offend Simpson at this moment. Even though the teacher was a pompous prig, he could probably tell O'Quinn where to find Leslie Gibson. "Sorry to interrupt your arithmetic lesson, Mr. Simpson," O'Quinn said, "but I'm looking for Leslie Gibson. Is he here?" As he asked the question, he realized the children in the room were staring at him. Their trusting yet curious faces reminded him of Avery, and that only increased his impatience.

"It doesn't matter whether Mr. Gibson is here or not," Simpson snapped. "You can't just barge in here and disrupt my lessons, O'Quinn. You don't know how hard it is to make these children concentrate in the first place. Why, when something like this happens, I do well to get their minds back on their work before the day is over!"

O'Quinn felt his hands clenching into fists and hoped he would not give in to the urge he felt. Tightly he said, "Just tell me where Leslie is, and I'll get out of your way."

"I'm here, Seamus," rumbled a deep voice from the doorway that led into the other classroom. Leslie Gibson looked at him with a puzzled expression on his bearded face. "What's the trouble?"

O'Quinn hurried toward him, threading his way among the children's desks. "It's Emily Burton," he said, "and Avery, too. They've been kidnapped."

"Kidnapped!" Leslie exclaimed, his features creasing into a shocked frown. "Who the devil—"

"That's about right," O'Quinn cut in. "Come on. I need your help."

O'Quinn and Leslie had taken a step toward the door when Thurman Simpson's voice cracked like a whip. "Mr. Gibson! May I remind you that you have a class to teach this afternoon? You have a responsibility to those children. I can't allow you to run off on some wild-goose chase with this pugilist friend of yours!"

Leslie looked from Simpson to O'Quinn. "You were telling the truth about the kidnapping, Seamus?" he asked.

"I was. It's a matter of life and death, Leslie. I promise you that."

Leslie nodded. "Sorry, Mr. Simpson," he said to the schoolmaster. "I've got to go."

Side by side, the two big men strode out of the schoolhouse, while Simpson yelped peevishly behind them, "I'll have your job for this insubordination, Gibson!"

When they were outside, O'Quinn said, "I hope you don't lose your job over this, Leslie."

The teacher grinned. "I didn't get fired for knocking Simpson on his rear end. I don't think anybody will want to get rid of me for this, either. Now what's happened?"

Quickly O'Quinn told him about the events of the morning. Leslie's frown deepened. O'Quinn spared no detail, including his punching McTeague. When he was finished, Leslie said, "I knew Avery and Nora weren't in school today, but I had no idea such a terrible thing had happened. What do you intend to do?"

As O'Quinn talked, the two men had been walking toward Texas Street. Now the prizefighter stopped, thrust his hand into his pocket, and pulled out a crumpled piece of paper. "The marshal forgot about this," he said. "It's the note from Rainey that tells how to get to the cabin where the prisoners are. I want you to take me there."

Leslie took the note, then glanced up and saw that they had stopped in front of the livery stable. He scanned the writing on the paper, then said, "I think I could find the place, all right, but didn't you say that Travis and Cody have already gone out there with a posse?"

"It's me that Rainey and Parker want, not some posse," O'Quinn replied. "I have to be there, Leslie. I can't just wait and do nothing!" The desperation in his voice was plain.

Leslie looked uncomfortable. "This is the kind of thing that's best left to the authorities, Seamus," he said slowly. "If we go out there, you could wind up badly hurt."

O'Quinn shrugged. "I know. Maybe even killed. But it's my life I'm risking. I can't stay here when Emily and Avery are . . . are . . ."

"I understand," Leslie said with a grimace. "I don't know Emily very well, but Avery and I have become good friends." He took a deep breath. "All right. I suppose we don't really have a choice."

A fierce grin broke over O'Quinn's face, and he clapped his friend on the shoulder. "Good! Now let's get going. I don't know how long McTeague is going to be out."

"You pulled your punch, I hope?"

"Of course. He'll be all right when he wakes up, except for a headache."

Leslie nodded and led the way into the stable. Five minutes later both men were mounted and riding out of town. They followed Texas Street to the west, their horses' hooves clattering over the bridge spanning Mud Creek. Ahead of them stretched the prairie, the Kansas Pacific tracks cutting through the plains. To the south, paralleling the railroad, was the Smoky Hill

River. The two big men urged their horses into a gallop as they rode beside the rails.

Somewhere up ahead were Emily and Avery. O'Quinn promised himself that he would see them alive again. Or he would kill Mitch Rainey with his bare hands.

The posse led by Travis and Cody set a fast pace on the ride west from Abilene. They hugged the line of the now leafless trees that grew along the banks of the Smoky Hill River. But as they neared the area where the cabin was located, the marshal ordered the men to slow their horses to a walk. If the kidnappers had posted sentries, as was likely, Travis did not want a large dust cloud to give away the approaching posse.

As they rode at the head of the dozen or so men hastily deputized in Abilene, Cody said to Travis, "I think I recollect this place, too, Marshal. It used to belong to some farmer, didn't it?"

Travis nodded. "He couldn't make a go of it, from what I understand, and finally gave up. The farm had plenty of water, since the river was right beside it, but the ground was just too rocky. The cabin sits on a bluff above the river."

"That's the way I remember it, too," Cody agreed. "I've ridden past it a few times. You think we can get close enough to the place without them seeing us?"

Travis rubbed his jaw thoughtfully and then said, "That's what I hope. There are some trees along that bluff; they might give us enough cover."

The two lawmen fell silent. When they saw the peak of the cabin's roof through the trees a hundred yards away, Travis called a halt. Gesturing to the posse, he ordered them to move into the stand of trees. Once the men were under cover, he swung down from his horse and turned to the Scotsman. "Orion, you and the others stay here and keep as quiet as you can. Cody and I will scout ahead a little."

"Aye," Orion acknowledged with a nod.

On foot Travis and Cody slipped through the trees. They were so close to the river now that they could hear its soft gurgle. They also heard the sudden whinny of a horse up ahead.

"That'll be them," Travis breathed. Crouching, he inched forward, then paused behind some brush. Cody knelt beside him. Travis moved some of the growth aside, and they were able to see the cabin, some fifty yards away.

Four horses were tied up in front of the ramshackle structure. Smoke curled lazily from the stone chimney, a sign that someone inside was probably brewing a pot of coffee. One man stood on the porch, a rifle in his hands. He appeared to be the only guard.

Travis whispered, "Do you know that fellow?"

Cody shook his head. "Don't recognize him right off at this distance. Reckon he's one of Parker's friends."

"That would be my guess. I can't see if they have anybody else on guard."

"Neither can I," Cody agreed. "You think we could rush the place?"

Travis studied the open area in front of the cabin. The trees and brush did not come as close to it as he had hoped. "I'm not sure," he said finally. "That's a lot of open ground to cover. I reckon we could charge them and roust them out, but those two youngsters would probably get killed in the process."

Cody looked speculatively at the bluff. After a moment, he said, "What we need is somebody to distract them for a few minutes while the rest of the posse comes to the front. Looks to me like a man could slip along the river and then climb that bluff right up to their back door."

"It would be a pretty hard climb. That slope's pretty steep, and it's rocky."

Cody grinned. "Shoot, I've climbed worse. Judah could tell you. When I was a little kid, there was this cliff close to where we lived—"

"I'll take your word for it," Travis cut in. "One thing, though. I don't want you providing the distraction. The rest of us will do that. When we start the ruckus, it'll be up to you to get in through the back and grab Emily and Avery. Can you do that?"

Cody considered Travis's suggestion, then nodded. "It's the only way they'll have a chance. You'd better give me about fifteen minutes to get into position. I'd signal you, but I don't know what I could do that wouldn't tip them off, too."

Travis agreed, and the two lawmen moved stealthily back to where they had left the posse. Once there, Travis quietly explained the plan to the other men. Orion put a hand on Cody's shoulder and squeezed. "Good luck, lad," he said.

"Thanks. I reckon Emily and Avery are the ones who'll need it the most, though." With a carefree wave to Travis that belied the grim nature of his mission, Cody left his horse tied in the trees and headed for the river on foot.

Travis pulled his watch from his pants pocket and flipped the case open. Fifteen minutes, Cody had said. That was what they would give him. And if he was not ready, this rescue attempt could quickly turn into a disaster.

# Chapter Thirteen

———————◆———————

THE TIME PASSED VERY SLOWLY. ACCORDING TO LUKE Travis's watch, they had been waiting for five minutes when he heard galloping horses approaching from the east. He spun around and hissed to Orion, "See who that is and stop the fools before they ruin everything!"

Orion ran toward the rear of the posse, carrying the shotgun that was his preferred weapon. He spotted two men riding through the trees and stepped in front of them, covering them with the gun. "Hold it!" he ordered in a harsh whisper, muffling the deep rumble of his voice.

Leslie Gibson and Seamus O'Quinn reined in awkwardly and gaped at him in surprise. They had not spotted the posse members hidden up ahead. Leslie cried, "Orion! I'm glad to see *you*."

"Hush, lad," the Scotsman rasped, lowering his shotgun and motioning for the newcomers to be quiet. "Wha' are the two o' ye doing out here? Especially ye, Seamus. Dinna McTeague say ye could no' come?"

"I guess you could say McTeague got his mind changed for him," O'Quinn quipped. Despite his wry comment, lines of concern were deeply etched in his face. "What's happened?" he asked.

Orion shook his head. "Nothing yet. We be waiting f'Cody t'get into position 'fore we rush the place."

O'Quinn frowned anxiously. "If you rush them, they're sure to kill Emily and Avery."

"Not the way Lucas has planned it," Orion told him. "G'down off tha' horse and come wi' me. Lucas kin tell ye all about it."

O'Quinn and Leslie dismounted and tied their horses to a sapling, then followed closely behind Orion to where Luke Travis was standing, staring at the watch in his hand. At the sound of their footsteps he glanced up and frowned in angry surprise when he saw who the newcomers were.

"Dammit, Seamus, I thought you were staying in Abilene," Travis snapped. "Where's McTeague?"

"I said all along he didn't have to come," O'Quinn replied. "But I'm here, and that's all that matters. I want to go in there, Marshal."

Travis took a deep breath. He suspected that O'Quinn had slipped away from McTeague somehow, maybe even got the jump on him and knocked him out of this fight for the moment. But this was no time to question the prizefighter. Cody would be climbing the bluff toward the cabin above by now.

"We already have our rescue attempt planned," Travis told O'Quinn. He explained it tersely, finishing, "If we don't hit the place when Cody said, things could get fouled up."

"But your deputy's not going to make his move until he hears the shooting when you charge the cabin," O'Quinn pointed out. "As long as nobody fires a gun, he'll wait for the right moment."

"True enough, but every second he waits there behind that cabin his chances of being spotted increase. He's got to take Rainey and Parker by surprise, or he won't do any good."

O'Quinn thought that over. Leslie Gibson stood by, a worried look on his rugged face. Finally, O'Quinn said, "Look, Marshal, Rainey's after me. I think it should be my decision whether or not I ride over there. I honestly think that I can get Emily and Avery out."

Travis looked intently at him for a long moment, then glanced over at Orion and Leslie. "What do you two think?" he asked.

"The man has a point, Lucas," Orion replied. "And he's right about Cody waiting until the shooting starts 'fore he busts in."

Leslie said, "It looks to me as though Seamus will be the only one taking any extra risks, Marshal. If anything goes wrong, the posse can still charge, and Cody can come in the back just as you planned."

Travis nodded abruptly. "All right," he said to O'Quinn. "I don't much like it, but you're right about it being your life. If you want to go in there, I won't stop you."

Despite his worry, O'Quinn was able to grin. "Thanks, Marshal. You don't know how good it feels to be *doing* something instead of just sitting and waiting."

"You'd better do it pretty quickly. Cody should be

just about ready now. I don't want him to be a sitting duck any longer than necessary."

"I'll go right now," O'Quinn said, turning and heading for his horse. He untied his mount and swung up into the saddle, then rode through the trees toward the clearing in front of the cabin. The posse members had overheard the conversation, and several of them muttered, "Good luck, O'Quinn," as he passed them. Leslie said, "Be careful, Seamus," a warning echoed by Orion.

Travis held the butt of his gun out toward O'Quinn and said, "You might need this. I've got a spare in my saddlebag."

O'Quinn shook his head. "I've never been any good with one of those, Marshal. My fists are the only weapons I've ever used. But thanks anyway."

Holstering his gun, Travis watched O'Quinn walk his horse through the brush and into the clearing. The next few minutes would tell the story.

O'Quinn could feel his heart pounding as he rode toward the cabin. He saw the man standing on the porch suddenly straighten and duck into the building, no doubt to warn Rainey that someone was coming. O'Quinn half expected shots to ring out, but the air remained still and quiet. It was a pretty day, he thought, warm for autumn. The sky was a clear blue. If it came to that, not a bad day to die.

It seemed to take forever to cross the open space in front of the cabin. As he rode forward, O'Quinn could see how the ground dropped away a few feet beyond the shack. That would be the bluff Travis had told him about. At the bottom of it was the river.

Finally, O'Quinn drew the horse to a stop a few feet from the porch. Resting his hands on the saddlehorn, he called out, "Rainey! Are you in there?"

For a long moment there was silence. Then a voice called from inside the cabin, "I'm here, O'Quinn. Where's McTeague?"

"In Abilene," O'Quinn replied. "You don't need him, Rainey. All he knows is what I've told him. He didn't see you and Gold and your thugs kill Dooley and Rutherford. You know damn well a judge and jury aren't going to listen to anybody but an eyewitness."

A cold laugh floated through the open window next to the door. "True enough," Rainey agreed. "But I wouldn't mind seeing McTeague dead anyway, just to make sure all the loose ends are tied up. That's not your concern, though, O'Quinn."

O'Quinn sensed there were several guns pointing at him. With his skin crawling, he called, "That's right, Rainey. All I'm worried about now is Emily and Avery Burton. I came out here like you wanted. Now le⁺ them go." He had raised his voice so that if Cody was indeed concealed behind the cabin, as he was supposed to be, he would overhear the conversation and know what was going on.

The cabin door swung open with a squeal of rusty hinges that tore at O'Quinn's tightly stretched nerves. When he saw who stumbled through it, he clutched at the saddlehorn to keep from flinging himself off the horse.

Emily and Avery stood on the porch, and crowding close behind them were Mitch Rainey and Willie Parker. This was the first time that O'Quinn had seen Rainey since that awful night in Chicago, but he had no trouble recognizing the man. Rainey was holding the barrel of a small pistol to Avery's head. His other hand gripped the boy's shoulder. Parker was behind

Emily, one arm around her waist and the other hand holding a revolver pressed into her side.

Both captives looked as if they had been roughed up, their clothes torn and disheveled. One sleeve and shoulder of Emily's dress had been ripped away, exposing her smooth, slim arm. O'Quinn saw purple bruises there, and anger surged through him. Trembling slightly, he managed to control it.

Despite what she had gone through, Emily held her head up, and her eyes were clear as she looked at O'Quinn. He saw sorrow in them and realized with a shock that it was for him, not for herself. He could tell that she wished he had not come; she would rather die herself than have him fall into Rainey's hands.

Avery hung his head, his eyes staring at the planks at his feet, his stance one of fear and defeat. Were it not for Rainey gripping his shoulder, he might have fallen.

O'Quinn heard a noise at the window and glanced up to see the two other men glaring at him, their rifles trained on him. Grinning, Rainey said, "That's so you don't try anything funny, O'Quinn. Those men will blow you right out of that saddle if you do."

O'Quinn sighed heavily. "I'm not going to try anything, Rainey. I came to see that my friends aren't hurt. Why don't you let them go now? You've gotten what you wanted."

"I haven't," Parker growled. "Not yet, anyway." He moved the arm that was around Emily's waist so that he could reach up and roughly stroke her breast. She paled but did not flinch or utter a sound.

O'Quinn felt his desperation and rage growing. "Come on, Rainey," he growled. "I'm not going to double-cross you. You keep your end of the bargain."

"Now that's a funny thing, O'Quinn," Rainey said,

his grin broadening. He moved the muzzle of his pistol away from Avery's head and aimed the weapon at O'Quinn's large frame. "I don't mind double-crossing you one damn bit. Darius always told me never to leave any witnesses behind. I think I'll just kill you, then let Parker and his men have their fun with the girl here. They've been very patient. I might even take a turn myself."

Avery's head lifted, his eyes widening as the horrible meaning of Rainey's words soaked into his stunned mind. Suddenly, surprising everyone, he twisted out of Rainey's grasp and spun around. Using all the courage, self-confidence, and skill he had learned during his boxing lessons from Leslie Gibson, Avery lashed out and knocked Rainey's gun arm aside. The pistol cracked, but the bullet went wild. Avery launched a punch, putting all of his weight into the blow and driving his fist into Rainey's stomach.

Rainey grunted and took an involuntary step backward, but he recovered quickly. Avery had accomplished a great deal with surprise and timing, but he lacked the sheer power to knock down a grown man. Furious, Rainey slashed at the boy with the gun. The barrel thudded against Avery's head and sent him sprawling off the edge of the porch.

Seeing Avery take action, O'Quinn made his move at the same instant. He flung himself out of the saddle, his vigorous lunge bridging the few feet so that he landed on the porch, and plowed into Emily and Parker. The collision loosened Parker's grip on the girl. O'Quinn's hand closed over the barrel of the gun and jerked it away from Emily's body just as Parker fired.

O'Quinn felt the bullet tear into him, but he had already thrown a punch at Parker's head. It landed with devastating force, slamming Parker back against the wall of the cabin. He still managed to hang onto the gun, though. With the last of his fading strength, O'Quinn pushed Emily off the porch and cried, "Run!" Then he collapsed, clutching at his middle and feeling the blood welling between his fingers.

Inside the cabin the two men standing at the window were trying to aim their rifles at the figures struggling on the porch when the back door was smashed open by a kick from Cody Fisher's booted foot. Cody leapt into the room and threw himself to the floor as the men whirled around. Their rifles blasted, but the slugs whined over Cody's head, through the space he had occupied a split second earlier. He triggered twice, the reports so close together they sounded like one. The bullets caught one of the men in the chest. He spun around and collapsed like a rag doll. Cody rolled to the side as the other man's shots chewed splinters from the rough planks of the floor. The Colt in his hand boomed a third time and sent the remaining outlaw staggering backward, clutching a lead-shattered shoulder.

On the porch, Rainey and Parker both recovered in time to see a dozen men on horseback burst through the trees on the far side of the clearing. Rainey jammed his pistol back in its holster and vaulted over the porch railing. He jerked the reins of one of the horses free and leapt into the saddle. Pulling the animal's head around savagely, he slammed his heels into its sides and galloped toward the river, heading east away from the cabin.

Parker chose not to flee. He was tired of running, tired of being pushed around. If he was going to go down, it would not be alone. He lifted his gun and lined its sights on Emily Burton, who was running across the front of the porch toward her fallen brother. There was no way Parker could miss at this range.

Before his finger could tighten on the trigger, a .44-.40 Winchester slug barreled into his chest, knocking him back and killing him instantly. He collapsed on the porch next to Seamus O'Quinn's bloody, motionless body.

Luke Travis levered another shell into the chamber of his rifle and drew a deep breath. Seeing what Parker was about to do, he had yanked his horse to a halt to steady his aim, but it had still been a lucky shot and he knew it. Emily was still alive, though, so he would take the luck and be thankful for it. He kneed his horse into motion.

The posse rode up to the cabin, guns out and ready, but silence had descended on the place. That quiet was broken by a groan from inside. Then Cody stepped through the door. He still held his Colt, but there was a grin on his gunsmoke-grimed face.

"There's one dead and one hurting pretty bad inside here, Marshal," he told Travis. "Neither one's going to be giving us any more trouble."

Travis dismounted and quickly stepped up onto the porch. He prodded Willie Parker's body with a toe and grunted, "Neither is this one." Then he knelt next to O'Quinn's crumpled form.

Leslie and Orion hurried to Emily's side. She was sitting on the ground cradling Avery's head in her lap. On the boy's temple was a gash from Rainey's gun barrel, and although it was bleeding freely, his eyes were open. "Durn it, Emily, let me up!" he cried. "Seamus might need some more help!"

Leslie knelt beside the boy and put a hand on his shoulder to help hold him down. "Just take it easy,

Avery," Leslie told him sternly. "You've done plenty to help. Besides, you're hurt."

Orion studied the cut and pronounced, " 'Tis bleeding a mite, but it dinna look too deep. I think ye'll be all right, lad, but we'd best get ye back t'town f'the doctor t'have a look at ye."

Emily, satisfied that Avery was all right and that the danger was over, looked up and searched the faces of the men crowded around her, trying to find O'Quinn. Then, suddenly, she saw him lying on the porch, saw the grim look on Travis's face as the marshal stood up and motioned to Cody to join him. As the marshal spoke quietly to his deputy, Emily stared at O'Quinn's pallid face and felt new horror welling up inside her.

"I saw a fella that I reckon was Rainey take off on the back of a horse, heading east along the river," Travis was saying to Cody. "Can you handle things here?"

"Sure." Cody nodded, slipping his pistol back into its holster.

Travis stepped off the porch and went to his horse. "I'm going after him," he said as he mounted up. "The rest of you stay here."

Before any of them could argue with him, he wheeled the horse around and galloped away from the cabin, riding on the bluff above the stream.

Hatless, his heart pounding in his chest, Mitch Rainey hung on tightly to keep from being thrown from the back of the racing horse. He was heading east toward the rail line, the only way he knew to go in this godforsaken prairie. If he was lucky he could jump on an eastbound train before any of those damned frontier lawmen caught him. More than ever, he wished he was back in Chicago. There he would have had no trouble fleeing from the law.

Everything had gone wrong. He had thought that kidnapping the girl and her brother would be a sure way to lure O'Quinn into a trap. That part of the plan seemed to have worked, all right, but then all hell broke loose.

At least he had seen O'Quinn go down with a bullet in him before being forced to run, Rainey thought with savage satisfaction. Without the prizefighter's testimony, the authorities back in Illinois had nothing with which to prosecute Rainey and Gold. If he could just get back to Chicago, he would be safe from the consequences of his actions here in Kansas. Gold had too much influence to let trouble like this catch up to his right-hand man.

Rainey swiveled his head and peered behind him as he rode, searching for any sign of pursuit. So far there was none. Evidently Parker and the others had put up enough of a fight to keep the posse occupied. Rainey grinned. He was going to get away; he could sense it.

When he turned back around in the saddle, he saw someone riding right toward him. The rider wore city clothes and a derby that threatened to fly off every time his galloping horse touched the ground.

*McTeague!*

Rainey reached for his pistol as he recognized the detective from Chicago. The two men were rapidly approaching each other and would be within firing range in a matter of seconds. Rainey's pistol got caught on the flap of his coat for a second, and that was enough to make the difference.

McTeague aimed his Remington and began squeezing the trigger. Three shots cracked as the detective pulled his horse to a stop with his other hand. Rainey triggered one shot, but his bullet came nowhere near McTeague. One of McTeague's slugs burned a furrow across Rainey's forearm. Another hit him in the side and knocked him out of the saddle. The third bullet missed, but the damage was already done. Rainey fell heavily to the ground as his spooked horse ran away.

Moving quickly, McTeague slid off his mount and walked warily toward the fallen Rainey, training his pistol on the wounded mobster. Rainey saw him coming and looked around frantically for his own gun, but he had dropped it when he fell and could not locate it. Pain and frustration coursed through him.

McTeague stopped a few feet away. For a moment he was tempted to finish the job, to put a bullet through Rainey's brain. But then his training and his devotion to his job won out. He took a deep breath and said, "Mitch Rainey, you're under arrest for the murders of Melvin Rutherford and Dooley Farnham, and for the kidnapping of Emily Burton and her brother Avery."

At that moment Luke Travis galloped out of a grove of trees fifty yards away. McTeague glanced up, worried for an instant that the newcomer might be Parker, but then he recognized the marshal. Travis took in the scene and slowed his horse to a walk. As he came up to the two men, he reined in and gave Rainey a hard look before switching his attention to McTeague.

"I'm a little surprised to see you out here, Inspector," Travis said. "I figured Seamus had knocked you out cold and left you back in Abilene. Judging from that bruise on your jaw, he must have at that."

McTeague reached up with his free hand and rubbed the sore lump where O'Quinn had hit him. "He was even more stubborn than I expected," McTeague replied. "When I woke up I managed to talk Dr. Bloom into telling me which way all of you had gone. I came as quickly as I could, but I'm afraid I'm not much of a horseman. I heard a great deal of shooting, Marshal. What happened?"

"We were able to rescue those two youngsters." Travis dismounted, reached across his saddle, and took a coiled rope from it. He gestured at Rainey with the rope. "What do you aim to do with this skunk?"

"Why, I'll take him back to Chicago with me, of course," McTeague responded, then looked anxious. "Is Seamus all right?"

Travis ignored the question. He glanced at one of the nearby trees, seeming to study a thick branch that extended out from the trunk. "We do things a little different out here," he drawled flatly. "This fellow kidnapped a woman, and that's a hanging crime, the way we see it." He began to fashion a noose as he strolled toward the tree. McTeague watched, surprised into silence, as Travis tossed the loop over the branch and went on, "Not only that, but Rainey just killed Seamus O'Quinn."

"Seamus is dead?" McTeague exclaimed, horror etched on his face.

At the same moment, Rainey burst out, "I didn't do it! Parker's the one who shot him!"

"You were part of it," Travis told him. "That makes you just as guilty in my book." He caught the noose and tugged on the rope, checking the strength of the branch.

"See here!" McTeague exclaimed, his dedication to the law overcoming the hatred he felt toward Rainey. "You can't just lynch this man without a trial."

"Can you convict Darius Gold without Seamus's testimony?" Travis asked him.

"Probably not," McTeague answered bitterly. "I'm

afraid Gold will go free. He'll be able to continue his reign as the boss of Chicago's underworld."

"Rainey's a killer and a kidnapper," Travis said. He turned to face McTeague, putting his back to the frightened Rainey. "Since you can't get Gold, we might as well see some frontier justice done for Rainey, right here and now."

Slowly, the marshal's right eyelid closed in an elaborate, meaningful wink.

McTeague's own eyes widened for an instant in understanding, but he quickly controlled the reaction. Hoping that Travis knew what he was doing, McTeague said bleakly, "I suppose you're right. We might as well string him up. Isn't that what you say out here?"

"That's right," Travis grunted. He stepped over to Rainey and bent to grasp his arm. He roughly hauled the criminal to his feet, then shoved him toward the dangling noose.

Rainey stared aghast at the rope that was awaiting him. He had never thought it would come to this. To die out here in this wilderness, while Darius Gold would go untouched back to his elegant, comfortable life.

"No!" Rainey rasped. He twisted around and lunged toward McTeague, but he was not attacking now. He grasped the detective's coat and babbled, "I'll tell you anything you want to know about Gold! He's the one you really want, McTeague! I can give you enough to convict him a hundred times over. Just don't let that crazy marshal hang me!"

McTeague stared at Rainey, his face grim but his eyes shining with triumph. "You'll confess to your own crimes and testify against Gold?" he demanded.

"Anything! Just get me out of Kansas!"

McTeague looked over at Travis. "What do you say, Marshal?"

"He's your prisoner, Inspector McTeague!" Travis replied with a broad grin.

At McTeague's request Travis examined Rainey's wounds and bound them with strips torn from the man's shirt. The makeshift dressings would suffice until McTeague could get Rainey patched up in Abilene. "Can I borrow one of your cells, Marshal?" McTeague asked.

"Be my guest," Travis told him.

"I want to get his confession written down and signed, while that memory is fresh in his mind." McTeague gestured toward the noose that was still hanging over the tree limb.

Travis swung into his saddle and went to retrieve Rainey's horse, which had wandered and was grazing in the brush about a hundred yards away. When they were all mounted, the sound of approaching hoofbeats made the two lawmen look around. Most of the posse, with Orion McCarthy at its head, came riding up. The wounded survivor of Parker's gang was with them, his shoulder roughly bandaged and his hands tied in front of him.

"I see ye caught up wi' the scalawag, Lucas!" Orion boomed, glaring at Rainey.

"Actually, it was Inspector McTeague who captured him," Travis informed him. "Rainey is the inspector's prisoner, Orion. Would you and the other men mind escorting them back to Abilene?"

" 'Twould be our pleasure." Orion waved a big hand at the other posse members. "Come on, lads."

A grin tugged at Travis's mouth as he watched the group ride toward Abilene. Then he turned his horse and cantered along the river toward the cabin where the battle had taken place.

When he reached it, he found Cody waiting on the porch. The deputy returned Travis's grin and said, "From the looks of it, you must have caught up to Rainey."

"So did McTeague," Travis replied. "He and Orion and the others are taking Rainey back to jail right now."

"McTeague!" a voice exclaimed from the doorway. "What the devil was he doing out here? Is he all right, Marshal?"

Travis watched Seamus O'Quinn step out of the cabin, supported on one side by Leslie Gibson and the other by Emily Burton. Avery was right behind them, a huge smile on his face.

"He's fine, Seamus," Travis answered the prizefighter's question. "Except for a goose egg on his jaw, that is. I reckon you know how that got there."

O'Quinn grinned sheepishly. "I suppose I do, Marshal. You think Jack will forgive me?"

"I expect he will."

A broad bandage was wrapped around O'Quinn's midsection. Cody had fashioned it from Emily's petticoat after cleaning the wound with a bottle of whiskey he found in the cabin. Like Travis, he had enough experience with gunshot wounds to do some temporary doctoring. And like Travis, he had been able to see that O'Quinn's injury was messy but not fatal. The slug had ripped through the flesh of his side, missing all the vital organs. It would leave another ugly scar to add to his growing collection.

"What happened to Rainey?" O'Quinn asked as Travis dismounted.

"Funny thing about that," Travis said dryly. "He decided that he wanted to tell McTeague about all the bad things he and Darius Gold have been doing. He's going to give McTeague a full confession, and he's going to testify against Gold back in Chicago, since you won't be able to."

O'Quinn frowned in puzzlement. "Since I won't be able to? I don't understand, Marshal. Cody said this wound wasn't that bad."

"Oh, it's bad enough. You're dead, Seamus, you just don't know it yet."

Cody chuckled, having an idea of what Travis was talking about. As the others stared, Travis explained the ruse he had used to get Rainey to confess. As the marshal talked, O'Quinn's frown gradually faded, and he finally let out a great booming laugh.

"And Jack thought you frontier lawmen weren't very smart!" he said between guffaws. Leslie and Emily had to warn him to be careful, or his amusement might start the wound bleeding again.

"I reckon anybody can make a mistake," Cody said. "Even an inspector!"

Brushing tears of laughter and relief from his eyes, O'Quinn then wiped his hand on his pants and extended it to Travis. "Thank you, Marshal," he said. "I've got an idea what you have in mind, and I think I'm going to enjoy being dead!"

# *Chapter Fourteen*

———◆———

ANOTHER WEEK HAD PASSED, AND A WINTRY WIND BLEW
through Abilene. But the warm, happy group that had
gathered in the Kansas Pacific station to say good-bye
did not notice the cold.

Seamus O'Quinn had his arm around Emily's
shoulders—Emily O'Quinn now, since the Reverend
Judah Fisher had married them in a private ceremony
the day before. The radiant bride had never looked
more beautiful, O'Quinn thought as he glanced down
at her. But then, he had that same thought every time
he saw her.

Avery and Nora stood beside them, dressed in
traveling clothes that O'Quinn had bought. All four of
them would be heading west as soon as the next train
came in. They had decided that they would find a
place to start over, a place to call their own, where
prizefights, killers, and grief would be only memories.

Luke Travis's quick thinking had given them this chance, and O'Quinn would be eternally grateful to the marshal for it. Shaking Travis's hand for perhaps the hundredth time, O'Quinn said as much, then went on to ask, "You'll be sure to let me know how the trial comes out, won't you?"

Travis nodded. "McTeague promised to wire me as soon as the verdicts were read. When you, Emily, and the youngsters are settled, get in touch with me and I'll let you know. Don't reckon you've got anything to worry about, though. Gold and Rainey will both hang, I'm sure of that."

"They deserve to," Leslie Gibson commented. He had taken part of the day off from school to bid farewell to his friend, despite Thurman Simpson's displeasure at the idea.

O'Quinn shook his head. "I don't care about that, and neither does Emily. There's been enough killing. As long as Gold and Rainey are put where they can't ever hurt anybody again, that's all that matters."

The others who were gathered there again congratulated the happy couple and bid them good-bye. Cody Fisher, his brother Judah, Aileen Bloom, and Orion McCarthy had all come to see the travelers off.

O'Quinn and McTeague had had their reunion several days earlier, a reunion that was also a farewell. Neither man would admit it, but they had grown fond of each other. From the bed in Aileen's office where he was recuperating, O'Quinn reached up and grasped McTeague's hand.

"You be sure and get Rainey back to Chicago," he admonished the detective. "And watch him, he's tricky."

"No need to worry about that," McTeague assured

him. "He's a beaten man, Seamus. He's not going to give anyone any more trouble."

"I think I'll stay dead anyway, as far as everyone in Chicago is concerned, since you don't need my testimony anymore. But if you ever need me, I reckon Luke Travis will know where to find me."

McTeague grinned. "You know, Seamus, you're even beginning to sound like a westerner."

"Not such bad folks after all, are they?" O'Quinn asked.

*No,* he thought now, *not such bad folks at all.* In a way he was going to miss Abilene and its people.

Travis pulled his watch from his pocket and looked at it. "Train ought to be here pretty soon," he commented.

At that moment, the telegrapher finished taking down a message and handed it to the clerk behind the window at the ticket counter. The clerk read it, then leaned out of his enclosure to call, "Sorry, folks. The westbound is running late. Won't be here for another forty minutes or so."

O'Quinn, Emily, and Nora looked disappointed at the news. Despite this bittersweet departure, they were anxious to get on with their new lives. But Avery Burton suddenly grinned.

He looked up at his brother-in-law and said, "Seamus, do you think I'd have time to go down to the school for a few minutes, since the train's going to be late and all?"

O'Quinn put his hand on the boy's shoulder. "I suppose you would." Understanding dawned on his face. "We've been so busy, you never got a chance to say good-bye to your friends, is that it?"

"Something like that," Avery agreed noncommittally.

O'Quinn looked at Emily. She considered the question, then nodded. "It would be all right, I guess. Just don't get your new clothes dirty, Avery."

"I won't," he promised. Quickly he left the depot.

O'Quinn watched him go, a thoughtful frown creasing his brow. If he remembered correctly, Avery had not had that many friends. The lad seemed awfully eager to pay one last visit to the school.

"I think I'll walk down there with Avery," O'Quinn decided. "Leslie, how about going with me?"

"Sure," the teacher agreed. "I really ought to get back to work, anyway."

Emily reached up to kiss O'Quinn's cheek. "Thank you for going and keeping an eye on him," she said. "Avery has always let himself get pushed around. I'd hate for him to have trouble on his last day here in town."

O'Quinn remembered the way Avery had turned on Mitch Rainey, and a smile tugged at his wide mouth. "I'll watch out for the boy," he said dryly.

The others went about their business, leaving Emily and Nora to wait at the station. O'Quinn and Leslie strode toward the school, their long legs carrying them to the school yard shortly after Avery had arrived. But as they neared it, the whoops and cheers of the students who had been outside at recess told O'Quinn that they might be too late.

"What the blazes is going on?" Leslie wondered, seeing the children gathered in a circle in the school yard. Thurman Simpson was dashing around the outside of the group, crying, "Stop it! Stop that barbarism this instant!"

As usual, no one was paying any attention to him.

O'Quinn and Leslie hurried into the yard and peered over the ring of shouting children. In the clearing in the center of the circle Avery Burton was trading punches with a taller, redheaded boy. Avery skillfully dodged some of the blows and blocked others, and the ones that got through did not seem to faze him.

"That's Roy Summers," Leslie exclaimed. "He's been tormenting the smaller children ever since I came here."

"It looks like he's about to get his comeuppance," O'Quinn grunted. This development came as no surprise to him. He had known when Avery left the train station that the boy was up to something. Avery had had the look of a man about to even a score.

Michael Hirsch moved among the students, busily taking wagers from them on the outcome of the fight. There was a grin on his freckled face. He would clear at least a dozen marbles and maybe a pocketknife or two from this bout.

Thurman Simpson finally stopped dancing around the group and contented himself with bouncing up and down, an agitated look on his narrow face. He had seen Avery march into the school yard and confront Roy Summers, but he had never dreamed a brawl would break out.

Slowly, it became clear to all the spectators that Avery was winning this battle. O'Quinn glanced over at Leslie and saw the proud grin on the teacher's face. Leslie had taught more than facts and figures to Avery; he had taught the boy the skills he needed to take care of himself—and Avery had learned as well to have faith in his own abilities.

Initially Roy's greater height, weight, and reach had given him the advantage, but Avery kept boring in, shrugging off the punishment and dishing out some of his own. Suddenly he feinted with his left, drawing a wild swing that left Roy off balance and wide open. Avery shot out his right fist, landing a blow directly on Roy's nose. The older boy sailed backward, his face bloody. He sat down hard, wailing and clutching his injured nose.

Avery stepped back and dropped his hands. "Fight's over," he said simply. He turned and walked away, the circle of children parting to let him through.

O'Quinn felt a surge of pride. Along with his new-found courage and skill, Avery had also acquired the maturity not to take advantage of a fallen opponent. Roy Summers had been stripped of his status as a feared bully, and that was all that Avery had set out to accomplish.

"Hooray!" called a female voice. O'Quinn turned in surprise to see that Emily had been watching the fight as well. Nora was with her, and the little girl was rushing forward to greet her victorious brother.

"I'm sorry, Emily," O'Quinn said quickly. "I shouldn't have allowed Avery to fight like that—"

"Nonsense," his wife replied. "I don't remember how many times Avery came home with a bloody nose because of that Summers boy. It's time he took some of his own medicine!"

O'Quinn grinned and embraced Emily, glad that she and Nora had followed them from the depot. Avery had taken care of their last piece of unfinished business in Abilene. Now they really could make that fresh start.

Far to the east, a train whistle shrieked faintly through the chilly air.

"That'll be the westbound," Leslie Gibson said with a smile. "You folks had better get back to the station." He held out his hand. "So long, Seamus."

"So long, Slugger," O'Quinn replied, gripping Leslie's hand firmly. "We'll come back to see you someday." The prizefighter's grin widened. "After all, we never did get to spar. You won the last time we mixed it up, and I figure I'm due for a rematch one of these days!"

# THE BEST WESTERN NOVELS
# COME FROM POCKET BOOKS

## Loren Zane Grey
- [ ] A GRAVE FOR LASSITER .................. 62724/$2.95
- [ ] LASSITER TOUGH ......................... 60781/$2.95
- [ ] LASSITER TOUGH ......................... 60781/$2.95
- [ ] LASSITER ON THE TEXAS TRAIL ...... 63894/$2.95

## Loren D. Estleman
- [ ] THE HIDER ................................. 64905/$2.75
- [ ] HIGH ROCKS ............................... 63846/$2.75
- [ ] THE WOLFER ............................... 66144/$2.75

## Norman A. Fox
- [ ] THIRSTY LAND ............................. 64816/$2.75
- [ ] SHADOW ON THE RANGE ................ 64817/$2.75

## Frank O'Rourke
- [ ] AMBUSCADE ................................ 63684/$2.75
- [ ] THE BRAVADOS ............................ 66212/$2.75
- [ ] DESPERATE RIDER ......................... 66213/$2.75
- [ ] GUNSMOKE OVER BIG MUDDY ....... 66210/$2.75
- [ ] HIGH VENGEANCE ......................... 63686/$2.75
- [ ] LATIGO ..................................... 63682/$2.75
- [ ] LEGEND IN THE DUST .................... 66214/$2.75
- [ ] THE PROFESSIONALS ..................... 63683/$2.75
- [ ] VIOLENCE AT SUNDOWN ................ 63685/$2.75
- [ ] WARBONNET LAW .......... 66209/$2.95

## William Dedecker
- [ ] TO BE A MAN ................. 64936/$2.75
- [ ] THE HOLDOUTS ............. 64937/$2.75

POCKET
B O O K S

**Simon & Schuster Mail Order Dept. WPB**
**200 Old Tappan Rd., Old Tappan, N.J. 07675**

Please send me the books I have checked above. I am enclosing $_____ (please add 75¢ to cover postage
and handling for each order. N.Y.S. and N.Y.C. residents please add appropriate sales tax). Send check or
money order–no cash or C.O.D.'s please. Allow up to six weeks for delivery. For purchases over $10.00
you may use VISA: card number, expiration date and customer signature must be included.

Name _____

Address _____

City _____ State/Zip _____

VISA Card No. _____ Exp. Date _____

Signature _____ 290-07